Emerald

Emerald

James Baddock

Walker and Company
New York

First published in the United States of America in 1991
by Walker Publishing Company, Inc.

Published simultaneously in Canada by Thomas Allen & Son
Canada, Limited, Markham, Ontario

Library of Congress Cataloging-in-Publication Data

Baddock, James.
Emerald : a novel / James Baddock.
p. cm.
ISBN 0-8027-1144-8
1. World War, 1939–1945—Fiction. I. Title.
PR6052.A3128E44 1991
823′.914—dc20   90-48859
CIP

Printed in the United States of America

2 4 6 8 10 9 7 5 3 1

AUTHOR'S NOTE.

Although 'Emerald' is a work of fiction, it is based extensively on incidents that took place in Berlin during the latter part of April, 1945. Many of the people portrayed in this novel are real, quite apart from Hitler, Bormann, Goebbels, Mueller, Philby, etc. General Hermann Fegelein was arrested on the night of April 27th, exactly as described in Chapter 6, and his mistress, who was also present in the flat at the time, did escape through the kitchen window. Although it is not known for certain whether this woman was a British agent, as I have portrayed her, there is considerable evidence to suggest that she was - Bormann was convinced that she was working for the British, once he had seen the contents of the valise that Hoegl took from Fegelein's flat (which were exactly as I have described).

The British did have a source of information in Berlin at this time - a woman - who had been supplying London with material concerning the Bunker inmates for several months. Although her actual identity has remained a secret to this day, one of the facts that is known about her is that she had Irish origins. Several survivors from the Fuehrerbunker, including Guensche, met Fegelein's mistress and they all agree that she came originally from the Republic of Ireland and that she had been the wife of an interned Hungarian diplomat. Neither Fegelein's mistress nor MI6's Irishwoman - if they were two different people - were ever heard of again after the end of the war.

Bormann was not the only one to be convinced that Fegelein's mistress was 'Das Leck'; a good deal of Mueller's interrogation of Fegelein the day after his arrest was devoted to the missing woman and the information thus gained would almost certainly have been passed on to the Russians in Mueller's subsequent defection. In addition, Albert Speer, who was familiar with Hitler's obsession with 'Das Leck', confirmed after the war that Fegelein would have been privy to the sort of information that was reaching London and so his mistress would have been ideally placed to gain access to it.

Thus, while the name 'Marianne Kovacs' is an invention of mine, I believe that, whatever her real name was, somebody very like her did live in Berlin during those last months of the war. She must have been a very courageous and remarkable woman. I can't help hoping she did, somehow, manage to escape from Berlin, but, unfortunately, her fate will probably remain a mystery.

Nevertheless, it would be nice to think she met her two knights in shining armour, after all....

PROLOGUE I.

THE BRITISH EMBASSY, BUDAPEST: FRIDAY, APRIL 4TH, 1941.

Martin Powell tied up another bundle of documents and placed it in the large cardboard box on his desktop; it was already nearly full. As he did so, the door opened and a young, bespectacled man came in with another pile of papers precariously balanced in his arms. Powell shook his head wearily. "How much more is there, for God's sake, Harris?"

Harris shrugged. "I've no idea, sir. Mr Slocombe hasn't even started on Room Twenty yet." He looked round for somewhere to set down the documents.

Swearing, Powell cleared a space on his desk and pointed to a large sack in the corner of the office. "That's ready for disposal."

"Right, sir." Harris hefted the bulky sack onto his shoulder and staggered out, leaving Powell staring thoughtfully at the new pile of documents. Most of it would be destined for incineration, but about ten per cent would have to be preserved and it was up to him to sort it out. Down in the underground Records Office, Slocombe, the Chief Records Clerk, would be performing a similar task, but the secret files that had been collected over the last twenty years or more were Powell's responsibility. Officially, he was a Senior Attache in the Embassy, but, in fact, he was the local field agent for SIS, the British Secret Service, and so it was his job to decide which of the files could be destroyed and which should be transported back to the United Kingdom.

There was precious little time to carry out such a massive administrative procedure. The latest news from London was that it would only be a matter of days before Whitehall broke off diplomatic relations with Hungary. Two days before, German troops had crossed the Austrian and Czechoslovakian borders into Hungary, supposedly in transit on their way to invade Yugoslavia. No permission had been granted by Budapest for this; it was thus tantamount to an invasion, except that the government was to be allowed to remain in power. Hungary was now no more than a Nazi satellite state, but Britain was powerless to intervene, despite the suicide of Count Teleki, the

Hungarian Prime Minister, the day before. The message that the Ambassador had received from London had been to the effect that as soon as the invasion of Yugoslavia was launched, Britain would sever all links with Hungary on the grounds that it was allowing itself to be used as a base for Nazi aggression. The latest estimate for this was April 6th or 7th and in the meantime, all non-essential records had to be destroyed - a mammoth task as Powell was increasingly coming to appreciate.

The telephone on his desk rang and he scooped it up hurriedly; more bad news, almost certainly. "Yes? Powell here."

"It's Mackay, sir. There's a woman here who would like to speak to you."

"What about, for God's sake?"

"She won't say, sir. Says it confidential and very urgent. She won't give her name, either, but reckons you and she met at the Swedish Embassy dinner a month ago and talked about the Eton Wall Game."

"Eton Wall Game?" muttered Powell, frowning in perplexity before he recalled the incident, but the realisation only brought further bewilderment; what the devil did Marianne Kovacs want with him? "Very well, Mackay, could you have her brought up, please? Not to my office, though - better make it Mr Ellingham's."

Her appearance as she was ushered into the office took him by surprise. He had a picture of her in his mind as he had seen her at the dinner: tall, slim, with long, reddish-blonde hair, startling green eyes with gold flecks and an excellent figure shown off to its best advantage by a black evening dress with a plunging neckline, but he scarcely recognised the woman who now stood in front of him. She wore a raincoat that had probably been expensive when new, but which now showed unmistakeable signs of wear and tear and a hat that all but concealed her hair, which had been pulled back into a bun on the nape of her neck. Her face was almost totally devoid of make-up; the elegant, sophisticated beauty had been transformed into a pretty, but anonymous, woman. "Do sit down, Mrs Kovacs," said Powell in English, indicating a chair in front of the desk.

"Thank you, Mr Powell." There was a faint trace of an Irish accent in her voice; if Powell had not already known that she had been born in Dublin, he would not have detected it at all.

"What can I do for you, Mrs Kovacs?"

Her green eyes stared at him with a disconcerting frankness. "I understand that you are the field agent for MI6, Mr Powell."

There was no visible reaction on Powell's face, but he could feel his stomach turning over. "Whatever gives you that impression, Mrs Kovacs?"

"Look, Mr Powell, I know that you're not going to admit anything, but that's not why I'm here anyway. Your status here is rather less of a secret than I imagine you would like it to be, but that scarcely matters now as you will be leaving within two or three days, does it? I'm telling you that I know who you are simply to make the point that I have access to diplomatic information that might well be useful to you - to Britain, that is - after your Embassy here is closed down." Once again, she fixed him with her direct gaze. "I'm willing to supply you with that information."

"I see," said Powell noncommittally. "What sort of information do you mean, exactly?"

"You know my husband, don't you?" There was a hint of scorn in her voice now; was it for Powell's obtuseness or for her husband? "He is an ambitious man. Already, he is ingratiating himself with the Pro-Nazi factions in the Government and I have no doubt that he will gain enough favour to move several rungs up the ladder - but he is less than discreet when it comes to discussing his work." She smiled, but with an edge of bitterness. "How else do you think I found out your identity, Mr Powell? The point is that Janos - my husband - gives me an entree to the highest diplomatic levels here in Budapest, so who knows what I might be able to pick up?"

Powell stared down at the writing pad on which he had been doodling; amongst the random whorls and squiggles, he had written "WHY?" in block capitals. Quickly, he scribbled over it. "This is a very interesting proposition, Mrs Kovacs, but I'm sure you'll appreciate that I'm not in a position to give you any immediate reply."

"I know that - but you can pass the message on, can't you?"

"Indeed, but-"

"Then would you? As soon as possible? Remember that you probably don't have very much time." There was a quiet desperation in her voice now; it seemed important to her that London's answer would be yes. "Tell them that I don't want any money or anything. Just tell them to think about my mother if they want to know why I'm doing this."

Powell stared at her for several seconds then nodded. "I'll certainly pass it on, but I can't guarantee anything, Mrs Kovacs."

"Good enough. You can contact me at this number." She took a

9

slip of paper from her handbag and passed it to him. "I don't think I can risk coming back here again, so you'll have to telephone me. If Janos answers, say it's a wrong number or something. If you manage to get me, just let me know whether London's going ahead and what arrangements you want to make - if he's listening, I'll just answer yes or no. All right?"

"Perfectly." Powell tried not to smile at her naive confidence; did she think this was all some sort of game?

"Good." She rose to her feet. "At the risk of sounding melodramatic, is there a back way out of here? I don't think I was recognised or followed on my way here, but I'd rather leave by a different route."

Again, Powell forced down a smile, but it was a sensible enough measure to take, if perhaps over-dramatic. "Yes, there is. I'll get someone to show you out."

"Thank you, Mr Powell." She held out her hand. "For all your help."

Powell stared at the door for some time after it had closed behind her then shook his head slowly, regretfully. He had little doubt that London would be only too delighted to take her up on her offer to spy for them, but it would almost certainly be her death sentence; she had been given no training whatsoever and amateur spies rarely lasted very long. Sooner or later they made an elementary mistake that gave them away to the security services and Marianne Kovacs would probably be up against the Gestapo within a matter of weeks.

She would be lucky to last six months.

PROLOGUE II.

BERLIN: NOVEMBER, 1941.

"Good evening, Herr General."

SS-Lieutenant General Hermann Fegelein turned around suddenly, as though startled, then smiled as he recognised the man who was talking to him: Major Otto Guensche, Hitler's Personal Adjutant. Like Fegelein, Guensche was in full dress uniform, as befitted a reception being held by Dr Josef Goebbels, the Reich Minister of Propaganda. As always, it was on a lavish scale, with well over a hundred guests at what had been described as "an informal gathering" - although everyone was wearing evening dress, of course. And, as usual, the guests were drawn from the very highest levels of society; without turning his head, Fegelein could see Albert Speer, looking strangely ill-at-ease, Hermann Goering, surrounded by his retinue of blond, handsome young pilots and Martin Bormann, who, despite the fact that he was engaged in conversation with a striking blonde woman, still managed to give the impression that he was missing nothing that was going on about him.

"Quite a gathering, eh?" Guensche commented, taking a sip from his glass.

"Indeed," Fegelein agreed, feeling a small glow of pride. He was a stocky man, of medium height, running slightly to overweight, with rather podgy features and dark hair slicked back from his forehead. Looking at him now, it was difficult to believe that he had once been a gentleman jockey. A year ago, he would never have been invited to such a gathering and he took it as concrete evidence that he was now regarded as a person of influence and power, someone to be reckoned with. Mind you, he had had to work for it, he reminded himself. Even to the extent of marrying that frigid bitch Gretl, simply because she was Eva Braun's sister - but that had ensured his place as one of Hitler's coterie and his entree to occasions like this....

"The Herr Doktor certainly knows how to lay on a party, doesn't he?" Guensche commented.

"He certainly does," Fegelein agreed again; he and Guensche had known each other professionally for several months now as both of them worked on Hitler's staff, but they also mixed

11

socially, having discovered that they shared a liking for the Berlin night life. "On your own tonight?" he added, conversationally.

"Afraid so," Guensche agreed ruefully. "But I hope to do something about it before long." He nodded significantly at a tall brunette who was talking to a Colonel, but whose gaze was wandering freely about the hall.

"Not bad," Fegelein agreed appreciatively.

"And yourself, Herr General? Is - ah - Frau Fegelein with you tonight?" Guensche's eyes glinted mischievously.

"Don't be damned silly," Fegelein retorted, smiling. "She's at home looking after the baby - as a good mother ought."

"Of course," Guensche agreed gravely. "So do you have alternative arrangements made?"

"I'm hoping to, yes."

"Don't tell me," said Guensche. "The tall reddish-blonde in black?"

Fegelein followed the direction of his look and nodded; the woman in question was one of a group of half a dozen or so standing a few yards away. She was undeniably very attractive, with a slim, desirable figure and long shining hair that tumbled over her bare shoulders; as he watched, she tossed her head back with a sudden, almost imperious movement. "That's the one. How did you know?"

"You've been staring at her for the past five minutes," Guensche grinned. "I have to admire your taste but she's a bit out of my league, I'm afraid."

"What do you mean?"

"She's Goebbels' current mistress," Guensche replied succinctly. "Has been for the last six weeks, which probably means that she's about due to be replaced if his previous track record is anything to go by; but I don't suppose she'd look at anyone below the rank of General." He shook his head in mock sorrow. "And I am but a mere major. But you, on the other hand-"

"Who is she?" Fegelein interrupted him.

Guensche shook his head. "I'm not sure of her name - I've never actually met her. Maria something-or-other, I think, but I wouldn't swear to it. She's the wife of some foreign diplomat, that I do know. Not that it would make any difference to Goebbels, of course, whether she was married or single, but I gather that her husband's been interned, so you can imagine what she had to do to escape the same fate." Guensche looked archly at Fegelein, who nodded.

"I can indeed."

"She must be quite something," Guensche continued wistfully. "The Herr Doktor has even given her a job in his Ministry." He chuckled lasciviously. "Maybe he summons her up to his office for a quick one every now and then."

"But you think she might be - ah - available?"

"Could be. Rumour has it that Goebbels is after that blonde with the big tits he's talking to at the moment."

"Interesting," Fegelein commented, looking over at the auburn-haired woman; she really was beautiful, he thought again, and the clinging dress enabled him to picture her naked with little effort. As he watched, the group split up and she was left talking to a Luftwaffe major, who hardly seemed able to believe his luck. "I think I'll go and introduce myself. If you'll excuse me, Guensche?"

"Of course, Herr General."

Fegelein saw her eyes flicker briefly in his direction before returning for a longer, more appraising look that became frankly inviting. "Excuse me, Major," he said curtly, ignoring the officer's angry glare which was instantly suppressed when he saw Fegelein's uniform. "May I have the pleasure of this dance, Fraulein?".

She smiled radiantly at him. "The pleasure will be all mine, Herr General." There was a perceptible emphasis on the word "pleasure" that was undoubtedly provocative and, as he took her arm, Fegelein realised that he was grinning like a Cheshire Cat. "You're General Fegelein, aren't you?" she asked, with the barest trace of an accent in her voice, but Fegelein was too flattered by the fact that she had evidently recognised him to pay any attention to it.

"That's right, Fraulein-?"

She ignored his question for the moment. "I thought you were. I've seen your picture several times at the Ministry." She looked frankly into his face. "They don't do you justice, Herr General."

"Why, thank you," Fegelein stammered, taken aback by her directness. They had reached the dance floor now and turned to face each other; as he slipped his arm around her slim waist, he was suddenly aware of her perfume - and of her closeness. "You haven't told me your name yet, fraulein," he reminded her.

"Not fraulein, I'm afraid - but you don't have to worry about my husband," she added, giving him such a sultry, blatantly erotic look that he felt himself beginning to breathe more rapidly. "I'm Frau Kovacs," she said and moved closer to him; he

13

watched, fascinated - and aroused - as she ran her tongue slowly, seductively around her lips.

"But you can call me Marianne," she murmured huskily.

CHAPTER 1.

THE FUEHRERBUNKER, BERLIN: FRIDAY, FEBRUARY 2ND, 1945.

With an abrupt gesture, Adolf Hitler reached out and switched off the radio. He glared at it for several seconds and then turned to the other two men in the room with him, Josef Goebbels, the Reich Minister of Propaganda and Martin Bormann, the Deputy Fuehrer. "Well, gentlemen?" Hitler demanded.

"They do seem to be remarkably well informed, my Fuehrer," Goebbels agreed glumly.

"Pah!" Hitler snorted. "And where are they getting the information, Josef?"

Goebbels shook his head again and looked thoughtfully at the silent radio as though it would provide the answer; Bormann said nothing.

"Time and again it's happened!" Hitler ranted. "The BBC seems to know more about what is going on here in Berlin than I do! Somewhere, there is a spy right here in Berlin, perhaps even in this Bunker for all I know, who is providing the British with information - isn't this abundantly clear to you?"

"It would certainly seem to be the case, yes, my Fuehrer," Bormann agreed dutifully.

"'Appears to be the case', Martin? Appears? What other explanation can there be? For weeks now, that programme has been broadcasting gossip and scandal about almost everyone except me! They're accusing both of you of keeping mistresses - did you realise that?"

Bormann and Goebbels managed to look suitably outraged, despite the fact that the accusations were perfectly true.

"And how do they know about my personal directives?" Hitler went on, not waiting for any answer. "I can't issue any orders without them being broadcast on that programme within three days!"

'That programme' was 'Soldatensender West', a radio programme that was broadcast nightly by the BBC. It claimed to be the product of a group of loyal but disgruntled SS officers and did, in fact, contain genuine Wehrmacht bulletins and military music, but its primary function was as a 'black propaganda' ploy. Its main interest was its juicy titbits of scandal involving the leaders of the Third Reich and, needless to say, it had acquired a huge, if secret, audience throughout Germany. Goebbels had often thought that it was a masterpiece, presenting enough substantial truth to make its more lurid, exaggerated claims convincing, but the obvious corollary to this was that the British must indeed have a very reliable source of information.

"What I want to know," Hitler continued, "is what is being done to catch this spy!"

"It's very difficult, my Fuehrer," Bormann replied, glancing nervously at Goebbels. "It may not be a spy. After all, a lot of the - ah - rumours that are used are fairly widely known throughout Berlin and so anybody could have passed them on."

"And what about Himmler's appointment as head of Army Group Vistula? Was that general knowledge throughout Berlin? But the BBC knew about it within forty-eight hours!"

"That's precisely the problem," Bormann continued. "The spy could be on the Reichsfuehrer's staff or he could be here in Berlin, or there could be several spies. Where do we start to look?"

"Listen, Martin, I will not have the British knowing what is going on here almost before it happens! I don't care how you do it but I want that leak stopped! I want that spy - or spies, if you prefer - caught and executed! Is that clear?"

Bormann nodded quickly, aware that Hitler was working himself up into a frenzy. "Certainly, my Fuehrer. I'll see to it at once."

"Be sure that you do!" Hitler spun on his heel and stormed out of the room, leaving Bormann and Goebbels staring at each other.

"Well, Reichsleiter?" asked Goebbels, with more than a hint of malicious glee in his voice. "You'd better get on with it, hadn't you?"

Bormann glared at Goebbels. Of all the Nazi leaders, Goebbels was the only one that Bormann was unable to manipulate, the only one who would dare to speak to him like that. "You think I haven't been investigating it already, Minister? I don't need to have such matters drawn to my attention before I act on them - unlike some."

This time, it was Goebbels' turn to glare. "Then I'll leave you to it. If you'll excuse me-"

Bormann winced as the door slammed behind the departing Goebbels, but then looked consideringly at the radio.

16

Unfortunately, Hitler was right; there was a leak and it was virtually certain that it was from someone close to the centre of power, but the very nature of the material being broadcast made it all but impossible to pin down likely suspects. When all was said and done, none of it was of earth-shattering importance, nor was it likely to contribute greatly to Germany's defeat, but there was no knowing how much more important information was reaching the Allies. Several weeks ago, Bormann had ordered an investigation into 'Das Leck', which was the name he had given to the source of information, but virtually no progress had been made to date. Now, of course, it would have to be stepped up in response to Hitler's demands, even though it had been fairly low on Bormann's list of priorities. He had enough on his plate at the moment....

Fortunately, there was a simple solution. He would place the matter in the hands of Ernst Kaltenbrunner, the head of the Reich Security Services, along with instructions to spare no effort in tracing 'Das Leck'. That should keep Hitler happy - and it might even find the spy.

Fegelein mounted the stairs to the second storey of the rambling apartment building off Kurfurstendamm and let himself into the flat that occupied the entire floor. "Marianne!" he called, pulling the door closed behind him. As always, he was struck by the sheer luxury of the apartment; everything - the suite of furniture, the velvet drapes, the paintings on the walls, the Persian carpet, the Chippendale bureau - everything exuded wealth and comfort. Any visitor would know that it belonged to a man of influence, taste and culture. Fegelein believed that he was all of these, preferring to forget that the furnishings had already been in the flat when he had bought it six weeks before. "Marianne!" he called again.

"Coming," a voice replied from the front bedroom. Moments later, Marianne Kovacs emerged, wearing a long, flowing nightdress of almost transparent black lace. "I've been waiting for you, Hermann," she said invitingly. "Where have you been?"

"The briefing went on longer than I thought," he said, suddenly dry-mouthed. "The Fuehrer was furious about Torun falling, although Jodl tried to dress it up as a tactical withdrawal, of course.... I like the nightdress."

"I hoped you would," she smiled, rotating gracefully on the rug to give him an all round view. Despite the fact that their affaire

17

was over two months old now, Fegelein still found himself delighting in the sight of her body and in her ability to arouse him, often with a single look. "A drink, darling?" she invited.

Fegelein sank down gratefully onto the sofa. "I'd love one. A cognac, I think."

Marianne smiled to herself. Fegelein thought that a taste for cognac was a sign of sophistication and so he would drink it at almost every opportunity, although he really preferred schnapps or beer. She brought him the drink and then sat on the sofa next to him, drawing her legs up beneath her. "Well, Hermann - tell me what's been happening."

"Not very much, I'm afraid. We've lost Torun, as I said, and I can't see Budapest holding out much longer - which might interest you, I suppose?"

She shrugged. "Not any more. As far as I'm concerned, I'm a German now. In any case, you know I'm not really all that interested in military matters. I-"

"I know, Marianne." Fegelein smiled roguishly. "You want to know all the scandal, don't you?"

"Well - yes," she admitted.

"There isn't much of that either, I'm afraid. Bormann's still got his mistress installed at his villa in the Obersalzburg, and Kempka's still with his Berchtesgaden tart. Nothing much else is happening apart from that."

"Has the Fuehrer decided whether he's going to go to the Alpine Fortress?"

Fegelein's face grew serious. "No, he hasn't. We'll have to think about what we're going to do if he decides to stay in Berlin."

She leaned towards him and put her arms around his neck. "You haven't changed your mind about taking me with you, have you?"

"Of course I haven't, Marianne."

"And your wife, darling?" she asked throatily, nibbling at his ear.

"How many more times do I have to tell you? Gretl means nothing to me - she never has. But when Hitler 'suggests' you marry his mistress's sister, what alternative do you have?"

"I know, darling. It's just that I like to be reassured now and again." Her fingers began to unbutton his tunic, deftly. "I mean, I'm only your mistress, not your wife - I'm bound to get a bit jealous of her sometimes."

"No need to be, Marianne," Fegelein said thickly as she

unfastened his shirt. "I haven't even slept with her since I met you."

"Do you honestly expect me to believe that?" she teased him.

"It's the truth - I swear it!"

"Well - I would hope that I was keeping you satisfied," she murmured.

"Of course you are," he groaned as he felt her cool fingers under his shirt.

"Good," she chuckled and then she knelt astride him on the sofa, reaching down to unfasten his trousers as her mouth pressed tightly against his.

It was after midnight before Marianne was satisfied that Fegelein was properly asleep; his breathing was regular now and he had begun to snore. Carefully, she eased herself out of bed, slipped on her dressing-gown, taking care not to disturb him, although she knew that the Nembutal that she had added to his cognac 'nightcap' would ensure that he would not wake until the morning. She paused by the bed for a moment, looking down at him with an expression of distaste before she padded silently out of the bedroom, closing the door behind her.

In the lounge, she made her way over to the sideboard and took a keyring from her gown pocket to unlock the bottom drawer. As she pulled it open, it gave a slight creak that made her wince. There was no response from the bedroom and she smiled to herself at the thought that an exploding bomb probably wouldn't wake Fegelein at the moment. Inside the drawer was a large wooden jewellery box which she unlocked and opened to reveal an assortment of rings, necklaces and brooches. She reached down into the bottom of the case and pressed one of the studs in the base; a concealed compartment flicked open, from which she took a small camera.

Fegelein's briefcase was still where he had left it when he had come in: next to the coffee table. She opened it, took out the documents inside and placed them on the bureau. She turned on the anglepoise lamp, positioning it so that it shone on the papers, then, with a practised efficiency born of countless repetitions, she began to photograph the documents.

SATURDAY, FEBRUARY 3RD.

Marianne showed her platform ticket to the inspector and went

19

through the barrier to the platform. The large station clock showed that it was a few minutes before eleven, which meant that the train from Dresden should be arriving within the next five minutes or so. Slowly, she made her way along the platform, pausing at the kiosk to look at the books and magazines before moving idly on, a woman waiting to meet someone off the train. Which might well be true in a way, she thought to herself; all she knew was that the instructions had specified this platform at eleven a.m. but, by now, she had enough confidence in her contact to know that everything would go smoothly.

This would be her tenth package in the last year. In her pocket was a manila envelope containing the film she had used last night to photograph the documents as well as several typed sheets on which she had written, in code, every scrap of information she had been able to glean in the last month or so. Exactly how much use it would be to London, she had no idea; it was difficult to see how knowing the gossip and scandal surrounding the leaders of the Third Reich would help the Allied war effort. Nevertheless, she knew that a good deal of it was used in BBC 'black propaganda' broadcasts and so they must be finding some use for it....

The Dresden train pulled into the station, jolting her out of her reverie and she went over to a stone pillar, apparently scanning the faces of the alighting passengers. The train had obviously been busy, judging by the throng of people as they made their way towards the barrier, but nobody approached her, or even seemed to notice her.

Her attention was suddenly distracted by a commotion at the ticket barrier; a burly man was arguing with the inspector and a knot of onlookers was forming around the incident. It was at this moment, when virtually everyone's interest was focused on the platform exit, that she had a fleeting impression of a man beside her and of the barest perceptible tug at her coat before he had gone. All she saw was a small figure in a nondescript coat slouching away from her.

She did not need to check her pocket to know that it no longer contained the envelope.

THE MINISTRY OF PROPAGANDA: MONDAY, FEBRUARY 19TH.

"Frau Kovacs?"

Startled, Marianne looked up from her work and then relaxed

20

slightly as she saw that it was only one of the records clerks. "Yes?"

"Er - it's nearly five o'clock." The clerk indicated the papers on Marianne's desk. "I have to return them to the archives."

"Yes, I know. I'm sorry - I hadn't realised the time." She smiled up at him apologetically, but he did not respond; he never had done in all the three months she had been working there. Carefully, she sorted the various documents back into their correct folders before handing them back to him, but, as always, he leafed through them, checking them against his list to ensure that they were all there. Not that there had been very much in that last batch; it had consisted of copies of various articles in 'The Times' that she had been translating into German. The work she had been doing earlier on in the day had been much more interesting. She had been given the German texts of propaganda bulletins that were going to be broadcast on the 'Deutschlandsender' network and which had to be translated into English. Often, by reading between the lines and by relating it to Fegelein's gossip, it was possible to deduce how much truth there was in each news item and she was sometimes able to insert key words into the translation that would alert London to the amount of credence that they should give to the broadcast. And for that, she - and London - had to thank Reichsminister Josef Goebbels, for giving her the job - even if she had been obliged to sleep with him to get it....

At least Fegelein was less demanding than Goebbels had been, she reflected. And a lot more talkative; she had been lucky to find him. He was so full of his own self importance that he was only too willing to talk both about his own work and that of others, so that he could impress her with the extent of his knowledge. There was also the consideration that he was very highly placed in the Nazi hierarchy; as the liaison officer between Hitler and Himmler, the head of the SS, he had access to a considerable amount of secret information and gossip about the leaders of the Third Reich, all of which he would pass on to her with malicious glee.

He was exactly the sort of man - vain, garrulous and gullible - who should never be allowed access to any confidential material. So much so, in fact, that, for a while, she had been worried that she was deliberately being fed misleading information by the Gestapo, until she realised that such a subtle approach was not their hallmark; if they suspected her of being a spy, she would have been arrested and executed long since. The fact of the matter was that Fegelein was the type of person who prospered in the regime Hitler had created, simply by being ingratiating and compliant. His marriage to Gretl Braun - Eva Braun's sister - had been a case in point; she had been pregnant at the time to another man, who had refused to marry her and had been packed off to the Russian Front, but as soon as Hitler had suggested to Fegelein that he might like to be her husband, he had almost fallen over himself to agree.

Carefully, she tidied up her desk and then made her way out of the large office she shared with three other translators, onto the landing. It was when she was halfway down the stairs that she saw the Gestapo squad in the lobby. Evidently, it was time for one of their random security checks and everyone was being stopped on their way out. There was no reason for any undue concern on her part as she never took anything incriminating out of the Ministry, but, despite this, she was aware of a dryness in her throat as she joined one of the queues that were forming at the street doors.

The search was perfunctory, however, involving only a brief scrutiny of her pass and a rummage through her handbag before she was allowed through. Her face carefully expressionless, she went out into the open air and was about to descend the steps to the street when she heard someone calling her.

"Marianne! Over here!" About twenty metres along the street was a staff car and standing next to it was a tall, fair haired man in the uniform of an SS-Major. She recognised him at once; Alex Rindt. The sense of relief that she had felt on having passed through the checkpoint was replaced by a gnawing anxiety. She knew Rindt and his attractive dark-haired wife Inga socially, but there was also the unpleasant fact that he was a Gestapo officer. Marianne generally tried to avoid him, though she had to concede that he was nothing like the traditional image of the Gestapo. On the contrary, he was an engaging individual whom she could have found very likeable under different circumstances.

Rindt gestured at the car. "Can I offer you a lift home?"

"That's very kind of you - thanks." He was probably only being pleasant, she told herself as she climbed into the back of the car, but it was not easy to dispel the feeling that she was being arrested....

As if divining her thoughts, Rindt smiled reassuringly as he sat down next to her. "Relax, Marianne - you're not being detained or anything like that. Bleibtreustrasse, isn't it?"

"Er - yes."

Rindt gave the directions to the driver and then pulled the

22

glass partition across so that he would not be able to overhear their conversation.

"Gives us a bit of privacy," he remarked, grinning boyishly.

"This is very kind of you, Alex."

"Well, it looks as though it's going to rain and I'd hate you to get soaked."

"I'm sure you didn't come over to the Ministry just to stop me getting wet."

"Hardly," he chuckled. "That would be a shocking waste of Gestapo time and property, wouldn't it? No, the truth is that we're checking all the Ministries today and I got saddled with the overall supervision so I thought I might as well arrange to be here at five o'clock when you came out. We haven't seen you for a while. Is everything all right?"

"I'm fine, thanks, Alex."

"Still with your - ah - friend?" he asked delicately.

"Yes, I am,"

"And how is the illustrous General? He's well, is he?"

"He seems to be, yes," she replied, stifling a smile at his irreverence. Rindt had always had scant respect for authority, according to Inga, but the reverse side of that coin was the fact that he had achieved his present rank on merit alone; he was a very capable counter-intelligence officer indeed. She had to be constantly on her guard with him, despite his pleasant, open manner. "And how is Inga?" she asked, trying to change the subject.

"She's fine," Rindt replied. "Actually, she's in Danzig at the moment - she went on Saturday. Her mother's decided to move to Berlin and Inga's gone to give her a hand."

"Aren't the Russians rather close to Danzig now?" asked Marianne hesitantly.

Rindt glanced sharply at her and then nodded. "I'm afraid so," he agreed reluctantly. "In fact, that's why her mother is leaving. But it should be safe enough - Inga will be there and back inside five days." Despite his words, Marianne could detect an undercurrent of concern in his voice; he was clearly not as happy about the arrangement as he made out. "Anyway, once she's back, you must come and see us," he continued, briskly. "We haven't seen you for ages."

"I certainly will, Alex. I'll look forward to it." Her voice sounded sincere, but she knew full well that she would not be taking up the invitation.

The car turned into Bleibtreustrasse and came to a halt.

23

Courteous as ever, Rindt jumped out of the car and came round to open her door; she climbed out and smiled gratefully at him. "Many thanks for the lift, Alex - even if it didn't rain."

He grinned. "My pleasure, Marianne. Hope to see you again soon."

"Give my regards to Inga, Alex."

"I will," he replied, climbing back into the car. "Auf wiedersehn," he called and nodded to the driver; the Mercedes pulled away.

Marianne watched the car until it disappeared from view round a corner and then she let out a long sigh of heartfelt relief.

FRIDAY, FEBRUARY 23RD.

Rindt stared unseeingly at the report in front of him; he had been trying to read the same page for the last ten minutes or more but he just could not concentrate on it. Partly, it was the negative nature of its contents, describing a fruitless surveillance of a house in Spandau that was supposed to belong to a courier in a Russian spy ring. The main reason for his preoccupation, however, was that he had heard nothing from Danzig for ten days now. Inga had telephoned the day after she had arrived to say that she was safe and would be returning as soon as they could find a berth on a train or on one of the evacuation ships that left Danzig every day. But there had been no word since. Had they been able to find transport, they would have been back in Berlin days ago. And, although he could get through to Danzig by using his Gestapo priority, he had not yet been able to reach Inga's mother's number.

Almost unaware of what he was doing, Rindt replaced the report on the desk and swivelled his chair around to look at the wall map behind him. It could only be a matter of days now before the Red Army finished their drive north-westwards through Pomerania and reached the Baltic, thereby cutting off Prussia - and Danzig - so that the only escape for Inga and her mother would be by sea; unfortunately, that alternative was fraught with danger. At the end of January, the *Wilhelm Gustloff* had been torpedoed and sunk with the loss of over five thousand lives. Ten days after that the *General von Steuben* had suffered the same fate, taking over two and a half thousand evacuees with her to the sea bottom.

24

Rindt stared helplessly at the map. There was nothing that could, or would, be done to slow down the Russian advance, because what was left of the German Army was trying to hold back the main Soviet thrusts towards the Oder and Berlin. Prussia would be left to fend for itself and inevitably would be over-run. The Russians had taken Elbing a fortnight ago - and Elbing was only thirty-five kilometres from Danzig....

The telephone rang and he snatched it up. "Rindt here."

"Herr Major, there is a call from Danzig for you. Will-"

"Yes!" Rindt almost screamed. "Put it through, for God's sake!" There was a seemingly endless delay as the call was put through.

"Alex?" Thank God, he thought; it was Inga!

"Yes, Inga, it's me. How are you? For God's sake, what is happening? Why are you still in Danzig?"

"I'm afraid there's been an accident, Alex-"

"Accident?" Rindt felt his stomach turn over.

"I've been trying to call you for days, but I haven't been able to to get through. It's mother. She slipped on some ice at the top of the steps outside her flat and fractured her hip. She's in hospital and she won't be able to move for several days yet."

"How long? How many days?"

"Ten days - a fortnight - something like that."

"You can't stay there for another fortnight! The Russians will have Danzig surrounded by then!"

"But I've got to, Alex! I can't just leave her here, can I?"

Rindt stared fixedly at the desktop, his thoughts racing. "Look, use the priority travel permits I gave you. Get her on a hospital train or ship at once - they'll look after her, but-" The line went dead. "Inga! Inga! Are you there? Inga!" Frantically, Rindt juggled the telephone cradle up and down. He knew it would be futile; there had been an ominous finality about the way the call had been cut off. "Inga...." Slowly, he replaced the receiver and stared sightlessly at the wall.

It was less than half a minute later that the door opened abruptly and a young Lieutenant strode in, flanked by two troopers. The officer saluted smartly. "Colonel Wentzler's compliments, Herr Major, and would you report to his office immediately?"

Rindt nodded emptily. He knew what had happened; someone had been monitoring the telephone call and had heard the reference to Danzig being surrounded. Wentzler would probably throw the book at him for divulging military information over the telephone. Rindt couldn't give a damn. As he rose to follow the young officer, he was overwhelmed by the utter conviction that he would never see Inga again....

POZNAN, POLAND: THURSDAY, MARCH 1ST.

NKVD Colonel Mikhail Semyonin sighed irritably at the knock on the door and looked gloomily at the pile of paperwork that had accumulated on his desk. Poznan had fallen a week before and Semyonin's Intelligence Unit had moved into the city within forty-eight hours. Since then he seemed to have done nothing but read and sign reports, generally relating to interrogations of suspected collaborators. And still it was coming in....

"Enter," he called out. As he expected, it was Major Grigoriev, his deputy; nobody else would have dared disturb him. "What is it, Grigoriev?" Semyonin asked testily.

"We've had a message from 'Spartakus', sir," said Grigoriev briskly, passing over a typed sheet of paper.

Instantly, Semyonin forgot about the reports; 'Spartakus' was the codename for a high-ranking Nazi in Berlin who had been supplying the Russians with top secret information for several months. Semyonin did not know Spartakus' true identity - that knowledge was restricted to less than half a dozen very senior officers in Moscow Centre - but he did know that any messages from him were to be acted on immediately. This signal was brief and somewhat bewildering; he looked at Grigoriev questioningly. "Is this all there is?"

"I'm afraid so, sir."

"Hardly helpful, is it? Still, I suppose he has his reasons. Do we have anyone assigned to Danzig?"

"Markushev, sir. He and his group are already in Elbing on standby. They've been given their list of interrogation subjects."

"And what's the current estimate for taking Danzig?"

"Probably at least four weeks, sir. They're not due to start the offensive for another ten days or so."

Semyonin looked at the signal. "Then this is hardly urgent, is it?"

"I don't suppose Spartakus knew that, sir."

"True. Well, get a signal sent to Markushev then, telling him to add this name to his list. Tell him to be careful, though - according to Spartakus, she's to be unharmed."

"Yes, sir. I'll get on to it. Er - if I might have the message back, sir? I'll need the details."

"Of course." Before returning it, Semyonin read the name once more; what the devil did Spartakus want with Frau Inga Rindt?

CHAPTER 2.

Marianne left the flat at just after six o'clock, carrying a bulky envelope under her arm and walked unhurriedly along Bleibtreustrasse and into Kurfurstendamm. As she made her way towards Tiergarten, she stopped every now and then to look in shop windows - not that there was very much in them, these days, she reflected ironically. Every time she did so, however, she glanced back along the street to ensure that she was not being followed; finally, satisfied that all was well, she boarded a tram for the Zoological Gardens.

The Zoo was only a pale shadow of what it had once been. Before the war, it had housed over two thousand animals but now there were barely a hundred and most of them were half starved. However, it was still a pleasant enough place in which to walk and nobody would think it strange that she should be idling away her time there, especially on such a fine evening.

She noticed with annoyance that the last bench by the duck pond - where the drop was to take place - was already occupied; the man in the seat looked vaguely familiar. A moment later, she remembered seeing him at a reception at the Irish Embassy about eight months ago. Clearly, this was the courier who was to pick up the package, but he had broken the accepted procedure, which was not to arrive at the drop until she had left. There was nothing she could do about it because she dared not abort the transfer, not with the incriminating material in the envelope. Without looking at him again, she sat down on the opposite end of the bench, placing the package on the seat next to her. She rummaged in her handbag for a packet of cigarettes and, while doing so, she knocked the envelope off the bench so that it fell out of sight behind the wooden backing. Ten minutes later, she stubbed out her cigarette, stood up and walked slowly back towards the exit; the courier would probably wait a while before picking up the envelope.

Less than two minutes after leaving the Zoo, she knew that she was being followed.

Klaus Schuller had been convinced that this afternoon had been a complete waste of time; then he had seen the attractive auburn-haired woman sit down next to MacDiarmid, the junior attache from the Irish Embassy whom he had been detailed to watch over the last few days. Schuller knew that MacDiarmid was not under any real suspicion of espionage, but a routine part of the training for new Gestapo officers was following foreign diplomats around Berlin, whether they were involved in any subversive activities or not. It was boring, but certainly better than the Eastern Front, especially when such a woman as this one appeared on the scene....

From his vantage point, thirty metres away, Schuller failed to spot the 'drop' itself; if truth be told, he had not even noticed that she had been carrying an envelope, let alone the fact that she had left it behind. However, his instructions had been quite specific as to what to do if the subject under surveillance made contact with anyone - he was to follow the 'contact'. Ignoring the question as to whether merely sharing a park bench with someone could be construed as a contact, Schuller decided to follow the woman; if nothing else, it would be a break in the monotony.

He followed Marianne out of the Zoo and into Kurfurstendamm; she seemed to be in no hurry at all, looking into several shop windows as she made her way along the street. Schuller stayed with her, stopping when she did, always staying at least twenty metres from her while congratulating himself on his surveillance skills; it was obvious to him that she had not the slightest inkling that she was being followed. Eventually, he was so confident that when she stopped once more, he decided to walk on past her, as his instructors had said should be done on occasion; besides, it would enable him to take a closer look at her.

As he was about to pass her, however, she suddenly turned and smiled at him. "Excuse me, but do you have a light?" He realised, belatedly, that she was holding a packet of cigarettes.

"Er - yes. Certainly." He produced the gold lighter he had bought only the week before and, with as much aplomb as he could muster, lighted her cigarette for her.

"Thank you," she smiled then frowned slightly. "Have we met before, by any chance?"

"I don't think so, fraulein," he replied uncertainly.

"Your face looks familiar. It's not like me to forget a face as - handsome as yours, Herr-?"

"Schuller. Klaus Schuller," he stammered, scarcely believing his luck. Things were looking very promising indeed....

"I'm very pleased to meet you - Klaus. My name is Luisa. Luisa Hansen." Her eyes were now openly inviting.

"Er -" he stuttered, hesitating before he took the plunge. "Where are you going at the moment, Luisa?"

She shrugged elegantly. "Nowhere in particular. Why?"

"I thought I might buy you a cup of coffee. I know somewhere near-"

"Come now, Klaus," she chuckled throatily. "Is a coffee all you want? You disappoint me."

"W-What do you mean?"

She nodded at a bombed-out shop on the other side of the road that had once been a tailor's. "Come with me for a minute, Klaus, and I'll show you exactly what I mean." Smiling invitingly at him, she began to cross the street. "Come on," she said, seeing his hesitation, "I won't bite. Well - not yet, anyway."

He followed her into the shop and through into what had been the store room at the rear; she walked to the back wall and turned to face him, slowly removing her coat.

"Nobody can see us here, can they, Klaus?" Her voice was husky, blatantly erotic, yet still he hesitated; she began to unbutton her blouse, still slowly, still with that sultry expression in her eyes. Suddenly impatient now, he moved forward and pulled her into his arms. Talk about being offered it on a plate....

As his lips pressed hungrily against hers, Marianne's right hand moved caressingly down his back. His fingers were fumbling with her blouse buttons as she slid her hand slowly into the handbag slung from her shoulder, searching for the handle of the kitchen knife whose blade she had painstakingly filed to a needle sharp point. Carefully, she drew the knife out of the bag and placed the tip against his side just under the ribs as his hand reached inside her blouse.... She held him tightly with her left arm, closed her eyes in fear and revulsion then drove the blade into his body with a strength born of desperation.

Schuller cried out and stepped back from her, looking down incredulously at the knife embedded in his side; she wrenched it out and plunged it into his stomach. Frantically, he clutched at the hilt, but again she yanked it out, staring at him with horrifed eyes; he lunged towards her, reaching out for her right hand, but she slashed downwards at his arm and saw blood spurt from his wrist. God, there was blood everywhere....

"You bitch!" he shouted, reaching for her again. "You cow!"

A third time, she stabbed him, in the chest, feeling the knife turn in her hand as it deflected off a rib, but she forced it home;

30

he let out an incoherent bellow of agony. For an endless moment, he stood motionless, his eyes wide, staring then his knees began to buckle under him and he fell forward; she stepped sideways out of his way, watching him as he slumped against the wall. He stayed there for several seconds, on his knees, trying vainly to pull out the knife. His breath rasped hoarsely out of his throat before he slowly toppled to one side, to lie face down, unmoving.

Marianne stared down at him, white-faced, feeling the gorge rising in her throat. He had been so young, barely more than twenty, and she had killed him, murdered him in cold blood....

Now pull yourself together! she told herself; he was a Gestapo officer, an arrogant, conceited bastard! The enemy, that's what he had been and a very real threat, especially if he had reported her to his superiors....

With shaking fingers, she buttoned her blood-stained blouse, fighting back a fresh urge to retch as she slowly drew on her coat. Trembling almost uncontrollably, she went through to the front of the shop to look around; there was no sign of anyone having heard the struggle. Even if they had, Berliners had learned better than to interfere; such shouts were generally from Gestapo victims and only a fool would attempt to intervene. Finally, satisfied that she had a few minutes at least in which to act, she went back to Schuller and, after several seconds' hesitation, she turned the body over so that it was lying on its back. She gritted her teeth and, her mind a careful blank, pulled the knife out, wiping it on his coat. Now, she reached inside his bloodsoaked jacket and took out his wallet, which she checked rapidly: several banknotes and a Gestapo identification pass. She placed the wallet in her handbag and searched Schuller carefully, swallowing several times to prevent herself from throwing up.... she could not afford to leave behind any clues whatsoever. Only when she was certain that Schuller had not scribbled down any notes that might have referred to her did she finally straighten up and look around the room.

Had she missed anything? If she were lucky, they might just put his death down to a simple robbery - if he had been working alone, which was a reasonable bet, based on what she knew about Gestapo training methods; and Schuller had been far too inexpert to be anything but a trainee. On the other hand, if he hadn't been alone, if another Gestapo agent had been present who could identify her....

There was nothing she could do about that except hope.... In the meantime, she had to dispose of the wallet and the knife before telephoning the Embassy to tell her contact what had happened, using one of their coded messages.... It was time to go.

In more ways than one, she decided, pausing for a moment to look back at Schuller. That had been too close for comfort; she should heed the warning. It was time to quit Berlin.

WEDNESDAY, APRIL 18TH: 2030 HOURS.

Fegelein saluted the sentries on duty as he emerged from the front entrance of the Reich Chancellery then rapidly descended the steps to the Mercedes staff car that was waiting for him. Somewhere to the west, he could hear the high-pitched wail of a siren, but he did not bother to look in that direction; he had already subconsciously noted the glow in the sky that indicated a fire that was still out of control, a legacy of the American bombers that had attacked during the day and which would now act as a beacon for the RAF planes that would almost certainly come tonight. After several weeks of virtually continuous air attacks, one ceased to notice their effect on the city, save that, every morning, there were more buildings in ruins, that road journeys tended to take longer because of the need to negotiate vehicles past piles of rubble or bomb craters or that the telephone lines were increasingly either busy or out of action. Berlin was being systematically battered to death - and yet he knew the worst was still to come.

Fegelein's lips were set in a grim line as he climbed into the car. The briefing had just finished in the Fuehrerbunker and the news from the battle fronts had not been encouraging at all. Two days before, the Russians had launched a massive offensive against the Wehrmacht defences along the Oder and Neisse rivers and, although the German troops were holding back the main Soviet attack on Berlin around Frankfurt-on-Oder, the news from the south was bleak. The Russians had advanced twenty-five miles or more after smashing through the defensive positions and there were virtually no German forces now between them and the southern outskirts of Berlin. Yet Hitler was still refusing to admit defeat or to come to a final decision whether to go to the Obersalzburg. The man was a fool, thought Fegelein; in a matter of days, Berlin would be surrounded and he would be trapped. Was that what Hitler really wanted?

The driver muttered something under his breath and Fegelein snapped out of his brooding reverie. The road ahead had been cordoned off and a young Lieutenant was directing traffic. Fegelein wound the window down and called out, "What's the delay, Lieutenant?"

The officer sprang to attention. "An unexploded bomb, Herr General. I'm afraid you'll have to detour round it. If I may suggest –"

"It's all right, Lieutenant. We know the way." He nodded to his driver and the car moved off.

Fegelein settled back in his seat and looked out at the darkened street. Night time was a blessing, he realised; it hid the worst effects of the bombing. Was that why Hitler preferred to remain in his underground Bunker, so that he did not have to see the destruction being wrought on his capital? Why didn't he face facts and leave the city, go to the Alpine Fortress and carry on the fight from there? Then he, Fegelein, could leave this rat-trap....

Nervously, Fegelein looked down at the briefcase on his lap, thinking of the almost inevitable consequences if it were to fall into the hands of the Gestapo. His position as brother-in-law to Eva Braun would not help him then; there was no doubt that Hitler would order his immediate execution. Yet he had to take some action, because to remain in Berlin would mean certain death, either in the final Russian assault or in one of their prison camps; Fegelein could imagine, only too well, how the Soviets would treat a man who had acted as the link between the head of the SS and the Fuehrer.

The car pulled up outside his apartment block and he climbed out, relieved to see that, once again, the street had escaped damage. Bleibtreustrasse had been lucky so far, in that most of its buildings were still intact. "0900 tomorrow, Eicke," he reminded the driver.

"Yes, Herr General."

Marianne was sitting in an armchair reading as he entered the flat; she looked up at him, startled. "You're back early, Hermann."

"It was a shorter briefing than usual," Fegelein replied, putting his briefcase on the coffee table. "Hitler's come up with another master plan to drive the Russians out."

Marianne went over to the drinks cabinet and poured him a drink while he lounged back in his armchair. "Is this plan as insane as the others?"

"Probably." Fegelein stared morosely at the fire. "But what is more important is that I don't think he's going to leave Berlin

33

after all."

"You mean - he's going to let the Russians take him prisoner?"

Fegelein shook his head. "I doubt it. I suspect he intends to commit suicide and I imagine all the rest of us will be expected to follow suit, like the faithful acolytes we are supposed to be. Well, not me," he added grimly and leaned forward to open the briefcase. Inside was a sheaf of photocopied documents, held together by a large paper clip, each one bearing a 'Top Secret' stamp. "These documents will be our way out, Marianne."

"What are they?" she asked, reaching out for them.

"Details of the ODESSA escape routes. Their organisation, safe-houses - everything we'll need to get us out of Germany and all the way to South America. I've also got blank travel documents, passports, money - everything."

Slowly, a radiant smile was spreading across her face as she leafed through the papers. "When do we go?"

Fegelein stared at the documents doubtfully. "As soon as I know Hitler is definitely not going to leave Berlin, I'll start organising it."

"Why wait until then, Hermann? Why not now?"

He shook his head. "Marianne - you don't understand. I could be shot just for possessing these papers, let alone for planning to desert the Fuehrer without orders. It would be madness to do anything until it becomes absolutely necessary." Fegelein stared at her, the fear evident in his eyes. "Some of the Bunker staff are going to be transferred in three or four days' time - Operation Seraglio, they're calling it. Perhaps I can arrange to be included."

"And where would that leave me?" she demanded icily. "They'll let you take your wife and child - but not your mistress."

"I could arrange something with Goebbels, perhaps-"

"Perhaps! Maybe! What happened to all those promises, then? 'Of course you'll be coming with me, Marianne - how could you doubt me?' Remember? I should have known better!" She leaped out of her chair and stormed over to the window, her arms folded angrily across her chest.

"Marianne-"

"Don't you 'Marianne' me! You're planning to leave me behind, aren't you?"

"I'm not, Marianne, believe me!" He rose to his feet and went over to her, putting his hands on her shoulders from behind. "I promise you that I won't leave Berlin without you. If you look in those papers, you'll see that there is a set of documents for you."

She turned round to face him. "Then let's use them now, while

34

we can still get out of Berlin!"

Slowly, he shook his head. "That is impossible, Marianne. If they caught us, they would shoot us, believe me."

"So you won't use those papers now so that we can escape?"

"I can't, Marianne! It's too much of a risk-"

"For you, maybe. Those papers might be my only chance of getting out of here, and you tell me to wait!"

"Just for a few days and then-"

"Well, in that case you can damned well wait as well, because you can sleep on your own - 'just for a few days'!" Her face like thunder, she pushed him away and strode out of the room, slamming the door behind her.

Silently, Marianne tiptoed back into the bedroom and slipped back into bed next to the sleeping Fegelein; she lay on her back, staring up at the darkened ceiling. She had not been able to carry out her promise, of course; there was only one way that she could be sure that Fegelein would be fast asleep while she photographed the papers, and that had been to allow herself to be placated by his apparently sincere promises, to stage a passionate reconciliation then, afterwards, to make sure that he enjoyed his doctored nightcap.... But that was not what was keeping her awake, her thoughts racing excitedly; it was the documents themselves. This was perhaps her greatest coup, in terms of detailed, substantiated information. She knew that her next move should be to pass the film on to Kiernan, her contact at the Irish Embassy, who would place it in the diplomatic bag immediately. Within forty-eight hours, seventy-two at the most, it would be in London. MI6 would be delighted....

But would they be sufficiently delighted to pull her out of Berlin, which she had asked them to do several times now? The Russians would soon conquer Berlin - what would they do to an MI6 agent if they discovered her? Or to a woman who had been the mistress of both Goebbels and Fegelein? Or to any woman, come to that; if only a tenth of the stories of the rapes and atrocities committed by the Russian troops were true, Berlin would still be no place for a woman when they took over.... always assuming that she was still alive by then, of course. She had more than 'done her bit' for Britain and now she wanted out - but how? London had not responded to her requests, while Fegelein was dithering as usual. There was no way that she could travel out of Berlin alone, even with the travel passes Fegelein had brought her and she could not ask the Irish Embassy for help any more - she was no longer an Irish citizen.

What she needed was a lever, she decided, a way of forcing London's hand, so that they would have to get her out of Berlin somehow. They would only do that if she gave them a very powerful reason.... Like the ODESSA documents.

Right. If London wanted that information, then London would have to come and get it.

And her.

CHAPTER 3.

"Sir Gerald is here, sir."

"Oh, good. Send him in, will you, Miss Paxton?" Sir Stewart Menzies sat back in his seat as Cathcart came in and sat down; the two men looked at each other with an icy formality that concealed a long-standing mutual dislike. Menzies had been 'C', the head of the British Secret Service, for the last five years and Cathcart had been one of his Deputy Chiefs throughout all that time, but from the moment that Menzies had taken over, Cathcart had made it clear that he did not approve of his new chief and that he should have been appointed as 'C' instead. Although Menzies had to concede that Cathcart had been superbly efficient at his job, he was still relieved that Cathcart was to be transferred to the Foreign Office in a few weeks's time. "Sit down, Gerald."

"Thank you, sir."

"Good of you to come at such short notice. I hope I didn't spoil your arrangements for the evening?" Both men glanced involuntarily at the ormolu clock on the wall; it was almost nine p.m.

"Not at all, sir."

"Good. It's just that we've had a signal from 'Emerald' - I thought you ought to see it as soon as possible." He held out a message flimsy to Cathcart, who read it rapidly.

"Good Lord," he exclaimed in consternation. "I see what you mean, sir," he continued thoughtfully.

"What I want to know, Gerald, is this. Could 'Emerald' actually have access to documents like this?"

Cathcart considered the question for some time before replying. "It's possible, yes, sir - but unlikely. We have to bear in mind the information she's sent us up to now. High level gossip, who's been having an affair with who, who isn't talking to who, all the scandals involving Hitler and his coterie. All very useful stuff, of course, from the propaganda viewpoint, even if we don't know how accurate it is, but none of it could really be called top secret."

"Very detailed, though, isn't it?" said Menzies. "I mean, she sent us details of a list of promotions for Dietrich's Panzer Army back in February, didn't she? That argues that she must have some access to military documents, especially if she's Fegelein's mistress."

"Certainly, sir, but this has been the first time she's ever obtained anything like this - what is it?" Cathcart looked at the flimsy again. "Details of the ODESSA escape routes and organisation? I'd imagine they'd be keeping those under lock and key, so if that's the case, how did she get hold of them? We know she can't actually get inside Hitler's Bunker herself - she presumably has to rely on whatever Fegelein takes home with him, or anything he lets slip in bed. And Fegelein, for all his exalted rank, is not much more than a messenger boy, so they wouldn't let him have much of any vital importance."

"So you're saying she's lying?"

"No - although she could be. I think she's exaggerating. I just can't believe that Fegelein, let alone her, could get hold of documents like these. She might have a summary or a digest about ODESSA, but no more than that. It's just way out of her league, sir."

"Well, if you're right and she is exaggerating, then why is she? I don't think she's ever been guilty of that before - and she's been sending us material for four years now."

"I know that, sir - if you recall, I was the one who set her running. In this instance, I would imagine that she wants us to get her out of Berlin. It won't be the first time she's requested it, after all. So she's given us an added incentive to pull her out now - these documents. I would say that she probably has some information, but not as much as she claims."

Menzies stared appraisingly at Cathcart. "In other words, you think we should leave her where she is."

"I'm afraid I do, sir. It would be an unjustified risk sending someone in to bring her out - and that's what we'd have to do. The Russians will have Berlin surrounded inside a week, so how would we get her out then? I wouldn't want any of our men falling into the hands of the NKVD. And that's ignoring the Gestapo and the dangers they present. 'Emerald' isn't important enough to justify the risk, sir."

"She's expendable, you mean." Menzies' voice gave no hint of his true feelings.

"Frankly, yes, sir. Her information - all the scandal in the Bunker - isn't much use to us now and I don't think we can risk any of our best undercover men just to bring out a summary of ODESSA activities. And we'd have to use our best men, sir, to have any chance of success."

Menzies nodded slowly. "I'm afraid I would have to agree with you, Cathcart - except that we can't be certain that you are right about these documents she claims to have."

"If she has them, why didn't she photograph them as she usually does? She's simply using this information as a lever so that we'll rescue her."

"I can't honestly say I blame her for that," Menzies commented. "I'd hate to be in Berlin at the moment. It's very understandable that she should want us to get her out. She may also be using this information to - ah - twist our arms somewhat, but that doesn't mean to say that she doesn't have it, does it? And if she has, then it would be well worth bringing her out, would it not?

"Think about it, Gerald. We know that a lot of top Nazis plan to leave Germany when the war is over and that this ODESSA network is organising their escapes. But we've got deuced little information about them - do we really want the likes of Goering or Himmler or Goebbels or, perish the thought, Hitler himself just disappearing to South America during the next few weeks?"

"Well, obviously not, sir, but-"

"The point is, Gerald, that even a digest, a generalised summary, no matter how non-specific it might be, could well be of use to us. And if Emerald's information is as detailed as this signal implies, then we cannot afford to lose the opportunity of laying our hands on it."

"I can see that, sir, but I still think it's an unwarranted risk. We'd have to send our men into a battle area with very little support, limited communications and with no clear-cut escape route. I doubt if even our best agents would have much of a chance of success, which is why I'm reluctant to make any attempt to bring Emerald out."

"I see," said Menzies slowly. "Isn't there a compromise you could use? Send in agents who are - well - expendable?"

"In that case, sir, they wouldn't be good enough to have any realistic chance of success."

"You miss my point. I mean use someone who has the ability to execute the assignment successfully, but who is not essential to us at the present time. Someone you have used in the past, but who is no longer directly involved in MI6."

Cathcart frowned thoughtfully. "I suppose that might be feasible," he conceded. "But who?" he added, almost to himself.

"Wasn't there someone who pulled off quite an audacious coup in Holland a couple of years ago?" Menzies said suddenly. "Stole a plane or something?"

Realisation dawned on Cathcart's face. "Yes, there was indeed, sir." He nodded slowly. "And he would be ideal."

GLASGOW DOCKS: FRIDAY, APRIL 20TH.

"Collins!" yelled the foreman, leaning out of the window of his dockside office. "Collins!"

A tall, dark-haired man, one of a party of men loading crates into the back of a lorry, looked up. "Yeah?" he called, even the one word betraying the fact that he was not a Scotsman, but a Londoner.

"Boss wants to see ye. Now!"

"Oh bugger," Collins muttered. "Now what've I done?"

"And get a bloody move on, ye Sassenach!" The foreman's accompanying grin robbed the words of all offence.

"All right, keep your bloody kilt on, will you?" The man grinned in turn then headed along the quayside, but as he approached the main office, his expression grew more thoughtful. There was a car parked outside the office, a Humber Snipe that looked ominously official and which filled him with a sense of foreboding as he pushed open the door. "You said you wanted to see me, Mr McTaggart?"

"Aye, son," said McTaggart, looking at him quizzically. He nodded towards the other man in the room, a tall, balding individual with ruddy, genial features. "Tae be more accurate, Mr Fitzgerald here asked if he could have a wee word with ye."

"Indeed I did, Mr McTaggart," said Fitzgerald smoothly, his voice pure Oxbridge; refined, cultured. "I asked if I could have a word with you in private, Mr - ah - Collins, and Mr McTaggart was kind enough to agree."

"Aye," said McTaggart hesitantly. "I'll leave you two to it, then."

"Thank you, Mr McTaggart." Fitzgerald waited until the door had closed behind the Scot before he spoke again. "Right - shall we drop the pretence, Cormack?"

"Cormack?" asked the Londoner, his face bewildered. "What are you talking about? My name's Collins - you musta gotten me mixed up with someone else, mate."

Fitzgerald nodded amusedly. "They told me you were a professional. I can see they were right, but it's pointless to carry on the charade. Your name is not Collins at all, to begin with. You are Captain Alan Cormack of the Royal Marines, assigned to SOE

40

and thence to MI6 - which is where I come from. You have been behind enemy lines no less than four times and on each occasion you completed your mission successfully. However, after your last operation in May, 1943, you absented yourself from the hospital in which you were being treated and, since then, you have been living under the name of Andrew Collins, using papers obtained on the black market. Need I say more?"

"No, you don't," said Cormack bitterly. "You've made your point. So why are you here? To arrest me as a deserter?" His London accent was far less pronounced now.

"Good Lord, no." Fitzgerald appeared genuinely amused. "If we were going to do that, we'd have done it ages ago - when we arranged for your false papers, that is." He paused and looked expectantly at Cormack, waiting for some reaction, but the other man's face was expressionless - as if he had already known about the papers, Fitzgerald realised.... "You see, we've been keeping an eye on you, just in case."

"In case of what?" Cormack asked, an edge in his voice.

Fitzgerald spread his arms in an expansive shrug. "Who knows? But we can hardly have men with your particular aptitudes running around the country unsupervised, can we?"

"Being able to kill people with my bare hands, you mean?" Cormack said bluntly.

"Indeed." Fitzgerald's composure did not falter in the slightest. "And, of course, there has always been the possibility that we might need those talents again."

"No," said Cormack flatly. "Forget it. I've had enough - you're not getting me into that again. Just go back to London and tell Guthrie and Cathcart to find someone else this time."

"Guthrie isn't with us any more," said Fitzgerald absently. "I've taken over his duties, you see, which means you're rather my responsibility now."

"Good for you. It makes no difference - the answer's still no."

"You haven't even heard what we want you for yet."

"I couldn't give a damn what it is. I'm not interested. You put me through the wringer once too often, so you can all go to hell." Cormack turned angrily away from Fitzgerald.

"As far as I can gather, the planning and execution of your last operation was entirely your own doing, so you can hardly blame us for that, can you? In fact, if I may say so, I was more than impressed by its sheer audacity."

"Yes, but you weren't bloody there, were you?" said Cormack, almost to himself. "You didn't see what it cost, did you?"

41

"The operation was a complete success, Cormack. The objective was achieved and, for that, all the credit must go to you."

"And all the responsibility!" Cormack spun round to face him. "Look, get it through your thick skull, Fitzgerald - I'm not doing it, whatever it is!"

"Just hear me out, will you, Cormack? At least listen to what I'm proposing and then you can say no if you wish. I won't deny that what we have in mind is hazardous - I'll admit that. On the other hand, it is perfectly suited to your abilities in that you speak fluent German and have shown yourself to be resourceful and capable when operating behind enemy lines."

"Behind enemy lines? What enemy lines, for God's sake? The war's nearly over. Where-" He broke off and stared at Fitzgerald suspiciously, a dawning comprehension in his eyes. "Bloody hell.... you're not talking about Berlin, are you?"

"I see that you are well-informed, Cormack, but I can't comment on that, of course."

"You want me to go into Berlin? You're off your bloody rocker, Fitzgerald."

"Flight Lieutenant Woodward doesn't appear to agree with you. He volunteered for this operation without any hesitation whatsoever."

Cormack stared at him. "Woodward? You're lying."

"Oh, come now, Cormack. You must know him better than that."

Cormack said nothing; it was true. Woodward would indeed volunteer if he were asked, out of his sense of duty. And that was how they were hoping to make him fall in line, by using Woodward.... Cormack's lips tightened in fury.

"So Woodward will be going regardless of what you do, Cormack. Of course, it would be better if both of you went - you made a damned good team in Holland, but-"

He got no further. Moving with a speed that took the other man completely by surprise, Cormack crossed the room, grabbed Fitzgerald by his collar and pushed him back against the wall, the impact knocking the breath out of his victim. "Listen, Fitzgerald, you get Woodward taken off this mission, d'you hear me? Because if you don't, I'll bloody kill you, and that's a promise."

Fitzgerald held up his hands. "Not up to me, Cormack. It's not my decision."

"Come off it, Fitzgerald. If you've taken over Guthrie's job, then you're running this operation, so don't try any of that flannel

42

on me, right?"

"It's the truth, Cormack! This operation has been approved by 'C' himself, and I don't get any say in the selection of personnel at all!"

Cormack stared at him for several seconds, his eyes blazing then, finally, he let out his breath in a great sigh and stepped back from Fitzgerald. Slowly, he shook his head. "Then why the hell do you want Woodward and me? He won't last five minutes on his own and-"

"That's precisely why we want you there, Cormack. You're the professional, you see-"

"Come off it, will you? I wasn't born yesterday, you know. You've got dozens of SOE and MI6 operatives kicking about, several of whom would be only too willing to take it on. Why us? A pilot with only one operation behind enemy lines under his belt and an old has-been who's - who's lost his bloody nerve. Can't you do better than us, for God's sake? Just what is going on...." His voice tailed off as realisation dawned slowly on his face; he stared at Fitzgerald. "Oh, you bastard...." he said softly. "You bastard - that's what's going on, isn't it?"

As if in a trance, he walked over to the window and looked bleakly out at the quayside. When he spoke, Fitzgerald found himself moving nearer to hear what he said, so low was his voice. "We're expendable, aren't we? You've been told to mount an operation, but you think it's a non-starter, so you want someone like me. Someone with a proven track record but who won't be missed if he makes a balls-up." He swung back round towards Fitzgerald. "That's it, isn't it?"

"As I've said, Cormack, it isn't my decision."

"You agree with it, don't you? You really don't care what happens to us, just as long as you can run to your master like a good little boy and tell him you tried."

"If you want to put it that way then, frankly, no, I don't care, Cormack," Fitzgerald snapped, his urbanity finally cracking. "As far as I'm concerned, when you walked out of that hospital you chickened out - couldn't take it. There's a word for that in my book."

"There are several words in my book for people like you, Fitzgerald. Armchair warrior is the least derogatory of them - how many times have you been behind enemy lines? How many times have you been shot at? How many men have you shot or knifed or strangled - killed with your bare hands, in fact? Well, Fitzgerald?"

43

"That's irrelevant, Cormack, and you know it. I'm not here to justify myself to you."

"No, you're just here to strong-arm me into taking this mission by using Woodward. OK, so I chickened out - but he didn't. Does he deserve this treatment?"

"I suppose not, but you could say the same about most of the men who have died in this war. They did their duty and they died for it - do you think Woodward will do any less than that?"

"Look, the whole thing's pointless!" Cormack protested. "Even if I do agree to go, I'm way out of training. Is there any point in launching a completely hopeless mission?"

Fitzgerald nodded, as if conceding the point. "You look fit enough to me. However-" He went to the door and opened it. "Phillips! In here for a minute, please," he called. Through the window, Cormack saw the Snipe's driver emerge from the car; he had to be at least six foot four and broad with it. As Phillips came into the office, Fitzgerald gestured at Cormack. "Sort him out, Phillips, will you?"

Phillips nodded and began to move towards Cormack, eyeing him up. "Now hold on a minute," said Cormack, holding out his hands, a bemused expression on his face. "What's going-"

It was all over in less than two seconds. Cormack leaped forward, his left arm spearing forward in a straight-fingered blow to Phillips' throat; the other man gasped and clutched at his neck then Cormack's right fist was driven like a piston into his solar plexus. Phillips dropped like a stone; Cormack winced and massaged the fingers on his left hand as he looked down at the doubled up figure on the floor.

"Out of training, are you?" asked Fitzgerald, smiling faintly; evidently, he was totally unconcerned about Phillips. "I'd hate to see you in peak condition." The smile faded. "Seriously, Cormack, from what I've seen of your record, I think you've got as good a chance of anyone of pulling off this mission. But Woodward will go whether you do or not - that much is definite."

Cormack stared at Fitzgerald for several seconds. "So you're putting it all on to me, aren't you? If I don't go then Woodward's as good as dead."

"But if you do go...." Fitzgerald left the sentence hanging in the air.

Cormack went to the window again and looked out; like Fitzgerald, he ignored Phillips, who was painfully dragging himself up onto his knees, still fighting for breath. Outside, it was coming on to rain - was that an omen? He could see McTaggart

44

talking to Hughie Wilson, the foreman, underneath one of the giant cranes, while, beyond them, he could just recognise Davie Anderson and Willie McBride - he'd been drinking in the pub with them only last night. Yet already they seemed part of a past existence....

"All right," he sighed wearily. "Let's go."

"You'll do it, then?"

Cormack turned back to face Fitzgerald. "Do I have any bloody choice?"

"No," said Fitzgerald softly. "I don't really think you do."

THE FUEHRERBUNKER, BERLIN: FRIDAY, APRIL 20TH.

"Bormann! Come in here!"

With an effort, Bormann stifled a curse; he recognised that tone of Hitler's voice only too well these days. The Fuehrer had read or heard something - probably utterly trivial - that had upset him and he would be demanding that Bormann do something about it this very instant. And Bormann would have to do precisely that, even though the chances were that Hitler would have forgotten all about it by tomorrow. But if he remembered and Bormann had done nothing, there would be hell to pay....

Sighing, Bormann replaced the document he had been reading in his 'In' tray and went through to Hitler's quarters to find the Fuehrer standing next to the radio set, listening to it. Bormann recognised the programme within seconds - 'Soldatensender West' - and knew why Hitler had sent for him.

"They're still doing it!" Hitler exclaimed petulantly. "They're still telling me what everyone is up to - why hasn't Das Leck been found?"

"I'm told that every line of enquiry has been followed up, and-"

"And nothing has happened! My God, do I have to do everything myself around here? Isn't there anyone I can trust to do anything properly? You've had two and a half months to find this spy, Bormann - so where is he?"

"I'm afraid I can't tell you that as yet, my Fuehrer," Bormann confessed. "But we are narrowing down the list of suspects. We now know, for example, that it must be someone here in the Bunker-"

"You told me this last month, Bormann! Is this the best you can do?"

Bormann winced inwardly. Increasingly, Hitler's memory was failing him, but there were still times when he seemed to have total recall of any situation and evidently this was one of those occasions.... "I'm sorry, my Fuehrer. These things take time-"

"Time? We don't have time, Bormann. Within a matter of days, Berlin will have fallen and I shall be dead by my own hand, as befits one such as I, but how can I leave this world knowing there is a spy here, in this very Bunker?"

Bormann stared at Hitler incredulously; this was the first time the Fuehrer had given any indication of his intentions regarding his own fate, but before he had a chance to reply, Hitler went on:

"I cannot run the risk of my earthly body falling into the hands of the Allies and there is always that possibility if this spy remains at large. I want him found!" Except for the last sentence, the entire speech was delivered in a calm, almost reasonable voice; Hitler meant every word. "I suppose I'll have to take over myself as usual," he grumbled. "Who is heading the investigation? Kaltenbrunner, isn't it?"

"Well, officially, yes, but General Rattenhuber is in effective charge," Bormann replied. Rattenhuber was the Chief of Security in the Bunker and was one of Hitler's personal choices, but now, at the mention of his name, the Fuehrer shook his head.

"He's not capable of dealing with this - and he's had long enough anyway. I want someone else called in, someone who knows what he's doing." Hitler suddenly nodded sharply. "Mueller - he's the man. If the head of the Gestapo can't find Das Leck, I don't know who can."

Bormann nodded enthusiastically. "An excellent choice, my Fuehrer. I'll contact him immediately."

Rindt poured another drink and stared blearily at the bottle; it was half empty already. Ah, what the hell.... Half of Berlin was drinking itself into oblivion waiting for the Russians to arrive - why shouldn't he join in with them? After all, he had a better reason than most.... He muttered a curse under his breath and wandered vaguely over to the armchair, practically falling into it, yet without spilling a drop of schnapps. Getting quite good at that, he thought, giggling, before he raised the glass to his mouth and threw half of it back in a single gulp. With the careful concentration of a man who is not yet drunk but who is rapidly approaching that state, he placed the glass on the coffee table before patiently counting the rings on its surface, most of them now dried, legacies of previous binges. Shocking waste of good drink, he decided; there must be nearly half a glass's worth on that table....

The thought made him look around the living room, at the unwashed glasses, plates and empty bottles that littered it. The place was a mess, he told himself admonishingly, but it did not seem to matter. Nothing mattered these days....

Danzig had surrendered on March 30th after a siege that had lasted just eight days; and there had been no word of Inga, none at all. He did not know if she were dead or a prisoner, only that she had not managed to get out of the city before it had fallen. She could be lying in a mass grave somewhere, or she could be in a Russian prison camp - and he had no illusions how she would be treated there. Even if the Russians were no worse than the Germans themselves had been in the Ukraine, Inga would probably be better off dead.... That was the worst part, not knowing; there were days when he was utterly convinced that she was dead and he almost felt relieved and there were others when he was equally certain that she was a prisoner and his mind was filled with lurid, horrifying images of what she must be going through.... On the other hand, at least that would mean she was still alive and that there was a chance, no matter how remote, that he might see her again.... If only he knew, one way or the other!

But he didn't, and the only way that he could forget was to drink and that was no solution at all, of course. The most that it could do was to numb the feeling of helplessness, of despair that was always with him, but the respite was only temporary, because if he drank too much, he became maudlin and, more than once, he had broken down into uncontrollable tears. It became a precarious juggling act, almost, trying to drink just enough and no more, but he thought he had the hang of it now.... he ought to, he told himself bitterly; he was getting enough practice these days.

The doorbell rang, cutting through his meandering reverie; he frowned and looked at his watch, focusing with an effort on its hands. Ten thirty; who the devil could it be at this time of night? With an effort, he hauled himself out of his chair and tottered over to the flat door. Taking a deep breath to try and steady himself, he opened the door.

He had never seen the man who was standing on the landing outside; he was of medium height and stockily built, with thick-lensed spectacles perched on the end of his nose. "Major Rindt?"

"Yes?"

"My name is Hentschel. May I come in?"

"Er - do I know you?"

47

"We have never met, Major, but I really think you'd rather hear what I have to say inside."

"Oh, very well. Come in." Rindt stood aside to let Hentschel go past then closed the door. "I'm afraid it's in a bit of a mess," he mumbled apologetically.

"It's of no consequence," Hentschel said flatly; he reached the middle of the living room and turned to face Rindt, staring at him with a peculiar intensity.

"Well, what can I do for you?" asked Rindt.

"Major Rindt," said the man softly, "I know what's happened to your wife."

Rindt stared at Hentschel incredulously; he was suddenly stone cold sober. "What did you say?" he asked, forcing himself to remain calm.

"I said I know what has happened to your wife, Inga. And her mother, Frau Kottke."

"And what has happened to them?" asked Rindt, his eyes glittering.

"They are both safe and well - although in captivity. I am assured they are being well treated."

"You are assured - who the hell are you?"

"You don't expect me to answer that, do you?"

Now, Rindt's control snapped; he lunged forward and grabbed Hentschel by his jacket lapel. "Oh, but I do. Who the hell are you?" he hissed venomously.

Hentschel appeared quite unperturbed. "Lay a finger on me, Rindt, and your wife will be dead within forty-eight hours. You have my word on that."

"Bloody hell...." Rindt said as realisation struck him. "You're working for the Russians," he said flatly.

"Took you long enough to work that out," Hentschel sneered. "Although I suppose you do have other things on your mind."

Rindt took a deep breath, consciously forcing himself to relax before he released Hentschel. "Where is she, then?"

"Still in Danzig."

"How do I know you're telling me the truth?"

"You don't," said Hentschel bluntly. He reached into his pocket and took something out. "You recognise this?" He handed it to Rindt.

It was a brooch that he had given her for her birthday two years before; he nodded slowly, feeling a bewildering mixture of relief and despair - relief that she was alive, despair because he knew why Hentschel had come to see him.... "It's hers," he said heavily. "But that's still no guarantee that she's alive, is it?"

"No," Hentschel agreed. "But can you take that chance?"

Again, Rindt stared at the brooch, remembering how she had laughed delightedly when he had given it to her.... and how she had thanked him later that night in bed. Hentschel was right, of course; he had to believe that she was still alive, which meant that he was completely in the Russian agent's power. It was now obvious why Hentschel had come; Rindt was going to have to choose between his country and his wife.... He sighed bitterly. "What do you want from me?" There had been no choice, really.

Hentschel nodded in acknowledgment. "Within the next day or so, you will be summoned by General Mueller and asked to act as his assistant in an investigation that he will be carrying out."

"Gestapo Mueller?" asked Rindt, startled.

"Naturally," Hentschel replied, a burr of irritation in his voice. "You will assist him in his enquiries to the best of your abilities, but you will of course be reporting the progress of the investigation to me at this number." He reached inside his coat and produced a slip of paper. "Memorise it and destroy it."

Rindt stared at the scrap of paper, trying to marshal his thoughts. "And if I do all this?"

"I would have thought that was obvious. Do as you are instructed and you will see your wife again. Fail to do so and you won't - it's as simple as that."

"I see," said Rindt sombrely, taking the slip of paper. "How often do I contact you?"

"Normally every twenty four hours, but if anything - ah - extraordinary develops then I want to know immediately, no matter what time of the day or night it is."

Rindt stared at him, puzzled. "What do you mean by extraordinary?"

"You'll know what I mean once Mueller has outlined the details of the investigation," Hentschel assured him cryptically.

Rindt waited for him to add to this, but once it was evident that Hentschel had said all he intended to, he asked, "How safe will the line be?"

"Perfectly safe, I assure you. You can be as open as you wish."

Rindt raised his eyebrows at this, but made no comment. Hentschel continued:

"You will be given further instructions if we think it necessary. You will of course carry them out to the letter."

"All right, all right - I know what I'm supposed to do," Rindt muttered peevishly. "You don't have to rub it in." His eyes met Hentschel's and the latter was struck by the naked malevolence in them; they seemed to say, one day, Hentschel, one day, you'll regret this.... With an evident effort, Rindt looked away. "How long?" he asked indistinctly.

"What do you mean, how long?"

"Before I see her."

Hentschel shrugged. "It's not up to me, but I would estimate within the next two weeks - if things go as planned."

"Two weeks," Rindt murmured. "I wish I could believe that.... but somehow, I can't."

"But what choice do you have?"

"None at all." Rindt shook his head. "None at all."

CHAPTER 4.

LONDON: SATURDAY, APRIL 21ST.

It was exactly ten o'clock when Cormack was shown into Fitzgerald's office overlooking Trafalgar Square. As he entered, a tall, brown haired man in RAF uniform leaped out of his seat in front of the large desk and strode across the carpet towards him, his features creased in a broad smile. "Alan! Good to see you."

"And you, Tony." They shook hands, each man thoughtfully appraising the other.

"You look well," Woodward said. "Pretty fit and healthy, eh?"

"I'm leading a virtuous life these days."

"So I heard."

Fitzgerald cleared his throat to attract their attention and gestured at their seats. "If we might begin, gentlemen...?" He waited until they were seated then began the briefing by passing them a large photograph. Cormack and Woodward stared at the face for several seconds, Woodward with increasing perplexity.

"She looks familiar," he commented doubtfully.

"Indeed she is - to you, anyway. You knew her as Marianne Driscoll before the war, Flight Lieutenant."

"Good Lord, so it is."

"Her name is Marianne Kovacs nowadays, although we generally refer to her by her codename - 'Emerald'."

"She's an agent, then?" asked Cormack, already knowing the answer.

"Indeed. In fact, she is our main source of information inside Berlin. For the past eight months, almost, she has been supplying us with a virtually continuous flow of information from inside Hitler's headquarters itself."

"And you want us to get her out," said Woodward bluntly.

Fitzgerald seemed taken aback by this brusque interruption, as though he might have expected it from Cormack but not from Woodward. "Er - quite."

"Who is she?" asked Cormack again.

Fitzgerald leaned back in his chair and steepled his fingers, clearly marshalling his thoughts. "Firstly, she's Irish. Born in

Dublin thirty-one years ago of an Irish father and English mother. Her father is a diplomat and was on the Embassy staff in Budapest from 1938 to 1941. During that time, Marianne met and married Janos Kovacs - in 1938 to be precise. What they call a whirlwind romance, apparently. In 1941, as we were on the verge of breaking off relations with Hungary and closing down our embassy in Budapest, she came to our man there and offered to work for us. We gratefully accepted, of course."

"Of course," Cormack echoed ironically; Fitzgerald glanced sharply at him before continuing.

"In 1943, Kovacs was transferred to the Hungarian Embassy in Berlin and Emerald went with him. We managed to install a contact for her in the Irish Embassy there and she began to pass information to us almost immediately.

"At first, it was nothing very exciting, mostly titbits of diplomatic gossip that she picked up at receptions and so on. Plus pillow talk from her liaisons."

"I thought you said she was married," said Cormack mildly.

"It had become a marriage of convenience. She and Kovacs appeared together at diplomatic functions but tended to go their separate ways in private. I imagine both were discreet in their affairs.

"However, in 1944, as I'm sure you both know, there was a breakdown in relations between the Nazis and the Hungarians. Kovacs was interned and placed under detention, which left Emerald on her own in Berlin. We thought we were going to have to write her off, but she rose to the occasion, as it were, by managing to get a job as a translator in Goebbels' Propaganda Ministry, working on their 'Germany Calling' programme. I think there's little doubt what she had to do to get that job, but she didn't stay with Goebbels for very long. Instead, she became the mistress of SS-General Hermann Fegelein."

"Who the hell's he, when he's at home?" asked Cormack.

"The liaison officer between Himmler and Hitler. In other words, he has access to both of them and, apparently, he likes to talk about what they're doing. He's one of Hitler's lackeys, really, more of a glorified messenger boy than anything else, but he's inside Hitler's HQ virtually every day. He's very much part of Hitler's circle, you see."

"So Emerald's been passing on information from Hitler's HQ?"

"Yes. It's mostly gossip and scandal, but it's all useful - we use the juicier bits in our own propaganda broadcasts."

"And now she wants to leave Berlin?"

"Exactly. She doesn't want to fall into the hands of the Russians."

"Why doesn't she go to the Irish Embassy for help?"

Fitzgerald shook his head. "She renounced her Irish citizenship when they went to Berlin. We didn't want any overt connection between her and the Irish Embassy so that we could protect our communication link."

"I see." Cormack looked at Fitzgerald. "So why this sudden panic to get her out? Why hasn't she been brought out before now?"

Fitzgerald looked abashed. "It was considered to be not worth the risk."

"Bloody typical," said Cormack disgustedly. "She's been risking her life for years for you lot and you're not even prepared to help her - until now, when it's probably too late. So why the last minute change of heart?"

"She claims to have obtained information that would certainly justify a rescue attempt - if she has it."

"Which is why you're fielding your reserve team," said Cormack bitterly. "You think she's lying but just in case.... Thank you for nothing, Fitzgerald."

"What is this information?" asked Woodward quietly.

Fitzgerald hesitated a moment then shrugged. "Details of escape routes that the Nazis are intending to use to escape from Germany when the war's over. Or even before then."

"Right," said Cormack briskly. "We know who and we know why. What about how? How are we going to get her out?"

Fitzgerald nodded at Woodward. "This is where you come in, Flight Lieutenant, at least for the access phase. We captured a fair number of Jerry aircraft in the Low Countries and the plan is for you two to use one of them to fly into Germany. If you can find a suitable landing space, fine, but failing that, you can simply bale out."

Cormack glanced at Woodward and something about the pilot's expression told him that he had his own ideas about that, but was keeping quiet about them for the time being. Fair enough, thought Cormack; he's the expert....

"Once there," Fitzgerald continued, "You make your way into Berlin. I'm afraid you'll probably have to cross enemy lines to do that. I should stress at this juncture that the Russians are not to be considered as allies in this operation.

"Once you have reached the centre of Berlin, you are to contact our agent in the Irish Embassy and he will tell you how to get in touch with Emerald. From then on, it will be up to you, Cormack, how you get out of Berlin. Perhaps stealing a plane would be your best bet - again." He permitted himself a brief smile.

"Very funny. Just because we managed it once doesn't mean we can do it a second time. Will we be able to arrange a pick-up by plane?"

"Of course. We'll have one on standby and we'll arrange several alternative locations."

Cormack nodded. "How long do we have? I mean, I'm pretty rusty now - I'd like a few days down at Bisley to sharpen up."

"I'm afraid we're up against a pretty tight time limit, Cormack. The latest Intelligence reports suggest that Berlin will have surrendered within the next ten days or so. I want you two to be in Berlin within five days."

"Oh great," Cormack muttered. "Just great." He looked sombrely at Fitzgerald. "And when do I do the walking on water bit?"

BERLIN: SATURDAY, APRIL 21ST.

"Major Rindt reporting as ordered, Herr General," Rindt said formally as he came to attention and saluted.

Heinrich Mueller, the head of the Gestapo, did not rise from his seat but simply gave the salute a cursory acknowledgment and pointed at the empty chair behind the desk. "Sit down, Major." As Rindt did so, Mueller studied him carefully, but if he noticed Rindt's gaunt, emaciated features or the haunted expression in his sunken eyes, he made no comment. "You're probably wondering why I sent for you, Major Rindt."

"Indeed, Herr General."

"I want you to act as my assistant in an investigation I have initiated on the orders of Reichsleiter Bormann and General Kaltenbrunner. It is a top priority investigation and you will be working directly under my orders. You will report to me and to me alone - is that clear?"

"Perfectly, Herr General."

"Good. Now the investigation itself," said Mueller. He looked at Rindt quizzically and asked, "Tell me - how often do you listen to 'Soldatensender West', Major?"

Rindt did not seem at all surprised by the unexpected question. "I don't listen at all nowadays, Herr General."

"But you know what I'm talking about?"

Rindt nodded. "Yes, I do, Herr General."

"What is your opinion of it?" Mueller persisted.

Rindt forced himself to respond; he had to take part in this investigation, like it or not and he could not afford to antagonise Mueller. "It appears to be remarkably well-informed as far as I can gather."

Mueller nodded emphatically. "Indeed it is, Major. So well informed, in fact, that the BBC must be receiving its information from someone inside the Fuehrerbunker itself." He looked expectantly at Rindt, who managed to look suitably impressed while he was wondering what difference such a breach of security could possibly make now the war was almost over. "Our job is to find this source," Mueller continued. "'Das Leck' is how we shall refer to him."

"Or her," Rindt murmured.

"Or her," Mueller agreed irritably.

"Why are you so certain the leak is inside the Bunker itself?"

"The nature of the information being used by the BBC. The material relating to the Bunker is too accurate for it to be someone on the outside. In other words, Das Leck is probably someone very close to the Fuehrer himself. What concerns us most, of course, is not so much the gossip that Das Leck is passing on, but that we don't know what other information he might be giving them. Every member of the Bunker staff will therefore have to be investigated, which is why I have chosen you to assist me, Rindt. Quite apart from your record to date, which I have to say is very impressive, there is also the consideration that you are an outsider. You do not know any of the Bunker personnel and so you will be able to be completely objective about the people you are investigating. To be perfectly frank, that is not something I can say about many of my subordinates."

Rindt nodded; he had been wondering why Mueller had chosen him.

"As my assistant, you will need a fair amount of leverage to open various doors in our enquiries and so I am promoting you to Colonel - that will give you sufficient rank to deal with most situations. If you run into any trouble, simply refer the matter to me. Is that clear?"

"Perfectly clear, Herr General."

"Good." Mueller opened his top desk drawer and took out a bulky file which he passed over to Rindt. "That contains a list of all the Bunker personnel as well as dossiers on each of them. Also included are the names of people who are such regular visitors to the Bunker that they could also be Das Leck. I think I hardly need tell you that you will have to be somewhat discreet in your enquiries."

Opening the file, Rindt saw what Mueller meant; the first names on the lists included people like Bormann, Goebbels, Himmler, Goering and Speer. "How many men will we have available, Herr General?"

"None," said Mueller flatly. "Although you can have access to any records or dossiers you please, only the two of us are to know the true purpose of this investigation."

Rindt ran his eyes down the list, which ran to over two hundred names. "How long do we have?" he asked.

"Until the Russians get here. A fortnight at the most, I would say."

Rindt shook his head despairingly. "Then we'd better start by making this list shorter if we can, Herr General."

"My thoughts exactly, Major - I'm sorry, Colonel. We'd better begin at once."

TUESDAY, APRIL 24TH.

Marianne stood at the window, staring down at the street below, but without taking in any of the scene; her thoughts were racing. Five days had now passed since she had sent her last message off to London and, so far, there had been no reply. Admittedly, there had not really been time for London to have done anything yet, but if they did not act soon, it would be too late. Russian tanks were already in the southern suburbs of Berlin, in Marienfelde and Lankwitz, while units of the Soviet Army had penetrated to the west of the city. Within days, Berlin would be completely surrounded, thereby making any escape from the city doubly difficult. Nor was that the only threat she faced, of course; she still had no way of knowing how the Gestapo's investigation into Schuller's death was progressing. She closed her eyes momentarily, remembering, then forced herself to evaluate the situation rationally. If they knew she had killed Schuller, they would have arrested her by now, but she had no way of knowing if anyone had seen him following her. Yet another reason to leave Berlin as soon as possible - but how?

The only other alternative to London providing help was Fegelein. He had been trying to make arrangements for them to leave ever since he had been left out of Operation Seraglio, but so far had met with little success; even if he did make any progress, Marianne knew that he would probably bungle the whole escape. To put it bluntly, Fegelein was not very bright; he owed his present position more to an animal cunning and a willingness to ingratiate himself with his superiors than to any real ability. Marianne was fairly certain that the difficulties in organising their escape were largely caused by the fact that nobody outside of the Bunker had any time for Fegelein at all; he simply wasn't important enough, or influential enough, for anyone to do him favours. Like it or not, however, it was becoming increasingly likely that she was going to have to cast in her lot with him....

Impatiently, she turned away from the window, went over to the cocktail cabinet and poured herself a drink. She raised the glass to her lips then paused; she had been about to down it in a single gulp and that would not do at all. Drinking would not solve anything although, apparently, that was the fashionable thing to do in the Bunker these days. Fegelein had described the sights he had seen in the officers' quarters with barely concealed relish. It was as if they were having one last epic spree of drink and sex before their world collapsed around them. Well, she decided, swilling the cognac gently around the glass, she was not going to go out the same way. If the worst came to the worst, and both London and Fegelein let her down, then she would damn well leave Berlin on her own, one way or another.

In the end, she mused, the only person you can really trust is yourself....

ALDERSHOT, ENGLAND: 2100 HOURS.

"Name?"
"Piet Vandamm."
"Age?"
"Twenty-seven."
"Date of birth?"
"March 14th, 1918."
"Place of birth?"
"Eindhoven."
"Rank in the Dutch Army?"
"Corporal."
"When and where were you captured?"
"May 10th, 1940, near Utrecht."
"When did you enlist in the Waffen-SS?"

"November 17th, 1940."

"Present rank?"

"Sergeant."

"Any brothers or sisters?"

"Yes. Two sisters."

"Names?"

"Helda and - and Marta."

Cormack sighed and threw the typed sheets on to the desk. "Now come on, Tony - you can't hesitate over your own sister's name, for God's sake. They'll be on to that like a shot."

"Sorry, Alan. I'll have another go at it."

"You do that. You've got to be word perfect on your cover - those bastards over there won't be messing about." He stood up and began to walk idly around the Nissen hut to stretch his legs; they had been sitting down for the last hour or more, running through their cover stories.

"I know that," said Woodward, a trifle huffily. "But let's face it, Alan, we haven't exactly been given an awful lot of time to get everything ready, have we?"

"No, we haven't," Cormack agreed slowly. "Which means we'll have to make damn certain we don't make any slip ups."

"By 'we', you really mean me, don't you?" Woodward asked, smiling faintly.

"Actually, I don't, Tony," said Cormack softly. "I'm more than a bit rusty myself."

Woodward looked thoughtfully at him for several seconds then asked hesitantly, "Alan?"

"Yes?"

"Look, I know it's none of my business, but-" he paused again.

"But what?" Cormack prompted him.

"Why did you do it? Walk out of the hospital? They were going to pin a medal on you, you know, before that."

"What, to tell everyone how big a hero I was?" Cormack asked bitterly. "And how true would that have been? And as for why I walked out - hell, you saw the state I was in when we landed. Do you think I could face being sent back again?" He wandered aimlessly around, looking at the floor and said, almost inaudibly, "I'd just had enough, Tony. I wanted out. I suppose they called it lack of moral fibre - and they're probably right. I did chicken out, when it comes right down to it."

"Don't be so bloody stupid, Alan. Without you the entire operation would have been a disaster."

"How else could you describe it?" asked Cormack heatedly.

"Five people dead, a whole network wiped out, and for what? A piece of equipment that's probably outdated by now. Just so that bastard Cathcart could score points off the SOE."

"Now you know that's not true. They needed that radar and you know it."

"They might have done, but did anyone stop to think about the price that was being paid for it?" He walked morosely over to the stove in the corner, picked up its poker and flipped open the lid. As he poked the flames inside he went on quietly, "All right, Tony, I know you're right. As far as the top brass were concerned, it was worth the sacrifice. But the point is, if you're the poor sod out there trying to carry out the operation and you begin to question what you're doing then you've had it. You can't afford the time for doubts.... or to become involved. And I did. Once that happens, you might as well jack it in."

Woodward stared at him. "If you feel like that, Alan, then what are you doing here?"

Cormack smiled crookedly. "That's a bloody good question, Tony. Maybe I'll tell you the answer some day." Suddenly, unexpectedly, he chuckled. "Maybe I just want to rescue the damsel in distress. She certainly looks the part, judging by the photos. Is she as gorgeous in the flesh, Tony?"

"I don't know about in the flesh," Woodward replied, grinning. "I never knew her that well, but yes, she is rather attractive, I must say."

"How come you know her?"

"I was at Winchester with her brother. I spent the summer of '37, it must have been, visiting them and I have to say that I was quite smitten with her." He grinned in self-mockery. "Alas, it was a case of unrequited love - she was four years older than me, you see."

"A shocking barrier to true love."

"Exactly. And she was going out with someone else, anyway. He ditched her the following year."

"The unspeakable cad."

Woodward grinned. "And I imagine he cheated at cards as well." His face grew more serious and thoughtful. "Although, if he hadn't thrown her over, she might not have married Kovacs. In the which case, we wouldn't have to be rescuing her, would we?"

"No," said Cormack slowly. "We wouldn't. I suppose that bloke's got a lot to answer for, one way or another-" He broke off as the telephone on the table rang. "Sounds ominous," he commented to Woodward as he picked up the receiver. "Hallo, Cormack here. Yes, go ahead.... yes, speaking...."

Woodward saw Cormack's lips tighten as he listened to the voice on the other end of the line then, slowly, Cormack replaced the receiver. He looked bleakly at Woodward.

"That was Fitzgerald. They want us back in London first thing tomorrow."

"I thought we were supposed to be having four days here," Woodward protested.

"So did I," Cormack replied grimly. "But we're not, apparently. At a guess, I'd say we are going to be sent in either tomorrow or the day after."

"Bloody hell," Woodward breathed, looking at the sheets of paper on the table. "In that case, I'd better get all this learned, hadn't I?"

CHAPTER 5.

NORTHERN GERMANY: 0100 HOURS, FRIDAY APRIL 27th

Cormack stood at the window, looking out at the darkened airfield then glanced at his watch - yet again. What the hell was keeping them? They ought to have been on their way fifteen minutes ago, but there was still no sign of the bloody plane .... "What the hell is going on?" he demanded impatiently.

"Relax, Alan," said Woodward's voice from behind him; without turning round, Cormack knew the other man would be leaning back in his chair at an impossible angle with his feet resting on the trestle table, the picture of relaxation, even down to the closed eyes. "If it all falls through, then we won't be able to go, will we - and would that be so much of a disaster?"

Despite his tension, Cormack found himself grinning. Woodward was absolutely right, of course; he could hardly pretend that he would be heartbroken if the whole thing were to be called off because of some last minute hitch, but if they were going, then he wanted to be off. Anything rather than this hanging about, kicking their heels....

Was that in case he changed his mind? he asked himself, scathingly. Too bloody right .... "Look, Tony, we should be on our way by now and the bloody plane isn't even here yet."

"Alan," Woodward said firmly. "We've only got two hundred miles to go - say forty-five minutes flying time, so it doesn't really matter if we're a bit late, does it?"

"No, I don't suppose it does," Cormack agreed heavily. He was annoyed with himself. Talk about letting Woodward see he was nervous - and they hadn't taken off yet. It was the waiting, he reasoned; if all had proceeded according to schedule and they had taken off immediately after the flight briefing, as planned, then he'd have been all right. Or so he told himself. But what if his initial reaction to Fitzgerald had been right - what if his nerve really had gone? Was he going to be up to this, after all?

And if he wasn't, then did he have the guts to pull out of it?

The door behind him suddenly opened and the tall Flight Lieutenant who had given Woodward the briefing came in. "Right, chaps," he said in the clipped Oxbridge accent that was already grating on Cormack's nerves. "Ready to go now. Sorry about the delay."

"What the hell caused it?" snapped Cormack.

"Engine trouble. We've got a replacement plane all sorted out, though. If you'll follow me?"

Cormack glanced at Woodward, who shrugged as he stood up; the last minute replacement was clearly of no consequence as far as he was concerned. Biting off the angry comment that had been on his lips, Cormack picked up the duffel bag that was lying on the table and followed the officer outside.

As they walked across the tarmac towards a large hangar a hundred yards or so away, Woodward suddenly turned to the officer and asked, "When did the replacement plane arrive? I didn't hear it coming in."

"Used one of the crates we had here anyway. Got plenty to spare you know."

"But that means-" Woodward broke off suddenly and glanced almost guiltily over at Cormack, who frowned at the evident consternation on the pilot's face; what had upset Woodward? "It's been properly equipped?" Woodward went on hurriedly.

"Of course. That's what caused the delay - fitting in the explosive charges."

"So where is it?" asked Cormack; there was no sign of the plane at all.

"Just round the side of the hangar. Just there, in fact," the Flight Lieutenant added, as the aircraft came into view.

Cormack came to an abrupt halt, a stunned expression on his face as he stared at the familiar two-engined silhouette. Too damned familiar.... "I thought we were supposed to be getting an Me110," he said flatly. "That's a bloody Ju88."

"As I said, the 110 developed engine trouble, so we used this one instead. They're very similar, after all. I gather you've flown one of these before, Woodward?"

"Yes, I have," Woodward replied, but he was watching Cormack intently, seeing the play of emotions on the other man's face.

"Then it should be no problem at all, should it?" the officer said, oblivious to Comack's reaction. "In fact, it's one of the later ones - higher speed, more manoeuvrable, the lot-"

Woodward barely heard him; his eyes were still fixed on Cormack who was staring at the aircraft, a mixture of fear and loathing on his face. This was why Woodward had specifically asked for the Me110 - anything but a Ju88 in fact - knowing that the sight of the Junkers aircraft would trigger off memories that Cormack would rather leave undisturbed....

Cormack suddenly took a deep breath and tore his eyes away from the plane. "OK by you, Tony?" he asked, his voice brisk, businesslike.

"No problem," Woodward replied.

"Then let's stop hanging about here, shall we? We haven't got all night." He began to walk rapidly towards the aircraft.

The Flight Lieutenant looked at his retreating back, a frown on his face. "Is he all right? Seems a bit edgy to me."

"So would you be if you were going where we are," Woodward snapped. "But you're not, are you?" He spun on his heel and went after Cormack, ignoring the sudden flash of resentment on the officer's face.

By the time Woodward reached the plane, Cormack was already pulling himself up through the cockpit hatch in the underside of the fuselage; Wodward clambered up the ladder after him and eased himself into the pilot's seat as the still indignant Flight Lieutenant removed the ladder. Cormack closed the hatch with an apparently nonchalant wave to the RAF officer then strapped himself into the observer's seat.

"You're sure this plane's OK?" he asked, seeing Woodward begin his pre-flight check; Woodward nodded abstractedly.

"It's basically the same as–" he broke off, glancing apologetically at Cormack. "As the one we came back in," he finished. "I can fly it - don't worry about that."

"Fair enough." Cormack subsided into silence and tried to focus his attention on Woodward as he ran through the seemingly interminable series of checks, muttering intonations under his breath. There was a look of complete concentration on Woodward's face and Cormack knew that, for the next few minutes at least, the outside world had ceased to exist for him.

Cormack wished he could say the same because the sight of the Ju88 had unnerved him more than he would have believed possible. Which was stupid, of course. It was only a bloody machine, when all was said and done - it wasn't as though he were being asked to use the same plane that had flown them out of Holland two years before, yet, despite this, he could not help feeling that this was, in some way, a bad omen. He had had to pay an appalling personal price to bring that other Ju88 back and he had never wanted to see another one in his life - yet now he was having to fly in one of the damned things again....

Suddenly, the starboard engine burst into life, startling him out of his reverie; moments later, Woodward started the port engine. He grinned across at Cormack, then spoke into the radio.

"Snowdrop to Tower. Pre-flight checks completed. Am now taxing to the runway."

"Roger, Snowdrop."

As the aircraft began to move off, Cormack realised that his heart was racing and that he was breathing rapidly; with a conscious effort, he closed his eyes and forced himself to relax. No good asking yourself what you're doing here, he told himself, because it's too bloody late to pull out now. You're committed, old son, so just get on with it.

He opened his eyes as the plane turned at the end of the runway and came to a halt. Woodward was systematically checking the instruments a second time, that look of utter absorption on his face again, the expression of a man in his own element. With a sudden flash of insight, Cormack realised that Woodward had no doubt of his own ability to fly them into the target zone - but what about after that, when the operation became Cormack's responsibility?

Jesus wept, he was going to pieces - he had to get a grip on himself!

"Snowdrop to Tower. Permission to take off?"

"Tower to Snowdrop.
 Go ahead."

Woodward reached out for the throttle levers but then hesitated; he looked across at Cormack in an unspoken question.

Cormack's voice was absolutely steady as he said quietly, "OK, Tony. Let's go."

0200 HOURS.

"Is that it?" asked Cormack suddenly, pointing through the perspex of the Ju88's cockpit canopy at the faint glow in the distance, dead ahead. "Berlin?"

"It had better be," said Woodward laconically. "If it isn't, we're off course."

Cormack shook his head in reluctant admiration. This was the first time he had actually seen Woodward flying an aircraft - on the way back from Holland, he had been in the fuselage section of the plane, separated from the cockpit by the fuel tanks - and he was impressed. Woodward's eyes were flickering constantly from the instrument panel to the map fastened to his thigh then in a rapid all round scan of the sky and finally back to the instruments. Gone was the careless bravado that had been Cormack's first impression of him all that time ago; it had been replaced by a cold, professional expertise. They had said that he was one of the

64

best pilots around and they had not been exaggerating.

"How far now?"

"Thirty miles - no more than that."

Cormack executed a rapid calculation. "About four minutes to go, then?"

"Yes. About time for you to do your stuff."

"Right." Cormack flicked his throat microphone over to transmit and spoke in fluent, rapid German. "Adler One to Brandenburg Control. Come in please, Brandenburg."

There was a delay of several seconds before he heard a voice in the headphones. "Brandenburg Control to Adler One. Go ahead."

"Request permission to land on the East-West Axis."

"State your flight origin, authorisation and purpose of flight, please."

"Flensburg. Authorisation Jagd four two. Carrying urgent despatches from Admiral Doenitz to the Fuehrer."

"One moment, please, Adler One. State your present position."

"On an open band? Don't be ridiculous. Landing in approximately five minutes."

"Adler One, we have no record of your flight plan or of your authorisation."

"Dammit, you fool, that's not my fault! Just get those landing lights organised and we'll sort it out when I get down!"

"I'm sorry, Adler One, but without the proper authorisation I cannot give you landing clearance."

"Who am I talking to?" snapped Cormack. "Your name?"

"I can't tell you that, Adler One - you know that."

"Well, for your information, this is Colonel Beitzen speaking and I am carrying vital documents for the Fuehrer's personal attention. The fact that you have no record of my authorisation or flight plan is probably because we have been out of communication with Berlin more or less continuously for the last two days - which is why I've been sent here with these despatches. Now I am not going to spend the next hour stooging around to be shot at by Ivan fighters while you get yourselves sorted out down there. So get those lights on, or I'll have you court-martialled! Is that clear?"

"We're over the outskirts now," murmured Woodward. "I've begun reducing height."

Cormack stared at the darkness ahead, willing the lights to come on. If they didn't, then it would be virtually impossible for Woodward to pick out the East-West Axis, the wide avenue that ran dead straight through the centre of Berlin, and which had been pressed into service as a landing strip now that Tempelhof

65

had been captured by the Russians. If the lights were not switched on, they might as well go home, beaten before they'd even started....

Suddenly, the Ju88 lurched to one side as Woodward wrenched at the control column, sending the aircraft into a steep bank to port. He opened up the throttles as he pushed the column forward and it was only then that Cormack saw the brightly lit tracer shells flashing past above them. Twisting round in his seat, he saw the gun flashes of a fighter behind them as it heeled over and came down after them.

Woodward had put the Ju88 into a tight corkscrew dive that was sending them plunging towards the city below, but the Russian fighter was following them down remorselessly, matching their turn and closing in on them at the same time.... Abruptly, Woodward yanked the stick to starboard, reversing the turn, still keeping the nose down in a headlong dive; Cormack stared horrified at the altimeter as the needle dipped inexorably towards zero. Woodward was going to fly them into the ground, for God's sake!

Then Woodward dragged the column back and the Ju88 levelled out; Cormack caught a glimpse of a grey ribbon of water that hurtled past, apparently only a few feet beneath them then the aircraft seemed to be flying along a narrow canyon, with buildings on both sides. Cormack glanced behind them then the Russian opened fire again from somewhere above them as Woodward hurled the aircraft first to one side then the other. The Ju88 shuddered as the tracer shells tore into the port wing and, within seconds, the port engine was ablaze, but Woodward did not seem to notice.

"There they are," he said calmly. Looking ahead, Cormack saw the two parallel bands of light: the East-West Axis. And there were the two huge Flak Towers that guarded the western end of the runway, sending delicate threads of tracer fire up at the fighter behind them.

"Undercarriage down," Woodward announced, with that same inhuman calm as the towers flashed past on each side. Cormack looked back a last time, to see the Russian wheeling away in a frantic bid to escape the anti-aircraft fire. It seemed to stagger under the impact of the shells and exploded with an eye-searing flash.

"Hold on," said Woodward. No sooner had he spoken than Cormack felt the bump of the wheels hitting the ground and he turned back to see the huge structure of the Brandenburg Gate coming straight at them. They were going to smash squarely into its base.... Woodward glanced once at the airspeed indicator and pulled back on a lever to his left. The aircraft seemed to sink down into the roadway and there was a sudden deafening screech of tortured metal as the aircraft slammed into the tarmac. Dimly, Cormack realised that Woodward had pulled up the undercarriage in a last ditch attempt to bring them to a halt in time. The Ju88 began to slew round to one side, but they were slowing, slowing....

Even before they had come to a stop, less than fifty yards from the Gate, Cormack had unfastened his safety harness and was sliding back the cockpit canopy. He bent forward and found the explosive device that was clamped to the side of his seat and armed it with a flick of its switch; Woodward did the same on his side as Cormack grabbed the suitcase that contained the radio.

Pushing it before him, Cormack scrambled out of the cockpit and dropped down to the road with Woodward only moments behind him; he had a duffel bag slung over his shoulder. "This way!" Cormack yelled and they sprinted over to the right, towards the trees that lined both sides of the avenue, diving flat as the charges detonated, the initial explosions being followed by a larger concussion as the fuel tanks went up, the flames leaping high into the darkness. Cormack and Woodward jumped to their feet and ran into the shadows cast by the trees; only then did they come to a halt and look back at the blazing aircraft.

"Well," said Cormack, his breath coming in great panting gasps. "We're here."

1200 HOURS.

Cormack paused in the doorway and looked around the smoky interior of the bierkeller, his haughty, condescending expression matching the uniform that he wore, that of an SS-Colonel. Several looks were directed towards him, almost all of them changing instantly to fearful respect, especially when they saw the coveted Knight's Cross at his throat. The bar was dimly-lit and crowded, with a small stage at the far end, where a bored looking stripper was going through her routine. Cormack was gripped by a sense of unreality at the scene before him; the city was surrounded by Russians - indeed, they were less than three miles from this very spot - and yet it was business as usual here. A second, longer look, however, revealed the desperation beneath the veneer of relaxed enjoyment. The conversation was a little too loud, the laughter a little too forced; over in the corner, a girl with too much make up was sobbing quietly while the man with her was trying to focus bleary eyes on the stripper.

Cormack strode over to the nearest table, where a young SS-Lieutenant and a woman were sitting; she looked at least fifteen years older than the officer. "I'd like to sit at this table," Cormack said quietly, dusting off the spare chair with his gloves. "By myself," he added.

"Of course, Herr Colonel. Of course." Hastily, the Lieutenant scrambled to his feet, but the woman remained where she was, staring speculatively up at Cormack.

"I said by myself," said Cormack, the merest hint of an edge in his voice; the woman shrugged and followed her companion over to an adjacent table.

A waiter hurried over. "A drink, Herr Colonel?"

"Thank you, yes. A cognac - and a real one, if you please. Also, I'd like to talk to Dominique, if I may."

"Of course, Herr Colonel. You show excellent taste, if I may say so."

"Say what you damned well please, but get that drink while you're doing it," Cormack snapped; the waiter scurried off.

A minute or so later, a petite brunette wearing a clinging red dress came into the bar through a side door and was directed to Cormack's table by the waiter. "You asked to talk to me, m'sieu?" she said in a pronounced French accent.

"I did, Dominique - but is there somewhere we can talk more privately?" He gave her a knowing glance.

"Well, I do have a room upstairs, m'sieu, but...." her voice trailed off.

Cormack reached into his pocket and produced a wad of banknotes. "Or I have cigarettes, if you prefer."

"Of course, m'sieu. If you'd care to follow me?"

The room was up a flight of stairs and was functional rather than decorative; there was a single bed, a battered dressing table and chair and a curtained alcove that, he surmised, contained a bidet. The girl began to unfasten her dress the moment she had closed the door.

"One moment," Cormack said in a low voice, speaking in French. "Cousin Jules sends his best regards and asks to be remembered to Yvette."

At once, her face lost its artificial sensuality and became brisk and businesslike. "Of course, m'sieu." She went over to the dressing table and opened the top drawer, taking out an envelope which she gave to Cormack. He nodded and rapidly opened it to find a single sheet of paper inside, which had been folded in half. There was an address written on it - 10/11 Bleibtreustrasse - and a telephone number.

"Do you have a lighter?" he asked the girl.

"Yes." She took one from her handbag and gave it to him. Carefully, he read the information once more, before he set fire to the paper and dropped it into an ashtray.

The girl had watched all this in silence, but now she spoke. "Do you have any message for cousin Pierre?"

"Yes. Tell him the present was just what I wanted."

The girl nodded. "I will, m'sieu."

Cormack nodded in turn and headed for the door; as he opened it, she called out:

"Good luck."

He paused in the doorway and looked back at her. "Thanks," he replied. "I think I'm going to need it."

GESTAPO HEADQUARTERS: 1230 HOURS.

Rindt was patiently reading through the file on Major Otto Guensche, Hitler's adjutant, wondering whether Guensche's known liking for the night life of Berlin made him a potential security risk when he heard a knock on the door. "Come in," he called, mentally breathing a sigh of relief - he had been ploughing through personnel files for the past four hours or more and seemed to be making no progress at all. No, this was not true, he decided; he was finding out a good deal about the inmates of the Fuehrerbunker, including things that the subjects probably fondly hoped were still secret, but very little of it had any value to Rindt and his search for Das Leck. Any break in the monotony was welcome at the moment....

It was a Lieutenant; Rindt could not recall his name offhand. "Yes?" he said simply.

"You said you wanted anything relating to surveillance on foreign embassies that might be out of the ordinary, Herr Colonel," the officer said hesitantly.

"That's right, I did," Rindt agreed. "So?"

The Lieutenant held out a folder to him; Rindt took it. "It concerns a murder enquiry, Herr Colonel, concerning-"

"Yes, yes, I can read, you know," said Rindt irritably. "Very well, Lieutenant. Dismiss." It was only after the other man had gone that Rindt realised just how abrupt he had been, but he felt no sense of guilt at his treatment of the officer - there was no time for that. Rapidly, he scanned the contents of the folder, which described, in clinical detail, how Klaus Schuller's body had been discovered in the back of a bombed out shop in Kurfurstendamm two weeks before. It related how he had been stabbed three times, while his right wrist had also been slashed, apparently by the same knife. Evidently, he had put up a struggle, but what had he been doing there at all when he should simply have been following a junior attache from the Irish Embassy as part of his training? His wallet had been stolen, but Rindt was dubious whether it was a simple robbery; MacDiarmid, the man Schuller had been tailing, had returned to the embassy without his shadower, so what had happened to Schuller in the meantime? And did it have any bearing on the investigaton anyway?

Rindt had decided to trace Das Leck from both ends; not only was he trying to determine how the information was being extracted from the Fuehrerbunker, but he was also attempting to establish how Das Leck was getting it out of Berlin. The neutral embassies had been as good a bet as any and so he had asked for all of the surveillance records to be studied for anything that might be significant. Several items had already surfaced, but had all proved to be dead ends; this would probably turn out the same, he thought resignedly. On the other hand, Gestapo agents were not murdered without good reason.... Had he been killed because he had stumbled on a rendezvous between MacDiarmid and an undercover agent?

Das Leck, perhaps?

Rindt turned and looked at the street map on the wall, tracing his finger along Kurfurstendamm until he found where the body had been found. It was some way from the Irish Embassy - had Schuller switched from MacDiarmid to someone who had met the Irishman? And had this someone realised they were being followed and had then killed him? Entirely possible.... But why there?

Suddenly, Rindt's finger stopped at a familiar street name: Bleibtreustrasse - where Marianne Kovacs lived. Less than half a kilometre from where Schuller had been murdered - and she had been born in Dublin, Rindt recalled uneasily. Was that the link to the Irish Embassy? She was Fegelein's mistress, after all - and Fegelein visited the Bunker at least twice a day. And she had also been Goebbels' mistress, ideally placed in fact, from the point of view of an Allied agent....

On the other hand, he had to admit that the evidence was purely circumstantial. There was absolutely nothing to connect her with Schuller's death - which might well be unconnected with Das Leck anyway. Nevertheless, it might be worth questioning her and....

The door to his office opened suddenly and Mueller strode in, grim-faced; Rindt's train of thought was shattered. "I think we may have found Das Leck," Mueller announced bluntly.

"Who?"

"One of Rattenhuber's men, a Major called Kremer." He threw a folder onto Rindt's desk.

Rindt nodded to himself; SS-General Rattenhuber was responsible for security within the Bunker and Kremer was one of his aides. "Why do you suspect him?"

"Because he's disappeared, that's why. He didn't report for duty today and there's no-one at his flat. He's gone and so is his wife. They've made a run for it."

"When was he last seen?"

"Six o'clock yesterday evening, when he went off duty."

Rindt glanced at the clock on the wall. "So he's had an eighteen hour start." His face was appalled.

"Exactly. So you'd better get moving, Rindt. Get a search instituted for him. I want him found - and quickly."

Rindt nodded, already reaching for the telephone on his desk; Mueller smiled faintly at his evident haste and turned to leave. If anyone could find Kremer, Rindt could....

As he waited for the switchboard operator to put him through, Rindt caught sight of the report of Schuller's death and recalled his suspicions concerning Marianne; he hesitated. In fact, the evidence of Kremer's guilt was not much more substantial than that implicating Marianne, when it came right down to it.... Hundreds, probably thousands of people were making a run for it to escape the Russians and who was to say that Kremer was any different?

But Kremer had disappeared and Marianne had not....

"Hallo, Rindt here. I want a search instituted for Major Helmut Kremer.... Yes, of course it's urgent." Impatiently, he closed the Schuller folder and pushed it to one side.

CHAPTER 6.

THE FUEHRERBUNKER: 1400 HOURS, FRIDAY, APRIL 27TH.

The silence around the briefing table had been dragging on for several minutes and was growing oppressive, but no-one dared speak until Hitler had completed his minute examination of the map. Not that there was anything that could usefully be said by anyone at this stage; the map told its own story. The Soviet ring of armour that surrounded the city was closing in inexorably, pushing through Siemensstadt and Moabit to the north, Lichtenberg to the east and Neukolln, Schoneberg and Schmargendorf to the south. The sound of the artillery bombardment was clearly audible even in the Bunker, a constant rumble only noticeable now and then.

With a sigh, Hitler stepped back from the table. He was unusually subdued this afternoon, as if even he knew there could be no further hope of an eleventh-hour miracle. His demands for massive counter-attacks by Wenck, Steiner or Heinrici were things of the past; if anything, he seemed to be revelling in each report of a Russian advance, in that it was bringing his personal Gotterdammerung that much closer. Suddenly, he gestured at the map. "There has been no report from Potsdamer Strasse," he said abruptly. "Surely Heinrich's own honour escort will have achieved something there?"

Understanding dawned on several faces at once. A few days before, Himmler had sent three hundred and fifty of his own SS escort into Berlin to help with the fighting. Although there was no denying that their combat experience was considerable, the fact remained that it had been no more than a gesture on Himmler's part in that there were far too few of them to make any difference whatsoever.

"Well?" Hitler demanded querulously. "I want a report! Fegelein, they are your-" He broke off, looking around the assembled officers. "Where is Fegelein?"

Guensche, Hitler's senior SS adjutant, snapped to attention. "I'll see if I can find him, my Fuehrer. With your permission-?"

Hitler nodded curtly and Guensche strode rapidly out of the room. There was a charged atmosphere in the cramped chamber now, a feeling of impending catastrophe; Hitler looked as though he were in the early stages of one of his formidable rages.

Within two minutes, Guensche had returned. "There's no sign of him at all, my Fuehrer. He does not appear to be in the Bunker at all."

"Oh, he doesn't, does he? Does anyone know where he is?"

There was a universal shaking of heads and muttered denials, but there was no denying the relieved expressions on many of the faces around the map table, now that it was obvious who was to be the object of Hitler's wrath.

"Then where is he? How long has he been absent from the Bunker?" demanded Hitler. "Now that I come to think of it, he was not present this morning, was he?"

"Er - I don't think he's been here for the past two days, my Fuehrer," said Guensche nervously.

"You're right, Guensche!" Hitler exploded. "Two days! What the devil is he playing at? I'll have his hide for this!" He snatched up the telephone on the table. "Get me Rattenhuber at once!" he barked. While he waited for Rattenhuber to come to the phone, he glared round at the others; nobody said anything at all. The thought of perhaps defending Fegelein did not cross anyone's mind at all; he was as good as dead now and they did not want to be dragged down with him. "Rattenhuber?" Hitler snapped. "Fegelein has not reported for duty here for two whole days. Why was I not informed of this?.... Well, order him to report to me at once. At once, do you hear?" He hurled the telephone down.

"Major Guensche?"

Guensche looked up from the folder he had been reading and leaped to his feet when he saw that it was General Rattenhuber; he had been more or less expecting such a visit ever since the briefing had finished ten minutes before with Hitler storming out in a rage - yet again. "Yes, Herr General?"

"I need your help, Major," said Rattenhuber bluntly. "Where the hell can I find General Fegelein?"

"I take it he's not at home, Herr General?"

"His wife hasn't clapped eyes on him for the last four days," Rattenhuber replied sourly. "The reason I've come to to you, Major, is because I gather that you and he often go out drinking together."

"Well - once or twice, Herr General," Guensche admitted.

"So do you have any idea where I can find him?"

Guensche hesitated; Fegelein had done him several favours in the past and so the Major was loath to become involved in this particular situation, but it was only too evident that Fegelein was in deep trouble and it would be foolish, if not downright dangerous, to side with him now. "Possibly, Herr General," he answered. "General Fegelein left me a telephone number and an address where he could be contacted in an emergency."

"I think you can regard this as an emergency, Major," said Rattenhuber grimly.

Glumly, Guensche nodded and opened his desk diary, from which he took a slip of paper. "That's the telephone number, Herr General," he said, handing it to Rattenhuber.

"Excellent. And the address?"

"It's in Charlottenburg. Number 10/11 Bleibtreustrasse."

1800 HOURS: BLEIBTREUSTRASSE.

SS-Captain Frick hesitated for a moment at the door of the flat then knocked firmly. When there was no reply, he knocked again and this time, the door was opened. A dishevelled figure stood in the doorway in his shirt sleeves, holding a half full glass; it was a couple of seconds before Frick recognised Fegelein - he was unshaven and evidently the worse for drink.

"Yes?" he demanded truculently.

Frick saluted smartly. "Captain Frick, Herr General. May I come in? I have a message from General Rattenhuber."

Fegelein stared at him uncomprehendingly for several seconds then nodded. "Oh, very well. Come in."

Frick turned to the two troopers who had accompanied him; a third was in the car outside. "Wait here." He pushed awkwardly past Fegelein and went into the lounge.

"A drink, Frick?" Fegelein asked, gesturing vaguely with his glass.

"Er - no, thank you, Herr General."

"Very wise, very wise." Fegelein downed the rest of his drink in a single gulp and went over to the drinks cabinet to replenish his glass. "I suppose Rattenhuber told you to come and collect me?"

"He said that I was to provide an escort for your journey to the Bunker," said Frick carefully.

"An escort?" Fegelein echoed, his speech slurred. "One way of putting it, I suppose.... An escort." He giggled then waved his

74

drink about in sudden agitation. "He phoned me three hours ago, you know? Ordered me - ordered me, mark you - to report to the Bunker within two hours. Damned impertinence! Who the hell does he think he is! He can't give me orders!" He leaned towards Frick confidentially. "I'm senior to him, you see," he explained. "So I ignored it, Frick. Ignored it." He peered at Frick. "Sent you here to arrest me, did he?"

"Of course not, Herr General. You know that would be impossible."

"Exactly! Can't have captains going round arresting generals, can we? Even Rattenhuber knows that and he's a cretin. So what did he tell you to do? Knock me out and bring me in handcuffed?"

"Of course not, Herr General!" Frick repeated doggedly. "I was merely asked to remind you of General Rattenhuber's request - he is simply passing on the Fuehrer's express wishes."

"Oh, it's a request now, is it? I see." Fegelein frowned vaguely and took two or three unsteady steps towards the window before turning back towards Frick. "Well, I'm staying right here, Captain. And do you know why? I'll tell you. It's because I'm getting out of this hellhole. Reichsfuehrer Himmler himself has placed a plane at my disposal and I shall be flying out in it tonight. If you've got any sense, Frick, you'll come with me. How about it? Send your men back to the Bunker and escape with me. You'll be well rewarded, you know - I can promise you that."

"I'm sorry, Herr General, but I cannot do that," Frick replied firmly.

"Your oath of loyalty, I suppose," Fegelein mumbled. He shrugged. "Suit yourself. Go back and tell Rattenhuber I'm staying here."

Frick stared helplessly at Fegelein, envisaging only too well the reception Rattenhuber would give him when he returned empty-handed, but he had been given no guidance what to do if Fegelein refused to budge - Rattenhuber had known full well that it was an impossible order to implement within the military code without Fegelein's co-operation. "Very well, Herr General," he said resignedly. "I'll tell General Rattenhuber."

"Be sure that you do."

2000 HOURS.

"Where the hell have you been?" Fegelein demanded angrily when Marianne arrived back at the flat; he was standing in the

75

bedroom doorway, swaying to and fro. Marianne thought he looked dreadful; his eyes were unfocused and he was still in his shirt sleeves. "What sort of a time do you call this?"

"I was held up at work - we didn't finish until half past six and it's taken me all this time-" She broke off. "Hermann, you look terrible. What have you been doing, for heaven's sake?"

"Drinking - what the hell does it look like?" He staggered over to the sofa and collapsed back onto it. "They're after me, Marianne.... all after me. But they won't get me.... won't. Got a plane coming to get me.... get us, that is.... just waiting for the phone call.... then we'll go."

Marianne stared at him dumbfounded: what the blazes was he babbling about? And what was he doing getting drunk anyway? "For God's sake, Hermann, you can't go anywhere in your present state!" She went over to him and took hold of his hands. "Now stand up!"

"All right.... all right." With an effort, he rose to his feet. "Should be telephoning me any minute, Marianne.... Our very own plane, you know.... just for us. Himmler will see we're all right.... Shows who your real friends are...."

"Look, what are you talking about? What plane?"

"Coming tonight.... been trying to phone you all day.... We can go tonight, Marianne, you and me.... just the two of us."

She was leading him towards the bathroom now. "Listen, have a shower, then get into your uniform. I'll make you some coffee." This was typical of the man, she thought disgustedly; he had finally managed to arrange an escape route and now he was jeopardising it all by just sitting around drinking when he should be getting everything ready - what did he use for brains, for God's sake?

"Phoned Eva...." he mumbled. "Did I tell you? My sister-in-law, the high and mighty mistress of the Fuehrer.... Not even she'd help me.... the bitch.... they say he can't get it up, our beloved Fuehrer - did you know that? Serve the old cow right.... You'll stick by me, won't you, Marianne? You won't leave me, will you?" There was a pathetic whine in his voice that made her curl her lip in disgust.

"Of course I won't, Hermann. Now get into that shower!" she shouted impatiently.

"Right. Whatever you say. Then I'll be properly turned out if they come back for me.... In my uniform...." He giggled suddenly. "Then I can tell them to piss off."

"They? What do you mean, they?" She stared at him, a sudden

76

chill gripping her heart. What the hell was he talking about now? What had gone wrong?

"I'm supposed.... supposed to be reporting to the Bunker. Not going to, of course.... must have missed me.... Sent some pup of a captain to fetch me.... damned cheek...."

"Oh, Good God...." Marianne breathed. Didn't the idiot have any idea what was happening? Was he really so drunk that he didn't realise that they would be back for him and that this time they would not take no for an answer? They could be hammering on the door at any moment and he could do was to sit her drinking himself into insensibility. For an instant, the thought came to her that she should just grab her belongings and run, leaving him to his fate.... No. Her one chance of escape was to be on that plane and so she needed Fegelein, like it or not. "Right, that settles it. We're leaving here tonight, whether you get that telephone call or not. Now pull yourself together!" With a final heave, she shoved him into the shower, still in his shirt and trousers, and turned on the water.

2200 HOURS: THE REICH CHANCELLERY.

Rattenhuber looked up at the armoured weapons carrier and turned to the Colonel standing next to him. "Right, Hoegl. On your way and remember - don't come back without him."

"If we can get through at all, Herr General," Hoegl replied gloomily. It had taken Frick an hour each way to make the four mile journey between the Chancellery and Bleibtreustrasse as the artillery bombardment en route had been particularly heavy; the Russians were now only a few hundred metres away and had unleashed a furious barrage that could only be the prelude to their final assault. The car had been blown onto its side by a near miss and Frick had eventually arrived back at the Chancellery on foot with blood pouring from his shoulder. Privately, both Rattenhuber and Hoegl doubted whether it was worth sending a Colonel, six men and a weapons carrier just to fetch Fegelein, but orders were orders....

"Just make damned sure you do get through," said Rattenhuber. "And don't take no for an answer. Bring him here."

"Easier said than done, Herr General. I can't arrest him, can I?"

Rattenhuber took Hoegl's arm and led him out of earshot of the other troopers in the carrier. "Listen, Hoegl - Fegelein is finished.

He'll be arrested for desertion when he gets back here, so there's absolutely nothing he can do to you. You're operating under the Fuehrer's direct orders, so forget about the military code and carry them out. Just don't come back without him - is that clear?"

"Perfectly, Herr General!" Hoegl saluted and strode back to the weapons carrier, jumping up into the seat next to the driver. A moment later, the vehicle was pulling away out of the underground garage.

BLEIBTREUSTRASSE: 2300 HOURS.

Cormack peered up at the street sign and nodded to Woodward. "This is it," he said. "Bleibtreustrasse."

"Which number is it?"

"Ten to eleven. Must be two buildings run into one or something."

"Then it's down the other end. This one's Number 75."

"It would be. Come on."

After leaving the bierkeller, Cormack had gone back to where he had left Woodward hiding in a disused cellar. Since then, Cormack had tried telephoning the flat from a phone booth, but each time, a man's voice - Fegelein's, presumably - had answered. Cormack had rung off without speaking.

They had decided to wait until after dark before venturing out, but they had still been obliged to make several detours to avoid checkpoints or defensive positions. Although Cormack knew that his SS-Colonel's uniform would discourage most soldiers from looking at his papers too closely - assuming they had the nerve to ask for them at all - he preferred to avoid the risk completely. It was already nearly eleven o'clock and they had only just reached their destination: had he perhaps been too cautious?

There also remained the problem of what to do about Fegelein if, as seemed likely, he was in the flat with Marianne. Unfortunately, Cormack knew that he had no real alternative there but to ensure Fegelein's silence.... Would he still be able to do it, after all this time? Bit bloody late to be worrying about that, he told himself sneeringly.

"Listen!" said Woodward suddenly, coming to a halt. Cormack heard it as well then, the sound of an approaching heavy vehicle; he gestured towards a darkened doorway and the two of them took cover in it only seconds before the vehicle came into view, rounding the corner they had left less than a minute before. As it rumbled past, Cormack recognised the shape of an armoured weapons carrier and swore softly under his breath; what the hell was it doing here? The question was soon answered - the carrier came to an abrupt halt outside a large, rambling building about thirty yards away and, without having to count off the numbers, he knew with a terrible certainty that it had stopped outside Number 10/11.

Hoegl was the first man to jump down from the carrier as it pulled up. "Right!" he barked. "Weissler, you stay here, the rest of you follow me!" He led the way up the stairs, two at a time, and paused outside the door of Fegelein's flat; he took out his Luger pistol and nodded to the sergeant beside him. The burly NCO hefted his Schmeisser and fired a two-second burst at the lock before smashing his foot into the door, sending it crashing back on its hinges.

As Hoegl strode into the lounge, it was as if the two occupants of the flat were frozen in a tableau, standing on each side of a round mahogany table. Fegelein was now shaven and wearing his uniform trousers and boots, although he had not yet donned his tunic, while Marianne was dressed in a cardigan, blouse and slacks. Between them was a woman's valise and Fegelein had a neatly folded shirt in his hand; it was only too obvious what they were doing. Hoegl had time to see the expression of terrified shock on Marianne's face before Fegelein stammered,

"Who are you? What - what the devil do you mean by this?"

"Colonel Hoegl at your service, Herr General," said Hoegl silkily.

Fegelein looked at the five SS troopers who had followed Hoegl in; each one held a machine pistol. None of these were actually pointing at him, but he knew that all each man had to do was to raise the barrel and he would have five automatic weapons aimed at him. And these were no inexperienced reservists - these belonged to the Liebstandarte Adolf Hitler and would not hesitate to shoot him if Hoegl gave the command. Nevertheless, he made one last attempt at bluster. "Well, Hoegl, what the hell do you mean by bursting in here like this?"

"I have been sent by General Rattenhuber to remind you that you are under orders from the Fuehrer himself to report to the Bunker. Indeed, you should have done so six hours ago."

"So what is this? An arrest squad?" Fegelein drew himself up to his full height. "You do not have sufficient rank to arrest me - Colonel."

"I am not here to arrest you at all, Herr General," Hoegl replied calmly. "I am here simply to escort you to the Fuehrerbunker so that you can comply with the Fuehrer's instructions."

"And if I choose not to accompany you?"

Almost absently, Hoegl flicked off the safety catch on his Luger pistol. "I have also been given orders covering that eventuality."

Fegelein's knees seemed to turn to jelly at these words, delivered in an almost bored monotone; in that instant, he had no doubt whatsoever that Hoegl would shoot him where he stood if he argued any longer. "Very well," he said, drawing in a deep breath in a bid to prevent his voice trembling. "I'll come with you. I'm sure there's no need for any - ah - unpleasantness, Colonel?"

"Indeed not, Herr General," Hoegl agreed.

"I'll - I'll need to collect one or two things."

"Of course, Herr General."

"Marianne," said Fegelein weakly. "Perhaps the Colonel would like a drink while he's waiting?"

Marianne stared incredulously at him, wondering if she had heard him correctly. It was obvious to her that he wanted her to slip something into Hoegl's drink, but did he really think that she would be able to do that without anyone noticing? "Er - yes, certainly. Herr Colonel?"

If Hoegl was surprised by Fegelein's sudden display of hospitality, he gave no sign of it; presumably, he interpreted it as a belated gesture of ingratiation on Fegelein's part. "Thank you. A cognac, please."

"A cognac," she repeated and picked up the tray containing the empty glasses from Fegelein's earlier drinking. "I'd better fetch some water," she said to no one in particular and went out, pulling the door closed behind her. The kitchen was at the far end of a short passageway and, as she opened the kitchen door, she glanced back, expecting one of the troopers to be following. She let out a sigh of relief when she saw there was no-one behind her. Once in the kitchen, she saw her handbag on the table - she had left it there earlier while she had made a coffee to sober Fegelein up - and, setting the tray down next to it, she looked quickly around; the numbed paralysis that had gripped her when Hoegl and his men had burst had vanished completely, to be replaced by a purposeful urgency. She would be a fool if she passed up this opportunity to escape, but she had to move fast; at any moment, Hoegl might decide to send one of his men after her, although it seemed they were only interested in Fegelein so far....

After a moment's thought, she turned on the tap to cover any sound she might make and, slinging her handbag over her shoulder, went over to the sash window behind the sink; she reached over and opened it, careful not to make any sound, before she climbed up onto the draining board and swung her legs out through the window. She turned around until she was facing back into the kitchen and pushed herself backwards, lowering herself down until she was hanging by her fingertips from the sill, her feet suspended a metre or so above the metal steps of the fire escape.

Taking a deep breath, she let go of the sill and dropped, stumbling forward as she landed, but she reached out and grabbed the rail to prevent herself falling. With no more than a momentary glance up at the window above, she turned and rapidly descended the stairs, down into the alleyway that ran behind the apartment block. When she reached the ground, she looked around, unable to believe that Hoegl would not have left someone behind the building to cut off any escape - but he hadn't. The alley was deserted.

Shaking her head incredulously, Marianne broke into a run, heading northwards, trying to put as much of a distance between herself and the apartment before they noticed she was missing.

The only thing was - where could she go now?

"If you please, Herr General," prompted Hoegl. "This is a matter of some urgency."

"Er - yes. Of course." Fegelein picked up his tunic and put it on, fastening it as slowly as he dared, wondering if Marianne had realised what he wanted her to do; if Hoegl was incapacitated, he might be able to use his rank to intimidate the troopers. Carefully, he adjusted his tie in the wall mirror.

"Come on, Herr General," said Hoegl impatiently.

Fegelein turned and glared at him. "I know you have your orders, Colonel, but there is no need for impertinence. Or insubordination."

Hoegl shook his head in exasperation and waited in fuming silence while Fegelein finished checking his appearance. Suddenly, a thought seemed to strike Hoegl. "Where is that woman? She's taking her time, isn't she?" The suspicion on his face gave way to certainty. "Baum, keep an eye on him." He spun on his heel and strode out of the room, through the door Marianne had taken.

He was back within thirty seconds, his face livid with anger. "She's gone," he said curtly to Baum, the NCO. "Climbed out through the window. There's no sign of her."

Fegelein stared at Hoegl, aghast. Marianne had made a run for it, leaving him to face the music on his own! After all he'd done for her! "You bitch!" he hissed under his breath. "You wait - I'll see you damned for this!"

"Shall I send two of the men to look for her, Herr Colonel?"

Hoegl shook his head. "No. By the time you get round the back, she'll be far away. She isn't important anyway - it's the General we were told to bring." He picked up the valise from the table. "Come on, Herr General," he said curtly. "We've wasted enough time, I think."

"Watch it," said Cormack softly. "They're coming out." The two men pushed themselves back into the doorway as a group of soldiers emerged into the street. One was wearing the uniform of an SS-General - it had to be Fegelein - and although none of the other men were pointing their guns at him, it was evident that he was virtually under arrest. Fegelein climbed up into the front of the carrier, followed by the Colonel who had been in charge of the detachment, while the rest of the men jumped into the back. The engine roared into life and the carrier moved off down the street, disappearing from view around a corner.

"No sign of Marianne," Woodward commented.

"No, there wasn't," Cormack agreed thoughtfully. "Right, you stay here, Tony, and keep a look out. If anything happens, press the doorbell twice, or kick over a dustbin or something."

Woodward nodded. "Will do."

Cormack looked both ways along the street and headed across it in a low, crouching run. Once again, he checked the street before he pushed open the door of Number 10/11, running rapidly up the stairs. He took out a Browning pistol from inside his tunic and pushed open the flat door, cautiously; all of the detachment had left, but it did no harm to be sure.

It only took a few minutes of searching for him to be certain the flat was empty. There was no sign of Marianne, nor any indication where she had gone; all he found was a German passport hidden in the dressing table drawer, with her photograph, made out in the name of Maria Kotze; Cormack pocketed it along with the wad of Reichsmarks he found below it. After a moment's thought, he lifted down an overnight bag from the top of the wardrobe and threw some of her clothes into it, ignoring the inner voice that was telling him that she had gone, disappeared for good....

Now what the hell was he supposed to do?

MIDNIGHT: THE REICH CHANCELLERY.

It was a few minutes after midnight when the weapons carrier arrived back at the Reich Chancellery and Fegelein was taken straight to his sleeping quarters by Hoegl and two troopers. Since leaving the flat, Fegelein had seemed to be in a state of shock, saying hardly a word throughout the journey and now, standing by the bed in his quarters, he did not appear to be aware of his surroundings at all; instead, he was staring blankly into infinity.

"I think it might be best for you if you were to get some sleep, Herr General," Hoegl suggested.

"Pardon? Oh - er - yes. I will. Thank you, Colonel." It was evident that Fegelein had little idea of what was happening to him at all; probably it was a combination of drink and shock that had done it, Hoegl decided.

Hoegl went out into the corridor, pulling the door shut behind him and turned to the two men who had accompanied him. "Right, Weissler, Baum, I want you to make damned certain that he doesn't leave that room. As far as you are concerned, he is under arrest. Is that clear?"

"Yes, Herr Colonel."

"Good." Without another word, Hoegl turned and strode briskly away, descending the stairs that led down to the tunnel connecting the Chancellery to the Fuehrerbunker. He was still carrying the valise he had brought from the flat; no doubt Rattenhuber would be interested in its contents. In accordance with his instructions, he made his way to the old map room, where he knocked briskly on the door.

"Come in," said a voice from inside. Hoegl went in and came to a stunned halt when he saw the group of men gathered around the conference table. Rattenhuber was there, as he had expected, along with Guensche, but it was the other three men who had provoked his astonished reaction; Martin Bormann, Josef Goebbels and Heinrich Mueller - their presence had been the last thing Hoegl had expected.

Collecting himself, he sprang to attention. "General Fegelein is confined to his quarters, Herr General," he reported to Rattenhuber as Bormann came rapidly round the table; without a word, the Deputy Fuehrer snatched the valise from Hoegl's grasp, opened it and emptied its contents onto the table.

"There," said Bormann softly. "What more do we need,

gentlemen?" He threw the items of clothing aside, to leave behind a collection of items that Fegelein would find very difficult to explain away. There were two thick wads of banknotes, one of large denomination Reichsmarks, the other of Swiss francs, an assortment of road maps, two passports, three gold watches and a large chamois bag which Bormann now opened. Inside this were several diamonds, amethysts and rubies, an opal, a diamond brooch, several gold rings and a pearl necklace. "I don't think there is any doubt about his intentions, is there?" Bormann continued.

"Evidently not," Goebbels agreed, his eyes glittering. "A deserter," he said, his voice dripping contempt.

"One moment," said Bormann suddenly, picking up the passports. One was Hungarian - and the other British; Bormann snatched up the second one. "My God," he whispered, opening it. Inside was Marianne's photograph above the name Marianne Driscoll. Quickly, he opened the other passport and swore softly as he saw an identical photograph; this time it was for Marianne Kovacs. Bormann spun round and held them out to Hoegl. "Who is this woman?" he demanded.

"She - she must be Fegelein's mistress," Hoegl stammered. "She was at his flat."

"Where is she now? Did you bring her here?"

"No, Herr Reichsleiter. She-"

"My God!" Bormann screamed, pounding the table with his fists. "You flat-footed idiot, Hoegl! Why didn't you grab her and bring her back instead of this damned valise!" He looked round at the others. "Don't you see? Fegelein is a traitor! This woman is British - an enemy agent. Fegelein went to bed with this spy and blabbered everything! She was Das Leck!"

Mueller nodded rapidly. "It would seem so, Herr Reichsleiter."

Bormann turned back to Hoegl. "Take your men back to the flat, Hoegl, and arrest her if she's there. For your sake, she had better be!"

"At once, Herr Reichsleiter!" Hoegl saluted, white-faced, and left, almost at a run.

"Idiot!" Bormann spat. "Incompetent fool!"

Greatly daring, Rattenhuber ventured, "His orders did only include Fegelein, Herr Reichsleiter. Nobody else."

"No excuse, Rattenhuber. No excuse at all. He should have used what little brains he has." He turned to Mueller once more. "Just to make sure he doesn't bungle it again, you'd better go there as well, Mueller." Bormann sighed. "Although I doubt if she's going to oblige us by being there."

0100 HOURS, SATURDAY APRIL 28TH: BLEIBTREU-STRASSE.

Mueller looked gloomily around the flat and shook his head slowly. The bird had indeed flown, that much was obvious; he turned and saw Hoegl standing by the sofa, his expression bleak. "How could you have let her go, for God's sake, Hoegl?"

"I don't know, Herr General," said Hoegl miserably. "I didn't realise she was of any importance."

Neither did I until now, thought Mueller, but he said nothing. He shook his head slowly and looked around the room again; it was only now that he noticed that the wood had been splintered around the lock of the bureau drawer and went over to it. "Did you do this, Hoegl?"

"No, Herr General."

Then who did? Mueller wondered. Both Fegelein and the woman would have had a key, surely, so it couldn't have been either of them. Someone else, then.... "Was it like this when you were here?"

Hoegl thought for a moment and then shook his head. "I don't think so, but I can't be certain."

Mueller stared at the damage for a moment longer. Probably it was nothing, but if it had been caused since Fegelein's arrest.... Rapidly, he rummaged through the drawer, but in vain. There was nothing to indicate where Marianne had gone, or who had broken into the bureau. Only Fegelein could provide any useful information now.

He picked up the telephone on the table and dialled. "General Mueller here. Get me General Rattenhuber, please.... Rattenhuber? I want Fegelein transferred immediately to Gestapo custody.... Yes, on my authority.... Take him to the cellar in the Dreifaltigkeit chapel and get him ready for interrogation.... Yes, of course I mean sharpened interrogation.... Good. Heil Hitler!" Mueller replaced the receiver and looked at his watch; right, he decided, grab a few hours sleep before starting in earnest on Fegelein in the morning.

Before that, however, he would have to get a search for the Kovacs woman under way. He would phone Rindt immediately.

It was well over a minute before the telephone was answered, but then Rindt heard Hentschel's voice, blurred and indistinct; probably he had been woken up. "Yes?"

"Rindt here."

"Ah, I see." Hentschel's voice was suddenly alert. "Go on."

"We've identified Das Leck," Rindt said crisply.

"Give me the name." Hentschel's reply was equally abrupt.

"Marianne Kovacs. She's-"

"Fegelein's mistress, yes, I know. Are you certain?"

"Mueller is and, judging by what he's told me, I think it's ninety-five per cent certain, yes."

"Good. Is she under arrest?"

"No. She - ah - escaped when Fegelein was arrested. It was only after she disappeared that Mueller realised who she was."

"Disappeared, you say?"

"Yes, but she can't get far - she doesn't have her passport or any documents."

"And there's no indication where she might be?"

"Not at the moment, no."

"I see." There was a long pause as if Hentschel were thinking about this latest development before he said, "Presumably, a search has been instituted for her?"

"Yes. All Gestapo units have been told to arrest her on sight."

"Right. Now listen to me carefully. You must ensure that you find her first. Once you have done that, you are to hand her over either to me or to one of my associates-"

"Now wait a minute!" Rindt protested. "That wasn't part of the arrangement! All I had to do was identify her for you and I've done that!"

"And now you have to do this, Rindt," Hentschel's voice said implacably. "Knowing her identity is no good to us unless we know where she is. The minute you have located her, then you make sure that she can be handed over to us."

"And how the hell am I supposed to do that?"

"If you can arrange to detain her personally, then you can deliver her to a prearranged rendezvous. Alternatively, simply let me know where she is and I'll arrange for her to be picked up."

"And what do I do if the Gestapo finds her first?"

"You are in a very powerful position, Rindt, as second in charge of the investigation. Surely you can think of something? Or shall I put it this way: we are now offering you a straight exchange. You give us this Marianne Kovacs and we will give you your wife."

"That's what you said last time," said Rindt bitterly. "How do I know you won't introduce more conditions the next time?"

"You don't," said Hentschel bluntly. "But as you so rightly said, what choice do you have?"

"You bastard, Hentschel."

"Just find Marianne Kovacs for us." The line went dead.

Rindt slowly replaced the telephone, his face ashen. He should have known they would do that to him.... deep down, if he were honest about it, he had, in fact, been expecting something like this all along. They had him exactly where they wanted him and they were not going to let him go until they had no further use for him. Stupid to have ever thought otherwise, he admitted bleakly; in their place, he would probably have done the same - but there had always been hope, no matter how forlorn.... until now.

Wearily, he rubbed his eyes; he had only just managed to drop into a troubled sleep when Mueller had rung him - was it only thirty minutes ago? - and he knew that it was pointless going back to bed now. In any case, he had to think: where would Marianne go?

Not to her friends, he thought, so she'll hide out somewhere overnight. Unless she makes a run for the Irish Embassy.... Rindt stood up abruptly and went to the wardrobe; he began dressing impatiently - of course that was what she'd do! What other choice did she have? He had to get a squad of men over there, waiting for her.

For perhaps the twentieth time, Marianne ducked back into the shadows of a doorway when she saw four approaching soldiers on the far side of the road. They were making their way cautiously along the street, constantly looking around, their rifles at the ready; all the patrols she had seen so far had been as watchful as this one, which meant that the Russians must be very close now. The crackle of small arms fire had often sounded as though it were coming from only the next street and Marianne would not have been at all surprised to see Soviet soldiers this time instead of Germans.

Not that it made any difference who they were, she thought bitterly, as she had no papers anyway; neither set of soldiers would stand on ceremony if they found her. She had to find a safe refuge and the only such place in Berlin now was the Irish Embassy as far as she could see. Although she was no longer an Irish citizen, there was a chance that Kiernan might be able to persuade the ambassador to give her sanctuary, if only for a few days. A chance - but only a slim one, if she were honest about it. She had no idea how much influence Kiernan had in the Embassy, nor how resolute the ambassador would be if the Gestapo demanded that she be handed over to them, but there was nothing else left for her now, nor had there been from the moment she had climbed through the kitchen window.

She could scarcely credit how easy her initial escape had been; presumably, they had only been after Fegelein but if they had not been interested in her then they certainly would be now, once that valise had been opened and its contents examined. From that moment, the hunt would be on and so the longer she took to reach the Embassy, the more likely it was that the Gestapo would be waiting for her when she eventually got there. It had taken her two and a half hours to come this far, because of all the detours she had been obliged to make to avoid the patrols.

She tensed suddenly. One of the soldiers was crossing the road and coming almost straight towards her. Looking rapidly around, she realised that there was nowhere she could go without revealing her presence and so she pressed herself back against the door, her heart pounding. The soldier came to a sudden halt, going down on one knee behind a telephone kiosk no more than five yards from her, on the pavement's edge and, slowly, he looked around, scrutinising the buildings opposite before checking his own side of the street. For one, heart-stopping moment, he looked directly at her and she was utterly convinced he had seen her but then his head turned away as he raised his arm, signalling his companions to move forward. Moments later, he was moving off, running past her and up the street.

Slowly, she let out her breath in a grateful sigh of relief and closed her eyes, aware of just how close that had been - but how long would her luck hold? She had to get to the Embassy. With a final glance at the soldiers who were moving steadily away from her, Marianne emerged from her hiding place and headed along the street.

When she reached the next junction, she looked up at the street sign and almost cried out in excitement. The Embassy was along the intersecting road, only about two hundred yards away - she had almost made it! One careful look around the corner and she was trotting along the road, her eyes picking out the Embassy, an imposing building set back from the roadway, with a small drive in front of it leading to a gate that was kept permanently open. And there was no sign of any Gestapo surveillance either, she realised, grinning exultantly....

But then there wouldn't be, would there, if they were laying a trap for her? The realisation was like a douche of cold water and she ducked instantly through a gateway, peering round its stone pillar at the Embassy.

There was still no indication of anybody waiting for her: no movement, no sudden flare of a match as someone carelessly lit a cigarette, but she resisted the almost overwhelming impulse to cover these last few yards in a headlong dash for safety. Having got this far, it would be utter folly to throw it all away now.... She stared intently into every patch of shadow that might conceal a watcher, but there was nothing to be seen, no flaw in the pattern. Gradually, her hopes began to rise.... perhaps the Gestapo hadn't thought to place the Embassy under surveillance after all, or maybe they had been held up on the way; whichever it was, it didn't look as though they were here yet....

Then she saw a figure detach itself from the shadows about twenty yards beyond the Embassy's gates and head across the street in a scuttling run into another pool of darkness and her heart sank. She stared longingly, sick with despair, at the Embassy, like a prisoner might look through his bars at freedom; the Embassy might as well be a million miles away, because it was completely out of her reach now.

The Gestapo were waiting for her after all.

CHAPTER 7.

SATURDAY, APRIL 28TH: 0300 HOURS.

Cautiously, Marianne picked her way down the steps, looking around the darkened interior of the cellar. In the centre was a pile of rubble where the roof had fallen in - presumably when the shop above had been flattened by a bomb - and the glare from a nearby fire provided enough light for her to see that the basement was empty. Whatever had been stored here had been removed, almost certainly by looters, but this did not concern her in the slightest; all she wanted was somewhere she could lie down and rest, even if only for an hour or so. She was utterly exhausted, nearly dead on her feet. And that was on top of the feeling of abject despair that had been with her from the moment she had seen the waiting Gestapo agents outside the Embassy - the man who had crossed the road had joined two others and had then gone on to another agent further along the road. It had been all she could do not to walk over to them and simply give herself up, but, instead, she had made her way back along the street, hugging the shadows, looking back again and again for any sign of pursuit. Since then, her only thought had been to keep moving, to put as much distance between herself and the trap and it had only been in the last fifteen minutes or so, as she had been moving almost like a zombie along Kleist Strasse, that she had realised just how tired she was. She had to find a hiding place, no matter how temporary and this was as good a place as any.... At least it looked dry.

For a moment, she stood at the foot of the steps, on the verge of collapsing where she was, but she forced her leaden limbs into motion, climbing awkwardly over the debris and rubble until she was in the pitch darkness at the back of the cellar. Only then did she sink down, propping her back against the wall, and close her eyes.

The minute she relaxed, she felt a dreadful weariness and lassitude descend on her; what was the point, she asked herself, of going on? All she was doing was merely postponing the inevitable, after all; she had nowhere to go and nobody to help her except Kiernan, but he was in the Embassy, out of her reach for good.... Her only alternative was to try and get out of Berlin on her own, but the very thought made her shake her head resignedly. Even with the forged documents Fegelein had provided for her, it would still have been virtually impossible, but with no papers at all it would be only a matter of time before she was arrested. And if she did somehow manage to evade all the German patrols, there were still the Russians to consider.

She clenched her fists in sudden anger and frustration. Damn Fegelein! Why hadn't he made a run for it earlier? Why had he waited until it was too late? And why had he been so unbelievably stupid as to stay away from the Bunker for two days - hadn't he known what would happen? If he had simply reported in as usual, nobody would have suspected anything and the two of them would have been well on their way out of Germany by now.... The imbecile!

And damn London as well for leaving her to fend for herself! She had worked for them for four years now, risking her life with almost every passing day and this was all the thanks she got.... Not so much as a message warning her to escape by herself because they were not going to send anyone for her. Nothing. They had simply thrown her to the dogs.... They were bastards, every one of them.

But worst of all, she thought bitterly, damn her own stupidity! How had she ever thought that Fegelein would be able to get her out of Berlin, for God's sake, when he could scarcely write a letter properly? And why had she ever trusted London to pull her out? A little considered thought on either count should have told her that she would be better off making her own plans instead of relying on a fool like Fegelein or on someone six hundred miles away whom she had never met.

And now, never would.

A sound from the front of the cellar snapped her out of her brooding reverie; someone was coming down the steps. Silently, she lay flat on the floor, praying that the darkness would conceal her if whoever it was were to look over the top of the rubble. As the thought came to her that, despite her despair, she was not yet ready to give up altogether, she heard a voice. It was that of a young woman - a girl, in fact; Marianne doubted if she was any older than twenty.

"Will here do?"

"I should think so," a man's voice replied. "What do you reckon, Hans?"

"Come on, let's stop pissing about. Let's get on with it."

"Right. How much was it you said?"

"You said - twenty cigarettes. Each," she added.

"No - between us."

"Oh.... all right then." The girl sounded resigned; slowly, Marianne began to relax. It was only too obvious why the three of them had come down here and so they would be unlikely to notice her - unless the girl brought them over the pile of debris. Fortunately, her next words dispelled that fear. "Who's first?"

"Me," said the first man, his voice eager; he sounded as though he were breathing heavily.

"Come on then, darling." The words were said so hesitantly, so fearfully that it was suddenly clear to Marianne that the girl was not used to this at all. In fact, she was hating every minute of it.... This was what Hitler had brought them to: a city which had once been one of the finest cultural centres in Europe was now a wilderness where teenaged girls had to do things like this just for twenty cigarettes....

"Don't take too long," said the one called Hans, chuckling. "It's my turn next, remember."

"Shut up, will you? I'm concentrating. Come on, fraulein, don't just lie there doing nothing - I've paid ten cigarettes for this."

As she tried to shut out the furtive sounds, the bleak thought came to Marianne that, before very long, she might end up the same way as the girl....

Dammit, no!

1000 HOURS.

Michael Kiernan could not help but feel apprehensive when he left the Embassy compound at just after ten o'clock; quite apart from the risk of being followed by the Gestapo, a possibility that had increased in likelihood since Schuller's death a fortnight before, there was now the added danger of the Russian artillery barrage, which had been especially heavy in the Tiergarten district. This was despite the fact that, as the Soviets well knew, most of the remaining Berlin embassies were in this area. Perhaps they felt that the embassy of any country that still maintained diplomatic relations with the Nazis did not deserve any immunity but the bombardment certainly did not make Kiernan's present task any simpler.

The telephone call to the Embassy had come less than thirty minutes before. Kiernan had not recognised the voice at all, which had spoken in fluent German, but the conversation had included the correct coded message that requested an immediate meeting. A reference to the zoo had been enough to tell Kiernan the location of the rendezvous, the main entrance to the Zoological Gardens, and he had slipped out of the Embassy as soon as he could find some pretext for doing so. Almost certainly, the caller had been the agent to whom he had sent Emerald's address via Dominique and if he wanted to see Kiernan personally then something must have gone very wrong - the original intention had been for Kiernan to have no direct contact with the London agents. Presumably, Marianne had not been at the flat when they had arrived there; if that was the case, it was difficult to see what he could do now to help.

Kiernan was so preoccupied that he did not see the two men in SS uniform who emerged from a side street until it was far too late to do anything about it. One was a Colonel, the other a sergeant; Kiernan felt his stomach turn over as the Colonel held out an imperious hand. "Papers," he demanded curtly.

Kiernan reached inside his jacket for his identification pass. "I'm a member of the Irish Embassy," he said coolly.

"Indeed?" The Colonel took the papers and stepped closer to Kiernan. His next words took Kiernan utterly by surprise: "Roger sends his regards." Kiernan stared at him, startled - the other man had spoken in English - but Cormack went on in German, "Forget about the zoo - someone could have been listening in."

Kiernan nodded in agreement; he was now recovering from his initial surprise. "You could be right," he agreed.

"They arrested Fegelein," Cormack said tersely. "Emerald's disappeared."

"Disappeared? Not arrested?"

"I don't think so. The point is, how do I find her?"

Kiernan shook his head. "You can't - not unless she contacts me. I could pass a message on if she does, I suppose - I could tell her to go to one of our dead letter drops, for example."

"Do that, would you?"

Kiernan nodded. "If she phones, yes. I'll tell her to go to the corner of Lutherstrasse and Kleiststrasse. The actual drop is the telephone box opposite Lutherstrasse. Can you find it? It's only about half a mile from here."

"I can find it, yes. When?"

"That depends when - if - she phones. Say six o'clock, then every three hours after that?"

Cormack stared thoughtfully across the street. He did not much like the idea of having to return to the same location every three hours, but there was no real alternative. "Fair enough. Let's just

93

hope she gets in touch with you, then."

"Amen to that."

"Right." Cormack handed the papers back to Kiernan. "You'll find a coded message in there - get it off to London immediately."

Kiernan nodded as he replaced the documents in his pocket. "I'll do that."

"Good. Now try to look annoyed - I've just told you to go straight back to your Embassy."

Kiernan nodded in understanding; he glowered at Cormack, spun on his heel and stalked away. On the far side of the road, a raincoated figure emerged from a doorway and began to follow him.

THE CELLAR, DREIFALTIGKEIT CHAPEL: 1130 HOURS.

Mueller glared across the table at Fegelein, who was sitting slumped in a chair, his head lolling forward and his wrists secured to the chair by handcuffs. "Listen, Fegelein, I want to know exactly how much you told that whore."

"Look.... I've told you everything I can remember.... How can I be expected to remember everything I've said to her?.... I just told her the gossip about what was going on in the Bunker." Fegelein lifted his head in an attempt at defiance. "Dammit, that isn't a crime, is it?"

"It is when you're passing on scurrilous rumours that could be of help to the enemy."

Behind Mueller, Rindt raised his eyebrows at this last remark; did Mueller really believe all that, or was he, even at this late stage, toeing the Party line? Did he really care, one way or the other, how much Fegelein had passed on to the British? In any case, all this was wasting time, from Rindt's point of view, in that it was not helping him to find Marianne; Mueller was asking the wrong sort of questions for that. Rindt shook his head minutely in frustration. If only he could have interrogated Fegelein before Mueller had arrived earlier that morning! Unfortunately, Mueller had left instructions that nobody was to talk to Fegelein before him and no amount of browbeating on Rindt's part had been able to persuade the officer in charge of Fegelein's guard detail to let him question the prisoner.

Fegelein had made no reply to Mueller's last statement; he was simply staring down at the floor in front of him. Mueller persisted, "And what about all those documents you took home for her to

94

photograph?"

"Photograph? Don't be stupid, Mueller. Neither of us owns a camera."

"Frau Kovacs does. We found one in her jewel box and it had been especially modified to take photographs in poor lighting. She is a spy, Fegelein - and you were giving her information."

"I didn't know she was a spy? How could I?"

Mueller shook his head almost sorrowfully. "Do you honestly think that will make any difference? Your only hope of escaping the death sentence, Fegelein, is to help us every way that you can."

"I've told you everything I know! What more do you want?"

"The two of you were planning to leave Berlin, were you not?"

At last, thought Rindt; unconsciously, he leaned forward in his chair.

Fegelein nodded. "Yes," he admitted. "I managed to get the passports for her-"

"I'm not interested in the passports, Fegelein. How were you planning to leave?"

"By plane. Reichsfuehrer Himmler placed an aircraft at my disposal."

"An aircraft?"

"Yes. We were supposed to meet it at the Brandenburg Gate at midnight last night."

"You were still in your flat at eleven o'clock. How did you expect to get there in an hour?"

"It would have waited until one o'clock," said Fegelein sullenly.

"And then?"

"The pilot would have taken us to Rechlin."

"Where were you going from there?" Rindt interrupted; he ignored Mueller's irritated glance.

"Munich. We were heading for Switzerland."

"Did Frau Kovacs know of these arrangments?" Mueller asked.

Fegelein frowned, trying to remember and then shook his head. "She knew we were waiting for a plane but not where we were supposed to meet it."

Neither Mueller nor Fegelein saw Rindt's momentary expression of relief; the thought had crossed his mind that perhaps Marianne had somehow reached the rendezvous and had then persuaded the pilot to take her, even without Fegelein. As things stood, however, it was a virtual certainty that she was still in Berlin. She could still be caught....

"Were there any alternative arrangements?" Mueller asked. "If you couldn't get there last night at all?" Fegelein's sudden hesitation was obvious; Mueller went on, "Don't be stupid. You must know that you'll never be there anyway now."

"Yes, there was. For tonight. The same place and time."

"And did Marianne know of that?" Rindt asked. "That there was an alternative?"

Fegelein shook his head. "No. I made no reference to it."

Mueller was looking speculatively at Rindt. Abruptly, he stood up and headed for the door. "A word with you, Colonel, if you please."

Outside, in the corridor, Mueller turned to Rindt and said, "Why all this interest in whether the Kovacs woman knows about the rendezvous, Rindt?"

Rindt hesitated. "Just a thought, Herr General. If she knew there was another rendezvous tonight she might try to get to it herself."

"Possibly - if she knew where and when it was."

"She could figure it out, couldn't she, Herr General? It only boils down to a choice between the East-West Axis and Gatow - the Axis is much closer."

Mueller nodded thoughtfully. "But if she can deduce that, how do we know she didn't catch the plane last night?"

Rindt pursed his lips. "I think it's unlikely, Herr General. She would have had to get there on foot last night, without any documents, so she would have had to avoid all checkpoints - I don't think she could have done it in two hours, which was all the time she had. But - she might try again tonight."

"She'd never be able to persuade a pilot to take her out - not by herself."

"I wouldn't bank on that, Herr General. She's a very attractive woman indeed - if the pilot was not especially willing to hang about and if she made the - er - persuasion tempting enough, she might be able to do it."

It was evident from Mueller's expression that he was not especially impressed by Rindt's arguments. "I don't think she would run the risk, Rindt. She'd stand a better chance just making a run for it."

Rindt was about to put forward further arguments to support his case when he stopped himself; he did not really want Mueller's involvement at all. "You're probably right, Herr General," he admitted. "All the same, if nothing comes up in the meantime, I'd like your permission to keep an eye on that plane when it lands tonight - just in case."

Mueller shrugged. "Very well - although I think it'll be a waste of time."

"You're probably right, Herr General," Rindt agreed dutifully. "But we can't afford to overlook anything, can we?"

1200 HOURS.

Marianne gave the operator the Embassy's number and looked both ways along the street. As always, there was a dismal throng cɩ people making their way past her, laden down with all the possessions they could carry - refugees making a last attempt to escape the advancing Russians, not realising that the city was surrounded, that they had left it too late.... None of these were paying her any attention at all, despite her undeniably dishevelled appearance; she had done her best to brush off the grime and dirt of the cellar, but it was still obvious that she had not slept in a bed last night. On the other hand, she did not look any worse than many others one could see around the streets and the only thing on these Berliners' minds was survival now. No, it was not the refugees that worried her but the possibility that a patrol might appear at any moment. What she would do if that happened, she had not yet decided; if she were simply to hang up and leave the telephone kiosk then that might look suspicious, but if she were to remain on the phone she would have no chance of escaping if they were to ask for her papers.... On balance, she would probably have to stay on the phone; it was a small miracle that they were working at all at the moment and she might never get another chance.

"This is the Embassy for the Irish Republic," said a voice in good German. "May I help you?"

"I'd like to talk to Herr Kiernan, please. Extension 127."

"One moment. I'll put you through."

The girl's two clients had not left for nearly two hours and, afterwards, Marianne had heard her sobbing quietly; she had certainly earned her cigarettes, Marianne had decided pityingly, but there had been nothing she could do to help her. It would have been utter folly to have revealed her presence and so she had waited until the girl had left, ten minutes after the men and only then had Marianne fallen into a troubled sleep. She had awoken with one thought immediately in her mind: telephone Kiernan. God only knew how he would be able to help now, but perhaps he could suggest something. Anything.

97

"Herr Kiernan here."

"This is Frau Emmerich speaking, Herr-"

"Listen. This is urgent," said Kiernan, cutting crisply across her. "I have a message for you. Cousin Victor will be catching the six o'clock train. Number Fourteen. It runs every three hours."

"Good God...." Marianne murmured under her breath. She stared unseeingly at the telephone cradle in front of her, a stunned expression on her face. It couldn't be true.... There had to be some mistake....

"Did you get that?" asked Kiernan urgently.

"Er - yes. You're sure it was Cousin Victor?"

"Absolutely sure."

"Thank you."

Abruptly, the connection was broken; Marianne did not know whether Kiernan had hung up or whether they had been cut off, but it did not greatly matter - she could not afford to delay any longer in either event. Her thoughts were racing as she walked rapidly away from the kiosk. So London had not abandoned her after all! 'Cousin Victor' was the codename for any agent from London, while the rest of the message had been crystal clear; she was to rendezvous with Cousin Victor at six o'clock, or three hours after that, at the phone booth in Kleist Strasse opposite Luther Strasse - Number Fourteen on the list of dead letter drops that she and Kiernan used. Crystal clear to her - but incomprehensible to anyone listening in. She noticed an elderly woman looking curiously at her as she passed, presumably wondering what she was smiling at and she forced her features back into a neutral expression, even though she felt like whooping for joy: they had come for her after all!

She wasn't beaten yet....

1800 HOURS.

Cormack shifted his weight restlessly, stretching out his left leg to ease the cramp before resuming his crouched position at the window that overlooked Kleist Strasse from the second storey of a half-demolished apartment block. From here, he could survey the street in either direction, while the telephone booth itself was almost opposite. He would be able to see Marianne approaching from some way off if she came along Kleist Strasse - if she came at all, Cormack reflected for perhaps the hundredth time. Three times now he had tried to contact Kiernan at the Embassy but the line had been dead on each occasion; there was no way of knowing if the message had reached her. Or if she was still alive....

He glanced over at Woodward, who was positioned at the west-facing window and received a mute shake of the head. Cormack wondered if his own face showed the same degree of tension as Woodward's; it would be understandable if it did. Although they were safe enough at the moment, holed up out of sight, they could not stay there indefinitely, not with the Russians drawing steadily closer. At any moment, there could be Soviet tanks rumbling past below - and they were both in SS uniform; Cormack doubted if they'd be given the chance to surrender. To cap it all, this was probably a fool's errand anyway; they should have got out of Berlin last night, if they'd had any sense.... What the hell were they doing here?

"Here comes trouble." Woodward's sotto voce comment broke into Cormack's thoughts; he scrambled over to Woodward's window and peered out. A German Army lorry was approaching, negotiating its way past the pothole and rubble and, as they watched, it passed by below them, coming to a halt about thirty yards away. Six soldiers jumped down from the back and a tripod mounted machine gun was lowered from the lorry, the sight of it confirming Cormack's worst fears.

"Shit...." he muttered savagely. "They're setting up a machine gun post."

"Oh, great...." Woodward murmured disgustedly. "Just what we needed."

The soldiers were working with practised efficiency, using sandbags and rubble to set up a low defensive wall that would provide cover against any attack coming down Kleist Strasse from the east, but the barricade still looked like a pile of rubble; clearly, these were seasoned troops. After ten minutes or so, the lorry turned and headed back the way it had come, leaving the six soldiers behind.

"Now what?" asked Woodward resignedly.

"You tell me," said Cormack softly. "Just hope they don't decide to post a look out up here."

"Bloody marvellous," Woodward muttered. It was a very real possibility, of course, because Cormack had chosen their present hide out for its excellent view of the street in both directions. "It never rains and all that."

Tensely, they watched the sergeant in charge of the detail post his men; one headed across the road and disappeared into a shop opposite. The sergeant looked thoughtfully around and Cormack muttered a soft curse as the NCO's gaze came to rest on their building; evidently he had come to the same conclusion as himself....

Then one of the soldiers called out to the sergeant and pointed along the street; Cormack looked in the direction indicated. "Oh, bloody hell, no."

"What?"

"It's her."

On the far side of the machine gun post, they could see a tall, slim woman approaching along the pavement; even at this distance, Cormack could see the long auburn hair. And she was heading straight towards the barricade; quite clearly, she had not seen either the soldiers or the machine gun.

But they had obviously seen her.

Marianne was hurrying, acutely aware of the fact that it was now after six o'clock and that there was no way of knowing whether the London agent would wait at the rendezvous; she was terrified by the fear that it would all go horribly wrong.... It had taken her over two hours to travel no more than a mile because of the constant detours to avoid patrols and checkpoints and now, in spite of telling herself to look casual, she was lengthening her stride in her haste to reach the rendezvous.

She did not see the machine gun post until it was too late; the sergeant in charge of the detachment seemed to materialise out of the rubble itself. "Excuse me, fraulein. Your papers, please?"

A hollow pit seemed to form in her stomach. "I - I've left them at home," she stammered, her voice shaking.

"You've left them at home," said the sergeant, looking her up and down slowly, appraisingly; without any warning at all, he sprang forward and grabbed her by the upper arm, pulling her behind the barricade. "Here, hold her," he snapped to two of the soldiers and pushed her towards them; they seized her and spun her round to face the sergeant, one of them holding each of her arms firmly.

"She's lost her papers, lads," said the sergeant, grinning, the expression on his face easily read. "No way of proving who she is."

"Nice looking bit, though," commented the corporal, licking his lips. He looked at the sergeant. "What d'you reckon?"

"Well, you know what standing orders are, Edelmann," said the sergeant. "We ought to send her to field HQ for interrogation."

"Why should they have all the fun?" Edelmann demanded. "We could interrogate her here, couldn't we?" He moved towards her, but the sergeant reached out an arm and held him back.

"Wait your turn, Edelmann." There was a leering grin on the sergeant's face. "I'm in charge here, so I get first go." He went over to Marianne and touched her cheek, ignoring the look of fear and loathing in her eyes. "You're right, Edelmann - she is a nice looking bit." His hand moved down to her breast.

"Don't touch me, you bastard!" she spat, squirming so violently that she managed to break free of one of the men holding her; she spun round and landed a stinging open-handed slap on the face of the second soldier before wrenching her other arm free. The next instant, her foot was lashing out at the sergeant's groin and it was only at the last moment that he dodged out of the way, taking the blow on his hip.

"You bitch!" he yelled and threw himself at her, the force of his rush knocking her off balance, so that she fell backwards with the sergeant on top of her. She twisted frantically underneath him, slashing at his face with her nails, but then he slapped her round the face with brutal force. "Right, you cow, you've asked for this!" He grabbed the top of her blouse and ripped it open.

"What the devil is going on here?"

The sergeant looked up, his face frozen in shocked surprise at this sudden interruption. Standing only five yards away was an SS-Colonel, his face set in an expression of fury. The sergeant's astonishment was mirrored on the faces of the other soldiers, none of whom, quite obviously, had noticed the Colonel's approach.

"On your feet, Sergeant!" Cormack barked, but the German hesitated, looking doubtfully at his comrades. "I said on your feet!" This time, the order was obeyed with evident reluctance. "I asked you just what was going on, Sergeant," Cormack said icily. "And I am still waiting for an answer."

"Nothing, Herr Colonel. She was resisting arrest."

Cormack flicked a glance at Marianne, who was rising shakily to her feet, holding her torn blouse together. "Why were you arresting her?"

"She had no papers, Herr Colonel." The sergeant's voice was more confident now, Cormack noticed; he was beginning to realise that he was only being confronted by a solitary man. It all hinged on how much respect he had for an SS-Colonel; by the look of it, not very much....

"And while you were so engrossed in all this, the whole damned Russian Army could have walked up!"

"I'm sorry, Herr Colonel," said the sergeant, not sounding sorry at all.

"You most probably will be," Cormack said ominously. "Right. If she has no papers, she falls under the jurisdiction of the Gestapo. I'll take her in for questioning. And I shall want a full report of this incident!"

The sergeant licked his lips nervously, but he did not look anywhere near as cowed as Cormack would have liked. The NCO looked around at the other men and replied, with a determined edge in his voice, "I don't think so, Herr Colonel. You just want her for yourself, don't you? Well, we saw her first - she's ours."

There was a general murmur of agreement amongst the others; two of the soldiers ostentatiously flicked off the safety catches on their rifles. There had always been bad feeling in the Army towards the SS and now, with everything collapsing around them, these men were seizing their opportunity to hit back.

"How dare you, Sergeant!" The NCO retreated a step before his wrath. "Hand the woman over at once!"

"And what will you do if we don't?" The sergeant sneered. "Put us on report? Or shoot us? Well, there's six of us and only one of you - remember that, Colonel!" He leaned over and picked up his Schmeisser, his eyes never leaving Cormack's.

"Now!" Cormack yelled and hurled himself to one side as Woodward opened up with the machine pistol from the window, raking the pavement in a withering burst of fire. The sergeant was thrown backwards by the impact of the bullets, arms outflung, as if a giant hand had picked him up and cast him carelessly aside; Cormack rolled away and up onto his feet. In three rapid strides, he had reached Marianne and pulled her aside, out of the line of fire as Woodward traversed the barrel, mowing down the astonished soldiers where they stood.

Abruptly, Woodward ceased firing, the sudden silence almost more shocking than the sound of the machine gun. Only one German was still standing, staring down at the sergeant's body lying at his feet. Cormack drew the Luger pistol from his belt and held it on the white faced soldier.

"Move over there!" he barked, gesturing towards the pile of rubble. "Move!"

Trembling, the soldier obeyed, gazing at the gun; he had no doubt whatsoever that the Colonel confronting him would use it at the slightest provocation.

"Right. Lie down on your stomach.... That's it. Now put your hands behind your head. Excellent." Cormack forced a note of gloating mockery into his voice. "I'm feeling generous today, so I'm letting you live. But don't try to do anything stupid or I'll change

102

my mind!" He turned to Marianne. "You - come with me!" Cormack pulled her roughly after him; she was shaking like a leaf.

Woodward appeared in front of them, the Schmeisser slung over his shoulder and carrying her suitcase, but she was too numbed by what had happened to recognise either it or him. Instead, she stared, horror-struck, at Cormack.

"Who are you?" she gasped. "You've just killed your own men!"

Cormack flicked a glance behind them and saw that the remaining soldier was still in earshot. "Quiet!" he snapped. "Or do you want to go the same way?"

"Where are you taking me?"

"I said quiet!" Cormack practically dragged her round the next corner and only then did he release her arm. "Sorry about that," he said, speaking in English for the first time.

She stared at him, open mouthed. "You - you're English!" Her eyes shifted to Woodward and widened still further. "Tony Woodward!" she whispered incredulously.

"The very same," Woodward grinned. "Your very own knight in shining armour."

"But - but-" She shook her head in bewilderment. "Bloody hell...." she whispered hoarsely, her tone now one of incredulous relief. "I didn't think anyone would come."

"How could you possibly doubt it, Marianne?" said Woodward nonchalantly. "We-"

"Look, leave all that for now, will you?" Cormack interrupted brusquely. "We've got to find a way out of this damn city."

2030 HOURS.

Marianne came back into what had once been the living room of an abandoned apartment off Kurfurstendamm to find Cormack and Woodward studying a map that was spread out on the table. They looked up at her approach. "Feel better now?" asked Woodward, smiling amiably.

"Much," she admitted. The first thing she had done once they had found the apartment in the half ruined block had been to change her clothes for some of those that Cormack had stuffed into her suitcase. The blouse and slacks she had been wearing had been dirty after the night in the derelict cellar, but it was the struggle with the sergeant that had been uppermost in her mind as she peeled off her ripped blouse and hurled it away. If Cormack hadn't shown up then.... she had pushed the thought aside resolutely. They were here; the miracle had happened and now, for perhaps the first time, she could believe she had a chance of escaping. But first, there was something she had to tell them and she might as well get it over with now.... "I'm afraid I've got some bad news for you."

Cormack looked at her, his expression unfathomable; she had already noticed this trait of this - never revealing his thoughts. "Bad news?"

"The film containing photos of the ODESSA documents - I haven't got it any more."

"And where is it?" asked Cormack, his tone of voice as opaque as his face.

"In the flat," she admitted quietly. "I didn't have time to take it with me. But I can remember most of what the documents said," she added, as a placatory gesture.

To her surprise, Cormack merely shrugged. "Then there's no problem, is there? No use crying over spilt milk, anyway."

Marianne stared at him disbelievingly; was he really as unconcerned as he seemed? She had just told him that the one thing they had come for was lost for good and he didn't seem to give a damn.... "But-" she began, before Cormack cut her off.

"Look, if you think I'm going to go back for the film, you've got another think coming. The Gestapo have probably got it by now, anyway."

"But - but wasn't that why you were sent here?"

"It may be why we were sent, but it wasn't why we came," said Cormack obliquely.

Dazedly, she continued to stare at him: now what the hell did he mean by that?

"Anyway," he continued briskly, evidently dismissing the subject, "what I'm worried about at the moment is how we're going to get out of Berlin. What plans did you and Fegelein have?"

"I don't know exactly," she confessed. "He said a plane was coming to collect us, but he didn't say where."

"You're sure he didn't?"

She thought for a few seconds and shook her head. "No, I'm positive he said nothing at all. He was pretty drunk and not making much sense, but he certainly didn't mention anything like that." She stared at Cormack. "Why? Were you thinking about taking the same route out?"

"It's a possibility," said Cormack noncommittally.

Woodward was examining the map intently. "It can't have been Tempelhof," he said, half to himself. "The Russians have already

104

taken that. And Gatow's been cut off, so it can't have been there either." He looked up at Cormack. "I reckon it's the same way we came in - the East-West Axis."

"Looks like it, doesn't it?" Cormack agreed. He turned to Marianne again. "Did Fegelein say anything about a contingency plan? If something went wrong with the rendezvous?"

She shook her head again. "No - nothing."

"There must have been one, though, Alan," said Woodward. "Twenty-four hours later, at the same place - that's what they do in the Moon Squadron if a pick-up goes wrong."

Cormack nodded. "Makes sense." For several seconds, he stared at the map, deep in thought before he began to fold it up, his movements suddenly brisk, decisive. "Right," he said. "Let's give it a go."

"Give what a go?" asked Marianne suspiciously.

"The likelihood is that there'll be another plane tonight sent in for Fegelein - we can use it ourselves," explained Woodward glibly.

"You can't be serious!" she protested incredulously. "If the plane is coming back, Fegelein will have told them all about it, believe you me - he'd do anything to save his own skin! They'll be waiting for us, won't they?"

"They could be," Cormack conceded, his eyes hooded, yet Marianne somehow sensed that he shared her fears. "But they won't be expecting us - Tony and me - will they? It's worth a try, anyway. And we won't be rushing in with our eyes closed either - what we'll do is take a good long look and if the area is crawling with the Gestapo then we beat a hasty retreat. The point is, if we can get that plane, we could be out of here in a matter of hours." As he spoke, a memory came back to him; two years before, he had said virtually those same words, just before they had made that suicidal raid on the airfield and that decision of his had cost three people their lives.... With an involuntary shudder of premonition, he forced his mind back to the present.

"You can't just steal a plane and expect to get away with it!" Marianne persisted.

"Oh, I don't know," said Woodward easily. "We're beginning to get the hang of it, actually." He flashed a conspiratorial smile at Cormack, but there was no response; in a flash of insight, Woodward knew why.

Cormack was wondering if history was about to repeat itself.

CHAPTER 8.

MIDNIGHT, 28TH/29TH APRIL: THE BRANDENBURG GATE.

Rindt stood next to his Kubelwagen, looking over at the Ju52 that was parked next to the Charlottenburger Chaussee; as Fegelein had said, it had been sent in a second time tonight to try and pick him up, although, of course, it was now too late for that. The pilot had been only too willing to talk once his plane had been boarded by Rindt's team - in fact, he had seemed relieved that he would not have to wait for Fegelein. All that remained to be seen was whether Marianne would appear to try and bluff her way aboard the plane, but Rindt, despite his earlier arguments to Mueller, was beginning to doubt that she would make any such attempt. It was fraught with far too many risks from her point of view and she would be much safer trying to escape from Berlin on foot, as Mueller had said, but the fact was that Rindt had nothing else to go on at the moment. There had been no reported sightings of her, nor had there been any leads where she might be - unless one counted the ambiguous report that he had received from the team that was keeping the Irish Embassy under surveillance. One of the attaches, a man named Kiernan, had left the embassy at just before ten o'clock that morning and had returned less than thirty minutes later. The only person he had spoken to, according to his shadower, had been a Colonel who had asked for his papers and had then apparently told him to return to the embassy. Had Kiernan been going out to meet Marianne and had he then been turned back? If that was the case, then Rindt would dearly like to get his hands on that Colonel.... at the same time, he knew that he was clutching at straws; the evidence that Kiernan had any connection with Marianne was merely circumstantial, at best.

What it boiled down to was this: Marianne had been missing for over twenty-four hours now and in that time, she could have succeeded in getting out of Berlin altogether. Or she could be dead - how would that affect the 'bargain' that had been struck with Hentschel? Rindt took a deep breath in a conscious effort to relax; his nerves seemed to be jangling, stretched to breaking point, and there was nothing he could do at the moment except wait.... and hope.

106

"Herr Colonel?" said a voice behind him; Rindt turned suddenly to see a young trooper saluting him.

"Yes?"

"Field Marshal von Greim has just arrived, Herr Colonel."

Rindt nodded. "You'd better tell the pilot." As the trooper nodded and left, Rindt shook his head in disbelief. Half an hour before, an Arado-96 aircraft had landed, its pilot having been given orders to pick up Ritter von Greim and his mistress, Hannah Reitsch, probably the best known test pilot in Germany. The couple had been summoned to Berlin from von Greim's headquarters near Munich only two days before by Hitler, but their journey had proved costly. In the last but one leg, from Rechlin to Gatow, half of their fighter escort of twenty planes had been shot down and then, flying the last stage into Berlin in a Fieseler Storch, von Greim had been wounded in the foot by AA shells, so that Hannah Reitsch had been obliged to land the plane herself. They had been whisked off to the Bunker, where, just before von Greim was carried into an operating theatre for surgery on his injured foot, he had been told by Hitler that he was now the new Commander-in-Chief of the Luftwaffe.... A man had probably been maimed for life and ten desperately needed fighters shot down just so that Hitler could tell von Greim of his promotion in person.... Madness.

A movement through the trees that lined the Charlottenburger Chaussee attracted his attention. An armoured vehicle had pulled up and its three passengers were emerging; one was on crutches and had to be helped by his two companions, one of whom, judging by her petite build, had to be Hannah Reitsch. The young pilot of the Arado appeared and went over to them, helping von Greim towards the tiny aircraft. The third man, who had arrived with von Greim and Hannah Reitsch, now returned to the vehicle and Rindt watched the two lovers and the pilot as they shuffled away. God only knew how that pilot was going to cope; he had confessed to Rindt that the Arado was only a two-seater and that they were going to have to squeeze Hannah in behind the pilot's seat. Rindt wished them luck....

Again, he looked at his watch and wandered over towards the Ju52. He might as well check that his men were in position; despite his growing conviction that Marianne would not appear, he had made his preparations on the assumption that she would. All he could do now was wait.

Cormack pressed his back against a tree trunk, peered around it and, satisfied that the coast was clear, beckoned to the others.

Silently, Woodward and Marianne emerged from the shadows and joined him. "There it is," Cormack whispered, pointing at the looming bulk of the Brandenburg Gate, about a hundred yards away through the trees. They were only fifty yards away from the East-West Axis itself and its hastily improvised landing strip.

"Any sign of the plane?" murmured Woodward.

"No. Which end of the runway would it be?"

"This end. The wind's from the west - he'd want to take off into it."

"Right. We'll head towards the Gate." Cormack took a long look around and made off in a low crouching run through the trees, barely visible even to Woodward who was watching him intently. After he had gone thirty yards or so, Woodward saw Cormack come to a halt and look around again; moments later, he saw Cormack's beckoning gesture.

"Let's go," he muttered to Marianne. They had taken perhaps half a dozen steps when the entire East-West Axis was bathed in light; cursing, he bundled her back into the shadows.

"What's happening?" Marianne hissed.

"Runway lights," Woodward replied tersely. "Someone's either landing or taking off." Suddenly, he pointed. "There." He gasped incredulously. "The stupid bastard's taking off the wrong way!"

It was true. The plane, an Arado-96, was accelerating along the runway, heading straight for the Brandenburg Gate, presumably to fool the Russian flak gunners but it seemed it would be impossible to clear the massive structure. "Go on," Woodward whispered. "Keep those throttles wide open.... Now pull back - get those wheels off the deck.... Go on! Go on!" In his mind's eye, Woodward was in the cockpit, seeing that huge arch hurtling towards him.... God Almighty, he wasn't going to make it....

And then the Arado was airborne, climbing away from the ground, but had the pilot left it too late? Woodward held his breath as the little plane clawed its way into the air.... It seemed it must hit the top of the Gate, but at the last moment, the pilot found power from somewhere and the Arado soared over it, just missing the sculpted charioteer on top of the arch; within seconds, it had disappeared from view. It could only have been a matter of feet.... Woodward nodded respectfully; whoever had been flying that plane had been one hell of a pilot.

Abruptly, the entire scene was plunged into darkness as the lights were extinguished and it was only now that Woodward began to wonder if that had been Fegelein's plane, so absorbed had he been with the take off itself. If it was, then they might as well

108

give up now....

He looked over to where Cormack was and saw him beckon once more; they reached him within seconds. "I hope to God that wasn't Fegelein's plane," said Woodward, voicing his thoughts.

"Doesn't really matter if it was," Cormack replied. "There's another one parked over there - see it?" He pointed through the trees to a point fifty yards away, where the trees had been cleared away completely to form a parking bay large enough to house a single aircraft. In the cleared area, Woodward could just make out the distinctive silhouette of a Ju52.

"Got it," he murmured. "Any sign of any Jerries?"

"Haven't seen any." Cormack was carefully scanning the area around the aircraft, but could see nothing. Not that this proved anything; if the Germans were, indeed, watching the plane, they would be well out of sight, whereas he would have to cross the open space of the parking bay in order to reach the aircraft.

He pondered the situation, knowing full well that he was merely postponing the moment of crossing that exposed stretch. It was at least an even chance that the Gestapo would be watching the Ju52; not for the first time, he asked himself what the hell they were doing here, when it could very likely turn out to be a trap....

The answer, of course, was simple; as he had said to Marianne earlier, they could not afford to miss any possible opportunity to get out of Berlin, but such rationalisations did nothing to quieten the fears that were knotting up his insides. Cormack did not want to cross these last few yards to the plane - but he damned well had to, whether he liked it or not.

"Don't move until I signal," he said softly. "And if anything happens, get the hell out of it." Taking one last look round, he headed towards the parking area, once more in a low crouch, his Schmeisser held across his body.

Suddenly, he dropped flat to the ground as someone came into view from behind the Ju52; he was wearing a pilot's helmet. Only to be expected, Cormack, he told himself scathingly, sneering at the stab of fear that had seemed to turn his legs to jelly: pull yourself together! Silently, he rose to his feet and slipped into cover behind a tree.

Yet again, he checked his surroundings, but there was still no sign of any Germans except for the pilot, who was standing only twenty feet away, his back now turned to Cormack. Slowly, Cormack reached inside his tunic and took out his silenced Browning pistol; holding his right wrist steady with his left hand, he lined up the barrel on the pilot, aiming between the shoulderblades. At this range, with a stationary target, he could not possibly miss.... his finger began to tighten on the trigger.

And stopped.

This was murder, pure and simple, cold blooded murder - shooting a man in the back. Don't be so bloody stupid, Cormack! he told himself. You've killed men before, you've shot them, strangled them, slit their throats - why this sudden attack of morality? Shoot the bastard!

But he couldn't.... Of its own volition, almost, his right arm was bringing the gun down, his hand already beginning to tremble uncontrollably. Jesus Christ, he thought bitterly, you really are in a state, aren't you?

Suddenly, the pilot turned round and, as though guided by some sixth sense, looked straight at Cormack. The German's reaction was instantanous; his hand came up, holding a gun, which must have been there all the time, concealed by his body.... Cormack fired two rapid shots, the bullets hitting the pilot in the chest within an inch of each other; the German fell tiredly backwards onto the grass.

Cormack dropped into a crouch again and pivoted round on one heel, executing a three hundred and sixty degree scan of his surroundings; there was still nothing to be seen. Slowly, looking all the while to left and right, he moved forward to the motionless figure of the pilot, who was lying on his back, arms spreadeagled, his eyes staring sightlessly upwards. He was wearing a Luftwaffe uniform - but did that prove anything either way? He could be a bona fide pilot who had been carrying a gun simply because it was night and a Russian advance party could appear at any moment - or he could be in the Gestapo.

Silently, Cormack moved towards the aircraft, his pistol held in a hand that was now rock steady. He was moving so that he turned through a complete circle every four or five steps, his eyes watching every pool of shadow. It had to be a trap, he decided - the pilot had reacted too quickly.... But the plane was still there; he could not just walk away and leave it.

He came to a halt next to the main passenger hatch and pulled it open, slowly, the Browning aimed up into the hatchway. There was a sudden movement in the shadows inside and he squeezed the trigger twice more; he heard a muffled cry and a heavy crash of someone falling but by then he was sprinting away from the aircraft.

And now there were figures all around him, materialising out of the darkness; he snapped off two quick shots at someone over to the left and heard the staccato clatter of a Schmeisser opening up in front of him and he knew he was as good as dead.... But the Schmeisser was cradled in Woodward's arms and he was raking the Gestapo agents with the same murderous accuracy as he had dealt with the soldiers earlier on; Cormack sprinted the last few yards and skidded to a halt behind the tree that Woodward was using for cover.

Woodward ceased firing. "I'll cover you!" he yelled. "Turn and turn about?"

Cormack nodded. "Right." He unslung his own Schmeisser and checked his gun as Woodward opened up again; another Gestapo agent threw his arms up in the air and fell backwards, while two others dived flat to the ground. "Ready?" Cormack said to Marianne, who nodded firmly. "Go!" Cormack and Marianne broke into a run, taking cover behind a tree thirty yards away. Moments later, Woodward came pelting after them but there was someone behind him; Cormack unleashed a brief burst of fire that cut down the pursuing German. As Woodward flattened himself against the tree trunk, Cormack looked around again and saw that they were only about fifty yards from a street with apartment buildings on the far side. "Keep going!" he hissed. "I'll bring up the rear." He saw the momentary look of protest on Woodward's face and gestured angrily. "Look, we haven't got time to argue! Get moving!"

Woodward hesitated an instant longer and nodded; Cormack slammed another ammunition clip into the breech and fired a burst round the tree as Woodward and Marianne broke into a run behind him. Seconds later, he was sprinting after them, emerging from the parkland and across the street to where they had taken cover in an alleyway entrance.

Again, Cormack reached inside his tunic and took out two grenades. "Get going!" he shouted to Woodward and Marianne. "These should stop them!" The three of them ran along the alley, but Cormack stopped after thirty yards or so and looked back the way they had come. Any moment now, their pursuers would reach the end of the alleyway; one after the other, he pulled the pins out of the grenades and lobbed them back along the passageway, just as the first pursuers came pounding into view. In such a confined space, the effect of the exploding grenades was devastating; the end of the alley erupted into flame and flying debris and Cormack poured a continuous burst of automatic fire into the dust and smoke. He could hear shouts and screams of agony above the harsh stuttering of the Schmeisser, but he deliberately shut out the sounds; he turned and ran after Marianne and Woodward.

The medical orderly sighed and straightened up slowly from his crouching position beside the motionless figure sprawled on the pavement. He looked at Rindt and shook his head slowly.

Rindt scarcely noticed; he was still staring blankly at the corpse. Seven men dead or wounded in what should have been a routine arrest of a single unarmed woman; who had those other two been? There had been no way that he could have foreseen that Marianne would have found help in her escape, but she obviously had - and highly expert help at that. And so she had escaped - again - and this time there was no saying where she had gone, because these two men had changed everything. They were almost certainly British or American agents, sent in to carry out this one specific task: to get 'Das Leck' out of Berlin. It was no longer a case of searching for a solitary woman wandering helplessly through the streets but of tracking down a highly trained team of agents who had probably already switched over to a predetermined escape plan. They were armed, would have brought false identification papers and would also have been carefully selected; the odds against finding Marianne had lengthened considerably now.

He closed his eyes in rage and frustration. Damn! Damn you, Marianne! And damn the British! But that was no good; they were simply doing what they had been ordered to do. They couldn't know what was at stake for him and even if they did, it would make no difference. In any case, they were not to blame: he was. Setting up the ambush had been his responsibility and it didn't matter a damn that the two men had taken them by surprise; he should have seen the possibility that she might not have been alone. The ambush should have been watertight, regardless of what help she might have found - but it hadn't been and if, as a result, Marianne escaped, then....

Whatever happened to Inga would be his fault.

"Damn!" he yelled and smashed his fist into the wall beside him.

SUNDAY, APRIL 29TH: 0130 HOURS.

Cormack threw himself flat to the ground as another shell exploded nearby, waiting until the pattering of earth and pebbles falling around him had ceased before looking cautiously around. Woodward and Marianne were still huddled in the doorway where he had left them, thirty yards or so behind him. There was no-one else in sight.

The street was a shambles, with hardly a building remaining intact, while the tenement block on the corner was blazing furiously, sending great gouts of oily black smoke up into the night sky and illuminating the entire road. Somewhere in the distance, Cormack could hear a fire bell ringing - surely they weren't fighting fires in this inferno? For every blaze they managed to put out, another dozen would be started by the relentless Russian bombardment and yet the fire service was still carrying out its duty.... Like trying to extinguish Vesuvius with buckets of water, Cormack thought, but without any trace of mockery.

Cautiously, he rose to his feet and moved off along the street, looking constantly about him for any sign of an approaching Russian patrol, because this was where they would be, he estimated. Since fleeing from the Brandenburg Gate, they had been making their way along Alt Moabit, taking cover or detouring along side streets whenever a German Army patrol had appeared and had crossed the Spree via the Moltke Bridge. In all that time, they had travelled barely half a mile, but Cormack guessed that they must be close to the Russian lines, judging by the crackle of small arms fire. He took cover in a doorway and beckoned the others to follow; they came running towards him, almost bent double, until they were safely hidden in the shadows.

Woodward opened his mouth to say something, then froze at the sound of vehicle engines above the incessant rumble of exploding shells. The three of them moved further back, Cormack and Woodward holding their machine pistols at the ready and no sooner had they done so than two Russian armoured cars came into view from the north, picking their way gingerly through the rubble that littered the street. Behind them came infantrymen, irregularly spaced and with their weapons held in front of them, clear testimony of their expertise in street fighting.

Suddenly a figure appeared in an upstairs window and threw a stick grenade that bounced in the road in front of the leading armoured car and rolled underneath it. The explosion lifted the car bodily off the road surface in a welter of flame and smoke. Two more grenades came arcing out into the street from the darkened windows and Cormack heard the clatter of gunfire.

The Russians were already scrambling for cover, raking the windows with sub machine guns, while the heavier machine gun on the second car was blazing away; all the Germans seemed to have, as far as Cormack could tell, were rifles. The leading Russian car was ablaze and its crew were scrambling out, yet none of the German bullets seemed to be hitting them.

The battle was hopelessly one-sided; the Russians were moving from cover to cover, remorselessly and it was only rarely that any of them went down - Cormack guessed that they were being confronted by nothing more than a Volkssturm unit, the German equivalent of the Home Guard - and they were brushing aside the resistance with almost contemptuous ease. Within a minute or so of the initial attack, they had closed in on the two buildings that housed the Germans, but then, unexpectedly, they stopped advancing.

Cormack did not have to wait long to find out why. A Russian T-34 tank was rounding the corner from a side road, its gun already lining up on its target. It fired and the front of the left hand building exploded outwards as the shell ripped into it and, seconds later, the second shot smashed into the other building. Slowly, majestically, both blocks came crashing down, collapsing inwards like a house of cards, sending up dense clouds of dust and debris.

"Jesus Christ...." Cormack whispered, awe-struck. They hadn't had a chance.... He watched incredulously as smoke-shrouded figures emerged from the wreckage, firing their weapons in a last gesture of defiance. To a man, they were cut down before they had gone ten yards.

Except one. A solitary figure came running out from what had been the side of the building and sprinted along the road towards their hiding place. For a moment, it looked as though none of the Russians had seen him, but then there was a burst of automatic fire and the fleeing German threw up his arms, falling forward and rolling over and over until he came to a halt only yards from the doorway. Cormack stared at the dead face and shook his head in disbelief; he could not have been any more than twelve years old....

"Come on," he hissed urgently and headed through the doorway into the wrecked building behind them. Carefully, they picked their way through the debris that littered the floor until they came to the back door, which had been blown off its hinges. Cormack led the way through the backyard and pulled open a rickety gate that gave onto an alleyway. Signalling the others to wait, Cormack trotted along the alley until he reached a street running at right angles to the one they had just left. There was no-one in sight; he beckoned to Marianne and Woodward to join him.

"Right," he said tersely. "Keep your eyes peeled - we must be right on the front line now."

And so it began again, the pattern that had been established over the last hour and a half, with Cormack advancing thirty or forty yards to the next available cover and calling up the other two once he was satisfied it was safe. Then another thirty yards. And another. Duck into a ruined building as a truck rumbled past, followed by infantrymen, dive flat to the ground when a shell exploded, turn into a side road at the sound of vehicle engines, a seemingly endless series of repetitions while all around them, Berlin was being torn apart.

It was the stuff of which nightmares are made, scenes from Hell lit by the leaping flames of the burning buildings that sent dense palls of smoke that enveloped them, tearing at their lungs as they fought for breath. Each street was strewn with rubble, wrecked vehicles.... and the dead and dying. Marianne literally fell over the body of a woman at one point as she stumbled through the smoke; she looked down to see what she had tripped over and almost threw up when she saw the horribly mutilated corpse. Woodward lifted her unceremoniously and virtually dragged her away after Cormack; for a moment, she thought he had not seen the dead woman - then he caught a glimpse of his face and its stricken, haunted expression and she knew that he had.... Was this really the Tony Woodward she had known before the war, in another world? She shook her head; it was as if she were with a complete stranger - but then was she the same Marianne Driscoll he had known?

Finally, Cormack called a halt at about two thirty, leading them into the lobby of an apartment block; only the ground floor was still intact. "Right," he gasped. "We'll take a breather. Ten minutes, then we're off again."

Gratefully, Marianne slumped to the floor, her back against the wall, gasping for breath. Cormack took out a map and spread it on the floor, shining a torch so that they could study it.

"I reckon we're somewhere about here," said Cormack, pointing to the map.

Woodward shook his head wearily. "We've come further than that, surely?"

"Afraid not, Tony, but we've got to be past the front line by now."

"Yes, but are we going to make the rendezvous at this rate?"

Cormack shrugged. "God knows - but there's damn all else we can do. Unless we can steal a car or something."

Woodward nodded gloomily and went over to join Marianne,

sitting down next to her. "You all right, Marianne?"

"Just about, Tony." She nodded towards Cormack. "He certainly doesn't believe in hanging about, does he?"

"Alan? No, he doesn't, I suppose. But he knows what he's doing."

"I'd got that impression already. It's you I can't get over, Tony. How did you come to be involved in anything like this?"

Woodward grinned sheepishly. "It seemed like a good idea at the time, Marianne."

She waited for a few moments but, when it was obvious that he was not going to elaborate, she said, "What is this rendezvous you mentioned?"

"A pick up. He sent a message through your contact at the Embassy to send in a plane to pick us up tomorrow night."

"So what were we doing trying to steal a plane tonight?"

"Alan doesn't believe in hanging about, as you said, Marianne," Woodward replied, grinning. "It was worth a try - especially as there's no guarantee that we'll make it to the rendezvous."

"Damn nearly got us all killed though, didn't he?"

"Ah, but he didn't though, did he? And if it had paid off, we'd have been home and dry by now."

"You seem to have a lot of faith in him, Tony."

Woodward nodded. "I suppose I do, actually. But-"

"Quiet!" Cormack hissed, gesturing urgently at them. "Listen!"

They could hear nothing but the distant rumble of explosions in the distance for several seconds but then they heard a voice that sounded as though it were just outside, in the street. Cormack flicked off the torch, barely in time; the street door opened and two figures stood silhouetted in the doorway. Abruptly, one of them switched on a torch, shining it around the lobby; the beam of light steadied as it picked out Marianne and Woodward. One of the newcomers said something in Russian to the other one, who brought up his rifle. There were two muffled coughs and the man with the torch staggered backwards as the bullets from Cormack's silenced automatic hit him in the chest. The torch dropped from his grasp, but before it hit the floor, Cormack had fired again, hitting the second Russian in the shoulder, sending him crashing into the door jamb. The Browning coughed once more and the Russian was thrown back against the wall before toppling forwards.

Cormack sprang to the doorway and looked outside; there was nobody else in sight, thank God. Letting out his breath in a long sigh of relief, he turned back to the others. "Right. We'd better get moving again." His voice sounded calm, matter-of-fact.

Shakily, Marianne rose to her feet, deliberately not looking at the two bodies on the floor as she stepped over them. Instead, she stared as if mesmerised at Cormack, who could kill two men in less than five seconds and yet show no emotion at all.... What sort of man was he? Blindly, she pushed past him.

Woodward picked up the map and followed Marianne out, but as he passed Cormack, the other man moved slightly so that his face was no longer in shadow and Woodward saw the look in his eyes. He was troubled; he had seen that expression too many times already in this war.

Cormack looked as though he were about to scream.

0330 HOURS.

It was an hour later that Cormack's wish was granted. They had reached Reinickendorf and were making better time as there were fewer patrols about. Despite this, Cormack never turned a corner or crossed a street without checking first. Once again, he peered round the next corner, but, this time, he ducked back hurriedly, gesturing to Woodward and Marianne, who flattened themselves against the wall behind him.

"What is it?" Woodward whispered hoarsely.

"A car. Just round the corner." Carefully, Cormack took a second look. The car was a Mercedes, presumably one that had been captured by the Russians, and was parked no more than twenty yards away. Someone was sitting in the rear of the car and, as Cormack watched, two Russian soldiers came out of the nearest building, each one carrying a suitcase. One of them opened up the boot of the car and started loading the cases into it; obviously, they were looting the building, a block of fairly comfortable flats, by the look of it.

He turned back. "Three men," he told Woodward tersely. "One in the back of the car. Ready?"

Woodward checked the magazine of his Schmeisser and pushed it firmly back into the breech. "Ready."

Cormack glanced round the corner again and nodded to Woodward before pivoting round so that he was facing the car. Woodward took two rapid steps to give himself a clear field of fire and, almost simultaneously, both Schmeissers opened up. The Russian soldiers were thrown against the back of the car before they slumped lifelessly down into the road. Cormack sprinted to the car to wrench open the rear door.

"Come on, out!" he yelled in German, gesturing with the Schmeisser. "Out!"

The passenger scrambled desperately out, his eyes wide in shock and fear. He wore the uniform of a Captain but Cormack scarcely noticed; grabbing the Russian by the tunic, he hurled him against the wall before stepping forward and slamming the gun butt into the back of the officer's head. The Russian collapsed on the pavement, unconscious.

"Into the back, Marianne!" he yelled, scooping up the dead soldiers' guns and ammunition clips; he slammed down the boot. Woodward was already climbing into the driver's seat and, within seconds, the Mercedes was accelerating away along the darkened street.

"Which way?" Woodward shouted urgently.

"Take the next right," Marianne answered without hesitation; Woodward nodded and spun the wheel, the tyres screeching as the car took the corner, still picking up speed. "Keep going," Marianne instructed, leaning forward onto the back of the driving seat and staring intently through the windscreen.

Cormack glanced at her and nodded to himself in unspoken approval while he pushed a replacement ammunition clip into the Schmeisser's breech - there was nothing wrong with her nerves, he decided and shook his head in amusement at the patronising assessment. Of course there wasn't anything wrong with her nerves - she wouldn't have survived this long as a spy if there were....

"Now left," said Marianne quietly. Woodward nodded again and wrenched the wheel over; the rear end slewed outwards, but he corrected for the skid and pressed his foot down on the accelerator, grinning hugely - he was clearly enjoying every minute of the breakneck drive. His expression changed abruptly, however, as he stamped on the brake.

There was a road block ahead, about two hundred yards away at an intersection, consisting of a jeep and a row of oil drums in a line across the road; Cormack saw all this in a single glance and yelled, "Keep going, Tony! Right on through!"

Woodward looked at him, a protest on his lips, but then nodded when he saw Cormack's expression and changed down a gear, jamming his foot to the floor again; the car surged forward, straight at the oil drums. If they were full, thought Woodward.... Jesus Christ.

As he wound down the window, Cormack was thinking virtually the same thing, but it was a calculated risk and, anyway, it was

118

too late to change his mind now.... "Lights, Tony!"

Woodward flicked on the headlamps, full beam; Cormack caught a momentary glimpse of two Russian soldiers holding up their arms to shield their eyes from the blinding glare and he leaned out of the window, squeezing the Schmeisser's trigger. The nearest Russian soldier spun away, arms outstretched as the bullets scythed into him; the second threw himself aside, out of the path of the oncoming car, a look of incredulous astonishment on his face. Cormack, Woodward and Marianne braced themselves for the impact as the oil drums seemed to leap at them.

At just over forty miles an hour, the Mercedes smashed into the drums - and scattered them like matchwood; Woodward fought the wheel as the car slewed round, but regained control when the rear tyre rebounded from the kerb. Cormack twisted round, still leaning out of the window and unleashed a burst of fire back behind them. A third soldier, who had been beyond the road block, clutched at his stomach and staggered backwards, falling heavily against the jeep before collapsing face down in the road. His face like stone, Cormack kept his finger on the trigger, traversing the barrel to and fro until the magazine was exhausted; by then, the checkpoint was receding into the darkness behind them. Slowly, he sat back in his seat and relaxed, his eyes closed as he drew in a long breath.

For almost a minute, nobody said anything until Woodward murmured, "Bloody hell...."

"Amen to that," Cormack agreed.

"Alan?" said Woodward hesitantly.

"Yes?"

"How did you know those oil drums were empty?"

"I didn't," Cormack replied bluntly.

"You what?"

"I didn't know. But it was a fair bet. They'd have had to move those drums every time they let a vehicle through - would you fancy doing that if they'd been full? Anyway, any full drums would have been at a fuel dump, not being used for road blocks."

"Fair enough," commented Woodward. "Makes sense. But what if you'd been wrong?"

Cormack shook his head. "Don't even think about it, Tony. Don't even think about it."

119

CHAPTER 9.

SUNDAY, APRIL 29TH: MORNING.

Dawn found them taking refuge in an isolated barn fifteen miles north west of Berlin, near the village of Pausin. Once they had reached the outskirts of Berlin, they had run into a constant stream of refugees pouring out of the beleaguered city; the congested roads had been in marked contrast to the almost eerie emptiness in the city itself, where the inhabitants who had decided to stay put had been hiding amongst the ruins. More than once, Cormack had bellowed at the refugees to get out of the damned way - couldn't they see he was on vital Gestapo business? A few had turned helpless, apathetic faces at the car as it had gone past, but most had not bothered to look up as they trudged wearily onward.... straight towards the Russian troops they were trying to escape. And so Cormack had taken the car past the seemingly endless line of people, deliberately closing his mind to their plight, telling himself that there was nothing they could do to help anyway....

Cormack turned the car off the road when the sky began to lighten and drove up a farm track until they found the barn. They covered the car with straw, just in case anybody should look through the door before they clambered up a rickety ladder to the upper level. As Marianne and Woodward sank down, exhausted, Cormack went over to the shuttered window above the door and opened it a fraction, looking out to see what sort of a vantage point it was; he nodded in satisfaction and turned to the others. "Right," he said quietly. "I'm going to pull rank for once." He came over to them and sat down, leaning his back gratefully against the wall; for the first time, Marianne saw how lined and drawn his face was. "You take first watch, Tony. Keep a lookout through that window - if anyone comes, it'll be along that track. Wake me in four hours." He closed his eyes and, within moments, seemed to be fast asleep.

Woodward glanced at Marianne and shrugged theatrically. "Better do as the man says, I suppose." He went over to the window; after a moment or so, Marianne joined him. She nodded over at Cormack.

"Is he really as unconcerned as he looks?"

Woodward shook his head gently. "He wouldn't thank me for

telling you, Marianne. That's something you'll have to find out for yourself."

"He seems to know what he's about, though."

"Oh, he does that. One of the best, so I'm told - I'm certainly not going to argue about that."

"You two seem to make a pretty good team."

Woodward looked surprised. "Do we? I suppose we do, actually."

"But you seem so different."

"What, because he didn't go to public school, you mean? Because his accent isn't what one would expect to hear in an officer's mess? To tell you the truth, I couldn't stand him the first time I met him - and the feeling was mutual. But - well, at the risk of sounding melodramatic, I'd trust him with my life. Hell, I already have, more than once."

Marianne looked at Woodward thoughtfully. "You like him, don't you?"

Woodward nodded. "I suppose I do, yes."

"But how can you? He seems a right bastard, to be honest."

"That's what I thought too. But-" he broke off, his expression suddenly far away, as though remembering.... Presently, he continued quietly, "He isn't a bastard, Marianne, believe me. And if anyone can get us out of here, he can."

Marianne was taken aback by the tone almost of hero-worship in his voice; Woodward, she remembered, never took anything - or anyone - seriously. "He's certainly created an impression on you, Tony. But-" she hesitated.

"But what?"

"It's you I can't get over. I thought you were a pilot in the RAF, not an undercover agent."

"So did I," said Woodward almost wistfully.

"I mean - I could always imagine you as a pilot, but not like this."

"The same applies to you, Marianne. I could never see you as a potential spy."

"Neither did I, Tony," she replied, her face serious. "You haven't seen what those Nazis are doing to the Jews. They're evil and they have to be stopped." She looked at Woodward. "I couldn't just sit back and do nothing once I realised what they were up to. It wasn't only that - I'm half English anyway, so I had to do something, or I'd have gone mad, I think."

Woodward stared at her, shocked by her words, remembering the girl he had met eight years before. Young, vivacious - a bit of a flirt, perhaps, but above all happy and outgoing. Now there was a haunted look in her eyes, as if she had witnessed horrors that would be with her for the rest of her life.

"They arrested Janos - my husband," she said quietly. "I can't say that we were very close by then, but he hadn't done anything at all against the Nazis - yet they threw him into Dachau."

"Dachau?" Woodward asked, evidently perplexed.

She laughed bitterly. "You won't have heard of if yet, but you will, believe me. You will. I once saw a document in the Propaganda Ministry that described how many Jews had been 'processed' that week. By 'processed' they mean killed - exterminated, as they put it. Over five thousand in one week - and they still felt there was room for improvement. Five thousand. Now do you see why I had to do it?"

"My God," Woodward whispered. "There've been rumours, but - I always thought they were exaggerated a bit for public consumption. You know, like the stories about the Huns eating babies in the last war."

"Believe them, Tony. I've listened to the BBC broadcasts and they don't measure up to anything like what's really going on. I know the Nazi leaders, Tony - I know what they're like - and they've got to be stopped. I'll tell you how revolted I am by them, Tony. If I'd had a chance to kill Hitler, I'd have done so, with my bare hands. They're loathsome. Absolutely evil."

"They're on the way out now, Marianne," Woodward reminded her gently.

"I know - thank God. And it's nearly all over. That's what I can't believe - that it really is all over. That I don't have to sleep with that bastard Fegelein or any of them again. That I can finally call it a day. I'm free at last...." Her voice tailed off and she stared across the barn without seeing any of it; she was far away, remembering, reliving the experiences of the past months.... Slowly, steadily, she began to cry, the tears streaming down her cheeks as she finally gave way to her pent up emotions. Reacting instinctively, Woodward put his arms round her and pulled her head onto his chest, gently stroking her hair.

"Oh God, Tony.... I can't believe it.... Tell me it's all over. Tell me I don't have to go through any more.... I don't think I could now.... Tony, I'm so scared!"

Dimly, Woodward could perceive just how rigidly she had kept herself under control for so long, simply in order to survive. God, how had she done it? What had she been through? Cormack must have known, Woodward realised suddenly, must have had an inkling of the pressures she was living under; was that why he was here? "It's all right, Marianne," he whispered. "It's all over now. By this time tomorrow, we'll be back home."

"Oh God, I hope so.... I hope so." Gradually, her tears were subsiding now. "Hold me, Tony.... please," she murmured indistinctly; two sleepless nights were finally taking their toll.

"It's all right, Marianne," he murmured. "We'll look after you, I promise."

She was already asleep.

LONDON: 1330 HOURS.

Fitzgerald was a few minutes late for the luncheon appointment, but his host did not seem to mind; he motioned him into the seat opposite him and, as he sat down, Fitzgerald could not fail to be impressed by his surroundings. This was the first time he had been in the Athenaeum, one of the more exclusive clubs in London, and he liked what he saw. He also appreciated his host's invitation, which hinted at coming preferment, especially from a man who was clearly destined for high places.

The conversation during the early courses was purely social, involving mutual acquaintances and it was only when they were sitting back smoking Havana cigars that the talk switched to professional matters.

"It's going to be difficult adjusting to peace, I suppose," Fitzgerald's host remarked. "Still, one good thing will come out of it - I hear SOE's pretty certain to be disbanded, providing 'C' plays his cards right."

"Really?" Fitzgerald felt a small thrill of anticipation. He was being made privy to matters of policy, which could only mean, surely, that he was being informally interviewed.

"Really. Which means that we'll regain control of our overseas networks. Damned stupid having two separate units for continental intelligence."

"It'll certainly make our jobs easier," Fitzgerald conceded. "Although I imagine that we'll have to see about re-aligning ourselves. Regarding the opposition, that is."

His host nodded. "Quite. The Reds may be our allies now, but we're already laying plans to penetrate their NKVD networks."

"Well, that'll be your pigeon, won't it?" Fitzgerald probed gently.

"Exactly." He smiled. "To be honest, my department has

123

already made its preparations - moved onto a more active footing, as it were. Which is why I wanted to talk to you, Miles. Obviously, my department will be expanding rapidly and - well - I need the best men available. Like yourself."

Fitzgerald looked suitably embarrassed. "Thank you, sir. I'm very flattered that you should think so."

"I've already spoken to 'C' and Cathcart and they've agreed to a transfer. I'd like it to be effective immediately, but that brings us up against a small problem. The Emerald operation."

"Ah yes. Of course," Fitzgerald said cautiously.

"Obviously, you have to complete that first, so - well - I'd like to know how long it's likely to take."

Fitzgerald hesitated. Normally, he would not discuss 'Emerald' or any other operation with anyone from another department, but what harm could it do now? "I think it should be completed during the next twenty four hours, sir. Successfully," he added.

"Good Lord. Well done, Miles. I'd heard it was a high risk affair."

"It was, sir," said Fitzgerald smugly. "But the team we selected has done wonderfully well. We had a signal from them this morning, actually. They've got 'Emerald' and we're sending in a plane tonight to pick them up."

"Not into Berlin itself, surely?"

"No, sir. It's to the north-west of the city, out in the country."

"Just as long as the plane isn't shot down on the way," said the other man gloomily. "I mean, our Russki friends don't know anything about it, do they?"

"We've tried to minimise that risk by using a Mosquito, one of the new ones that can do over four hundred miles an hour. Forty-five minutes there, the same to get back, so it seems a reasonable bet."

His host nodded. "Sounds as though it's all cut and dried, Miles. My congratulations. Just out of interest, who is this 'Emerald' anyway? Must be quite a remarkable agent to mount such a rescue mission."

Fitzgerald hesitated. "To be frank, sir, I'm not at liberty to tell you that."

The other man nodded approvingly. "I'm glad you said that, Miles - you're quite right not to tell me, of course. I'd have been disappointed with you if you had."

Fitzgerald smiled, relief plainly written on his face; evidently, the question had been some sort of test.

"So - all being well, Miles, you should be free to transfer after

124

tomorrow?"

"I hope so, sir."

"Excellent, excellent." He glanced at his watch. "Ah well, Miles, duty calls, I'm afraid. I've got to go and visit 'C' at his country domain in two hours, so I'd better be off." He rose to his feet. "No, no, don't get up, Miles. Finish your cigar." A thought seemed to strike him. "Tell you what. As you're about to become one of my senior men, why don't you come round for dinner sometime this week? Bring Elizabeth with you, of course. Thursday suit you?"

"Thursday will be ideal, sir." It wasn't actually, he reflected, but it was nothing that couldn't be cancelled.

"And you can stop calling me sir," said the other man, with the charming smile that was becoming famous throughout MI6. "Call me Kim - everyone else does."

"Thank you - Kim."

Fitzgerald smiled happily as he watched his host depart. Although this was not a promotion, he was convinced that this transfer would be a step forward in his career prospects. It would do no harm at all for him to hitch on to the coat-tails of such a rising star in the MI6 firmament. There was no doubt about it; Harold Philby, better known as "Kim", was going to go a long way in British Intelligence.

GERMANY: 1430 HOURS.

Cormack was sitting at the window, looking out at the track when he heard a movement behind him. His head snapped round, too quickly; his nerves were still on edge, he realised - it was only Marianne.

"Hallo, Captain," she said softly. "Mind if I join you?"

"Go ahead," he said in a neutral tone. "Did you manage to get some sleep?"

She nodded. "I was exhausted."

"I'm not surprised. And Tony?"

"Sleeping like a baby."

Remembering his own fitful rest, Cormack grinned sardonically. "Best thing for him." He looked at her thoughtfully. "I gather you knew him before the war?"

"Yes, I did. He was at the same school as my brother and he came over to stay with us one summer - 1937, it must have been."

"So did you get to know him well?"

"Well, not really, no." She seemed to hesitate before going on. "I was going out with someone else at the time and, anyway, Tony was four years younger than me." She smiled faintly. "When you're twenty-three, you don't pay much attention to nineteen year old boys, really. Not the done thing."

"No, I don't suppose it is." Again, he gave her a speculative look. "This someone you were going out with - he wasn't the bloke you eventually married, was he?"

Marianne glanced sharply at him before she grinned wryly. "You don't miss much, do you? No, he wasn't."

"You married Kovacs the following year?"

"Yes, I did," she said slowly. "The biggest mistake of my life."

"Why?" Cormack asked bluntly and then his expression softened. "I'm sorry. It's none of my business, is it?"

"No, it isn't," she replied equally directly. "But I don't see why I shouldn't tell you. It was a mistake because I didn't love Janos. It started off as an attempt to get Martin jealous - he was the one I was going out with when Tony knew me - and then I began to think that Janos was the one for me. I suppose I mistook his charm for sincerity and when he asked me to marry him I didn't hesitate for a minute. Mind you, he was damned good in bed." She chuckled at Cormack's startled reaction. "Have I shocked you, Captain?"

"Surprised me, rather than anything," Cormack replied. "Takes a lot to shock me," he added, almost to himself.

"The trouble was that Janos liked variety - one woman wasn't enough for him, you see. So I suppose that I started giving tit for tat and after that it all went downhill very rapidly."

"So why didn't you leave him?"

"And do what, Captain? Go back to Dublin, where I would doubtless be told to go back and be a good wife? In any case, there was no need. After a while, he went his way and I went mine - we were both happy enough with the arrangement and it meant I could carry on a lifestyle that was - well - difficult to give up." Now, she looked almost challengingly at Cormack. "No doubt you disapprove, Captain. No doubt you think I'm a grasping bitch - and you're probably right. I can't say I'm especially proud of it, to be honest."

"Let he who is without sin," murmured Cormack. "I can't exactly hold myself up as a paragon of virtue, so who am I to criticise you, Marianne?" There was a bitter smile on his face now. "I suppose we've all had to do things during the last few years that we aren't too proud of. We have to learn to live with them. Or go under."

"Or find a reason for doing them. In the end, I think I only stayed with Janos so that I could carry on passing information to London - and once he told me we were going to Berlin, that settled it." She took a deep breath before continuing, "At least, that's the way I justify it to myself."

"Don't sell yourself short. Nobody becomes an undercover agent just so that they can live in luxury, Marianne. There's not much luxury in a Gestapo interrogation cellar. Ask Tony - he'll tell you."

"Tony? He's been questioned by the Germans?"

Cormack nodded. "And he didn't say one word. He's got guts - I've got to give him that."

She shook her head disbelievingly. "I still can't believe he's mixed up in something like this. It's not how I remember him at all. I met him once after he joined the RAF and he seemed exactly right as a pilot. You know, the romantic image you have of one - somewhat of a daredevil, treating it all as a bit of a lark. I never saw him as an undercover agent."

"He isn't, really," Cormack said quietly. "He shouldn't be here at all, if truth be told - he just isn't cut out for it."

"Then why is he here?"

"Because someone asked him to volunteer, that's why. The good old traditions of duty, play the game and all that." Despite the words, there was no trace of mockery in Cormack's voice; instead, there was a note almost of grudging respect. Suddenly, he grinned mischievously, the expression transforming his face. "And, of course, once he knew it was you we were coming to get, wild horses couldn't have stopped him."

"What - the knight on a white charger?" She chuckled and nodded. "Yes, that sounds like Tony. You and he get on pretty well, don't you?"

It was as if a shutter had dropped behind Cormack's eyes. Marianne noticed his reaction and understood immediately; he was not prepared to talk about himself, not directly. Habit, a result of his training, or was he a very private man? "Yes, I suppose we do," he replied eventually.

Hastily, Marianne changed the subject, aware of a sudden strain in the atmosphere. "This pick-up tonight - it will be all right, won't it?"

"It should be," he replied abruptly, his eyes hooded.

There was a silence that lasted for several seconds before she said, "You're a hard man to get to know, aren't you, Captain?"

"Goes with the job." His voice was now off-hand, frankly discouraging.

Her mouth tightened. "Look, Captain, if you want me to go, just say so, will you?"

Cormack's eyes were instantly contrite. "I'm sorry. I didn't mean to be rude. It's just that-" He broke off, his eyes holding hers and she had the overwhelming impression that he was about to throw aside his mask and let her see the real Cormack behind that opaque facade, but then he looked away and the moment was gone as if it had never been. "Could you go and wake Tony, please? We'd better see about looking for a landing field."

Marianne did not move for several seconds, but continued to stare pensively at Cormack; then, with a vague feeling of regret, she nodded and went to wake Woodward.

BERLIN: 1900 HOURS.

Rindt was sprawled out on the sofa, dozing fitfully when he heard the peremptory knock at the door; he felt absolutely exhausted, which was hardly surprising, considering the amount - or lack - of sleep he had managed over the past ten days or so. Mueller had driven him remorselessly in the search for Das Leck, although it had been unnecessary, of course; Rindt had known full well what was at stake, from his own personal point of view. Even in the isolated moments when he had been able to stagger back to his flat, he had not been able to relax, not when Das Leck had still to be found.

And still she was at large, damn her! The Gestapo were combing the city for her - or rather, as much of the city as they could still reach, and Rindt doubted if the remaining Gestapo agents were even making any serious attempt to find her at this late stage; they would be planning their own escapes if they had any sense. Imitating their leader, no doubt, thought Rindt disgustedly - Mueller had not been seen at Gestapo HQ since midday and nobody had any idea where he was. Probably half way to Switzerland by now, thought Rindt morosely as he hauled himself to his feet and went to answer the door; he was so exhausted that it was only when he was about to open it that it occurred to him to wonder who it might be.

It was with no great feeling of surprise that he saw that it was Hentschel; it was as if he had been expecting this all along. Without a word, Rindt stepped aside to let in the other man and closed the door, his actions those of a sleepwalker.

"Are there any clues where the Kovacs woman has gone?" asked Hentschel without preamble; not for the first time, Rindt was impressed by the extent of the other man's knowledge. He had not

128

been able to contact him since the incident at the Brandenburg Gate the night before, yet Hentschel seemed to know already what had happened. He must have a very high ranking source of information....

"None at all," he replied.

"But she has help?"

"Yes. Two men. Probably British."

Hentschel nodded, as if it confirmed some previously held theory. "Very well. You are now being given new instructions - you are to come with me."

"Where to, for God's sake?"

"Through the lines, Rindt."

Rindt stared at him. "You mean - over to the Russians?"

"That is exactly what I mean."

"But - but why? What do they want with me? I thought you wanted me to find Das Leck and hand her over to you."

"Which you are now very unlikely to do, are you, Rindt? It seems highly probable that, if she is still alive, she will be in an area that we now hold. In any case, we shall control all of Berlin within the next seventy-two hours and so, quite frankly, we no longer need you here."

"Then - what the hell is this all about?" Rindt's bewilderment was evident.

"Like you, Rindt, I simply obey orders - and I have to take you to my superior." For the first time since Rindt had known him, there was the merest hint of a smile on Hentschel's face now. "And I imagine that you will also have to meet an agent called 'Spartakus' - I suspect you will be very surprised to discover his identity." The smile faded. "However, we're wasting time. Get whatever things you need and come with me."

2200 HOURS.

Rindt stood in the entrance of the Stadtmitte U-bahn station and looked carefully along the Friedrichstrasse, following the direction of Hentschel's gaze; the Russian agent seemed to be concentrating on a point forty or fifty metres away, on the opposite side of the street, although Rindt could not see anything to justify such interest. All he knew was that they had been waiting here for the last fifteen minutes or more, which probably meant that whoever Hentschel had intended to meet was late.

Or dead....

Rindt could not allow himself to pursue that thought too far, because if Hentschel's contact was dead or unavoidably detained, then it might mean that they would be unable to cross the front lines and Rindt knew that this was his only hope now of seeing Inga again. For some reason, the Russians wanted him - probably just for interrogation purposes - but they had not discarded him entirely, as he had feared they might. There was still a chance.... He had to hold on to that, no matter how forlorn the odds. The only alternative was just to give up and if he did that then he was betraying Inga as well as himself.... But there was an image that had come into his mind several days before and would not go away; it was of himself as a puppet, fastened to strings that were being pulled by a huge, faceless figure.

But what else could he do?

Suddenly, Hentschel seemed to tense beside him, bringing Rindt out of his reverie; he looked along the street again and saw a flashing of light from the shadows across the street. Moments later, it came again, twice in rapid succession, followed by a pause and then two more flashes.

"There they are," said Hentschel triumphantly; he seemed light-headed, exuberant now - in fact, he had been ever since they had left Rindt's flat. Not surprising, perhaps, Rindt thought, vaguely.... Hentschel was going home, his job well done.

Quickly, Hentschel checked the street and said to Rindt, "Follow me when I signal." With a last glance each way, Hentschel began to cross the road but then Rindt heard the high pitched wail of a mortar shell in its descent; the 'Stalin Organs' as they were called. Instinctively, Hentschel threw himself flat in the road and there was a deafening crash as the shell exploded on the roof of a building fifty yards away. Rather shamefacedly, Hentschel picked himself up and had just set off again when a second shell exploded directly beyond him, slamming into the upper storey of an apartment block. The front wall seemed to sway before it slowly toppled forward.

Rindt came out of the entrance in a headlong sprint towards Hentschel, who was standing as if transfixed, looking up at the falling masonry; Rindt slammed into him like an express train and wrenched him to one side as the rubble crashed down, missing them by inches as they sprawled in the road.

"Move!" Rindt yelled, scrambling to his feet and hauling Hentschel up after him; the agent was staring, white-faced at the debris only feet away until Rindt literally dragged him away, back across the street. "Do you want the rest of the damned building to fall on top of us?"

"No - no. Of course not," said Hentschel shakily, still unable to take his eyes off the spot where they had just been. "You just saved my life, Rindt," he said hoarsely.

"No," Rindt replied, panting. "Not yours."

Hentschel nodded in understanding. "Nevertheless, I would still like to thank you, Rindt." He held out his hand and, after a moment's hesitation, Rindt took it. Then, Hentschel turned away as he saw two raincoated men who had emerged from the shadows and were now walking towards them; his face broke into a tired, but triumphant, smile - evidently, these were the men who had been sent to meet him. Beside him, Rindt watched the approaching men in silence, as one part of his life ended and another began....

These were the puppet masters.

CHAPTER 10.

SUNDAY, APRIL 29TH: 2230 HOURS.

Cormack turned the car off the road and drove up a narrow track that led through a small wood to the edge of a large field that would serve as a landing strip. He and Woodward had surveyed it earlier while it was still light, and Woodward had asserted that there would be ample room for a Mosquito to land and take off.

"Right," said Cormack quietly. "Let's get the landing flares into position."

They climbed out of the car and took some magnesium flares out of the duffel bag. Cormack walked towards the western end of the field, while Marianne and Woodward headed in the opposite direction. It was fairly obvious that Woodward was quite smitten by Marianne and was trying to make an impression on her; Cormack wished him luck. There was no jealousy on his part, despite Marianne's undeniable attractions - not after what had happened two years ago.... With a wistful smile, he pushed the memories aside; there was no time for them at the moment.

He finished placing the flares and looked at his watch: ten fifty-five. At the far end of the field, he could just make out the figures of Marianne and Woodward; he signalled to them and lit the flare at his feet before running over to the other one. Simultaneously, two bright glows sprang into existence at the other end of the landing strap so that, from the air, the Mosquito would see a large rectangle of lights.

Almost immediately, he heard the approaching roar of aircraft engines throttling back as the Mosquito came into land and, by the time he had rejoined the others, the aircraft was already touching down, earning a nod of professional approval from Woodward as it rolled to a halt a hundred yards away.

"Come on," said Cormack, grinning hugely, the expression lighting up his features. They picked up their baggage and trotted towards the waiting plane, which had now turned round, ready for an immediate take off. As they approached, Cormack could see the hatch opening for them and was almost overcome by an urge to whoop for joy. Glancing across at Woodward, he could see an exultant smile on the other man's face: they had done it, had pulled it off....

But then Woodward came to a dead stop, his whole attitude that of a man straining his ears to hear a faint sound; his expression changed to one of incredulity and he yelled, "Get down! Get down!"

Reacting to the whiplash tone of command, Cormack and Marianne threw themselves flat to the ground and it was only then that Cormack heard the sound that Woodward had detected, the high-pitched scream of aero engines coming rapidly closer. The next moment, the entire field was bathed in an incandescent glare as a starshell burst overhead and he saw the aircraft - three fighters diving in, just above the treetops. The night was rent by the vicious stutter of the planes' cannons spraying wicked lines of tracer shells across the field towards the motionless Mosquito.

The first aircraft screamed past overhead and Cormack caught a momentary glimpse of something falling from it and curving lazily downwards. At the same instant he realised that it was a bomb, it exploded in a blinding flash just behind the Mosquito, whose engines were already revving up. The port wing and the tail exploded into flames and now more tracers were ripping through the fuselage as the second aircraft made its attack.

The Mosquito was moving now, although the entire rear part of the plane was ablaze. There still might be a chance that the pilot could get into the air, but that last, slender hope was dashed when the second attacker dropped its bomb and banked away, climbing and turning for another strafing run. The bomb exploded within feet of the Mosquito and blew the starboard wing off, lifting it up into the air and snapping it. The Mosquito spun round as the port wing ploughed into the ground, strewing blazing fragments of wreckage across the grass. Almost without realising it, Cormack leaped to his feet and sprinted towards the burning plane, with Woodward close behind him, before the remains of the Mosquito came to a halt. The third fighter came diving in, its guns clattering viciously, the bullets ripping up the earth in a line towards the two running men. Instinctively, Cormack hurled himself to one side and rolled clear of the bullets as the fighter swept past overhead; he was back on his feet in an instant, running towards the Mosquito. Perhaps they could still pull someone out.... He leaped up onto the port wing and wrenched at the cockpit canopy. Woodward pushed him aside, operated the release mechanism and slid the canopy back.

The flight engineer was obviously dead, his head and chest a mass of blood where the tracer shells had torn through him. The pilot was still moving feebly, trying to unfasten his safety harness.

133

Woodward dropped down into the cockpit and unclipped the catch, before lifting the pilot out of his seat and up towards Cormack, who reached down and hauled him out, ignoring his low moan of agony. Carefully, he lowered him down onto the wing while Woodward bent over the navigator.

Cormack manhandled the pilot down onto the grass, slinging him over his shoulder. Moments later, Woodward clambered out of the cockpit, shaking his head in response to Cormack's mute look of enquiry; the back of the navigator's head had been smashed to a pulp. Muttering an oath, Cormack headed away from the plane in a stumbling run and was about fifty yards away when the port fuel tank exploded, the concussion hurling him forward onto the grass.

Gasping, he lifted himself up onto his knees and crawled over to the pilot, who was lying on his back, his eyes open, but unfocused. "Oh, shit...." Cormack murmured and gripped the man's wrist, feeling for a pulse; after several seconds, he sat back on his haunches and shook his head in despair. It had all been for nothing - the pilot was dead.

Slowly, he turned to look at the flames behind him, his face bleak. Another two minutes, that was all they had needed, just another two lousy minutes and they'd have been away, safe.... Two lousy minutes. He rose to his feet and gazed up at the starshell sinking out of sight behind the trees. "You bastards!" he hissed, trembling. "You bastards.... Bastards!"

"Alan!" Woodward's voice was like a whiplash. "Alan, we've got to get moving! There'll be soldiers here any minute - now come on!"

Cormack looked quizzically at him. What the hell was he talking about? It was all over, didn't he realise that? What was he trying to tell him?

Abruptly, Woodward's hand lashed out and caught him a stinging slap across the cheek. Cormack stared at him, incredulously and Woodward brought his arm across to hit him a second time. Effortlessly, Cormack raised his arm to parry the blow; he nodded at Woodward.

"It's OK, Tony. I'm all right now." He drew in a deep breath. "And you're right - we can't hang about." He turned towards the car and said, without looking back. "Thanks, Tony."

"Any time," Woodward replied awkwardly, but Cormack was already running towards the Mercedes, gesturing urgently to Marianne. She jumped into the back, followed by Woodward, while Cormack slid into the driving seat and pressed the starter, spinning the wheel rapidly to turn round in the confined space.

With a squeal of tyres, he headed back along the track, the headlights picking out the dark trees as they raced past. Cormack's face was like stone, his eyes expressionless as he drove, pushing the car to its limits along the winding track, taking some of the bends almost sideways in his determination to reach the road before any vehicles appeared to block their escape.

They were almost there, with less than fifty yards to go, when they skidded around a corner and saw two jeeps coming towards them; Cormack changed down and pressed the accelerator to the floor. The Mercedes shot forward, straight towards the leading jeep and they saw the driver throw up an arm to shield his eyes from the glare of the headlamps. The jeep swerved aside to avoid a head on collision and the Mercedes roared on past, only inches away, with Cormack now aiming the car at the second jeep.

Out of the corner of his eye, he saw Woodward leaning out of the passenger window, aiming a Schmeisser at the jeep hurtling towards them. He loosed off a burst of fire. The jeep slewed round as the driver instinctively tried to avoid the fusillade of bullets and slammed into the trunk of a tree, rebounding back towards the oncoming Mercedes. Cormack yanked the wheel to the right and felt the back end skidding; it caught the jeep a glancing blow and then they were past, with the road coming up fast. Tyres screaming, the Mercedes slewed crazily out onto the road, almost going into a hundred and eighty degree spin. Cormack somehow kept control and pushed his foot flat to the floor again.

"Damn...." he murmured, looking into the rear view mirror; about fifty yards behind were more jeeps, who must have been backing up the first two. "There's two more behind us, Tony."

Woodward cursed and twisted around in his seat. "Can you lose them?"

"God knows." Cormack spun the wheel to take them around the next bend, still keeping his foot on the throttle, but as they sped along the narrow lane it gradually became evident that the road twisted and turned too much for him to be able to use the Mercedes' superior speed to pull away from the jeeps. They were not closing the gap, but if either had a radio they could easily summon up reinforcements.

Looking ahead, Cormack saw that they were driving into a wooded area and about a hundred yards ahead there was a right angled bend to the left, with the road beyond completely obscured. "Get your gun ready, Tony - OK? And be ready to jump out when I say so." Cormack was already braking, but the car still heeled sideways as they took the corner. He straightened the wheel and

135

pressed more firmly on the brake, bringing the Mercedes skidding to a halt; he hit the door handle and pushed the door open, leaping out on one side with Woodward doing the same on the other. Cormack turned to face the bend and reached inside his tunic for the Browning automatic.

The first jeep swung into view around the bend and both men opened fire, Cormack squeezing off four rapid shots at the windscreen while Woodward raked the jeep with his Schmeisser. The jeep's driver let go of the wheel, clutching at this chest at the same instant as his foot pressed convulsively down on the accelerator, sending the jeep catapulting off the road, its engine roaring as it slammed squarely into a tree trunk. The second jeep came hurtling round the corner, straight into a murderous hail of fire. The front nearside tyre blew out, sending the jeep into an uncontrollable spin; the back wheel caught a tree stump on the verge and the jeep flipped over, cartwheeling crazily into the trees. There was a sudden flash and it burst into flames; seconds later, the fuel tank erupted into an incandescent fireball that completely engulfed the jeep.

"God Almighty," Woodward breathed, staring at the blaze and shaking his head.

Cormack ignored the comment. "Come on," he said brusquely. "Let's get the hell out of here."

Fifteen minutes later, Cormack pulled off the road, driving in amongst the trees by the roadside before coming to a halt, but he did not switch off the engine for several seconds. Instead, he was gripping the wheel, white-knuckled, staring fixedly through the windscreen; eventually, he released his vice-like hold on the steering wheel and sat back, letting out his breath in a long sigh. Woodward glanced across at him and saw that his eyes were closed; he was also breathing deeply as though he were consciously trying to relax. Suddenly, Cormack spoke, without opening his eyes, taking Woodward by surprise.

"What sort of planes were they, Tony?"

Woodward stared at him; what the hell difference did that make now? "I don't know for certain. Probably Lavochkin La-5s, but-"

"Russian, you mean?"

"Oh yes, definitely."

"Oh, bloody great...." Cormack murmured. "Then that settles it. They were waiting for us."

136

"What do you mean?"

"Think about it, for God's sake." Cormack still had not opened his eyes and sounded infinitely weary. Defeated. "We had those landing lights on for two minutes at the most. What are the odds of Russian fighter bombers just happening to be flying past at that particular moment? And then, no more than - what? - three minutes after that, we run into four jeeps, also Russian, heading straight for that landing field. Did they just happen to be in the area as well? Not to mention whoever fired that starshell. Stretching coincidence a bit far, isn't it?"

Woodward nodded reluctantly. "It does seem they were expecting us. But how could they possibly have known?"

"Someone back in London, Tony. There must be a leak there - the Russians must have been tipped off and nobody else but London knew of the pick up."

Woodward nodded slowly; no other explanation made any sense. "That means they must know who we are and why we're here."

"Oh, doubtlessly. I imagine it's Marianne they're after." Cormack sat forward in his seat. "What is more important is that we can't risk any more signals to London."

"Bloody hell," Woodward murmured as the implications sank in. "Up the creek without a paddle, good and proper."

"Are you sure about there being a leak?" asked Marianne from the back seat. "It could just have been pure bad luck back there."

"It could have been, yes," Cormack agreed. "However, I'm not prepared to run the risk of arranging any more pick ups through London."

"So what are you going to do instead?"

"Good question," Cormack acknowledged. "I wish to hell I knew the answer. Get the map out, Tony, will you?"

Woodward unfolded the map and Cormack shone his torch on it. "Right," he said, pointing at the map. "We're here, somewhere between Berge and Friedenstadt, slap bang in the middle of the Russian Army, I would imagine. The Americans are on the Elbe - here - at Magdeburg, which is about sixty miles as the crow flies, but we've also got what's left of the German Army in the way as well as the Russians. We'd have to go through two front lines, which could be tricky."

"Where's the British Army?" asked Marianne leaning over the back of the seat.

"Too far away. The last we heard, they were attacking Bremen. They've probably taken it by now, but they can't be any closer than a hundred and fifty miles."

"So what the devil do we do?" asked Woodward. "Head for Magdeburg and chance it?"

"We could always head north for the coast," replied Cormack thoughtfully. "OK, it's just over a hundred miles, but we've got enough petrol in the tank and in the jerricans in the boot. We wouldn't have to worry about battle lines so much - we'd be in German held territory most of the time, and we've got our SS uniforms, not to mention our travel documents. On top of that, things will be pretty chaotic, what with the Russians coming from the east and our lot from the west, so it'd be easier to bluff our way through."

Woodward nodded. "So what do we do at the coast? Steal a boat and get across to Sweden?"

"Why not?"

Woodward drew in his breath slowly, studying the map. "Magdeburg's still closer."

"I know it is. But the Americans don't know anything about us, so if we try to sneak through battle lines in SS uniforms, they're just as likely to shoot us as take us prisoner."

Woodward nodded slowly in reluctant agreement. "Very true," he conceded. "So we go for the coast?"

"I'd say it was our best bet, yes. We'd better aim for this stretch here, between Lubeck and Rostock. I don't want to go too far east in case we run into the Russians."

"Rostock?" Woodward frowned. "That rings a bell somewhere. What was it now?.... Something to do with escape routes, I think.... Got it. There's an escape route for shot down bomber crews through Rostock to Sweden, rather like the Lifeline route in the Low Countries. It's run by a bloke called.... Voeller, I think it is."

"Tony, you're a bloody marvel. That settles it, then. We get up to Rostock and contact this Voeller." He looked at his watch. "It's just after midnight, so we've got five hours at any rate before it get light - we could get quite a chunk of our journey out of the way by then." He leaned forward and pressed the starter. "Rostock, here we come."

As the car pulled away, Marianne leaned back in the rear seat; she was studying Cormack intently. She had seen what had happened back at the landing field and he had seemed to have been in utter despair, yet now he seemed positively buoyant; was this all an act? It was only too evident to her now that he was not the cold, ruthless undercover agent she had taken him to be, but a man living right on the edge of a breakdown. Her wish had been granted in that she had seen through to the real Cormack beneath

138

the veneer of professional detachment, but the knowledge had unnerved her.

Because this was the man she and Woodward had to rely on, like it or not.

ROSTOCK: 0500 HOURS, MONDAY, APRIL 30TH.

Cormack leaned back against the side of the fuselage, eyes half-closed. He could feel nothing at all in his left leg below the knee; Lena must have given him just about the full dose. He was faintly drowsy; it was suddenly very tempting to close his eyes, let it all slip away, just for a few seconds....

He sat up with a start. For God's sake, this was no time to doze off....

Forcing himself to concentrate, he looked across at Lena, who was leaning out of the open hatchway, peering anxiously beyond the tailplane.

"What's happening?" he asked, suddenly angry at his own immobility.

"There's been shooting over by the hangar and some explosions, but I can't see much else."

"Schelhaas?"

Wordlessly, she shook her head. Then she tensed. "There's a car coming towards us!"

Jesus.... Cormack leaned forward and twisted himself round, gasping at the pain in his ankle. Slowly, he began to drag himself across the deck, cursing his useless leg. He had to see what was going on.... He picked up his Sten and hauled himself to the hatchway.

"There's Vim!" Lena exclaimed excitedly. "Over there!"

Cormack was lying on his stomach now, his head by the hatch; he saw it all. Schelhaas was sprinting towards the plane, with the car hurtling towards him; the Dutchman suddenly turned and saw the Kubelwagen. He skidded to a halt and brought his machine gun up.

Before he could fire, however, the Kubelwagen's lights came on, full beam, transfixing him; he put his arm in front of his face in a reflex action to cut out the glare. There was a long burst of fire from the Spandau in the back of the car that tore into Schelhaas, ripping him open from hip to shoulder; he reeled and staggered backwards driven by the impact of the bullets, yet he would not go down, even though his chest and stomach was a mass of blood. And the Kubelwagen was going straight at him....

Probably the driver had intended to hit him all along; the car smashed into Schelhaas at over forty miles an hour, throwing him high into the air as he cannoned off the bonnet, before falling to the ground behind the Kubelwagen in a limp, boneless fashion.

"Vim!" Lena screamed. "Vim!"

"Alan!"

"I'm here, Lena.... Don't worry...." But that hadn't been her voice; it had been Woodward's.... What the hell was going on? He ought to be flying the bloody plane....

"Alan!" Woodward said again, urgently, and now Cormack's eyes flickered open in realisation. They weren't in the plane at all - Woodward was driving a car and it wasn't Lena sitting beside him, but Marianne.... Jesus Christ, how many more times did he have to live through that in his dreams?

"Yeah, Tony?" he muttered thickly.

"Another checkpoint, by the look of it." Woodward was already slowing down; he nodded ahead of them, through the windscreen. The sky was just beginning to lighten and the group of vehicles was plainly visible about a hundred yards ahead.

"Where are we?" Cormack asked, looking at his watch.

"Nearly at Rostock - another couple of miles, I'd say."

Cormack nodded. They had made good time during the hours of darkness, despite the lines of refugees that had slowed them up more than once, as had being stopped at several checkpoints along the way. There had been surprisingly little trouble at any of these, not even concerning Marianne's presence; the officers manning the checkpoints had obviously assumed that she was Cormack's mistress and that they were escaping from the advancing Allies, but none had dared argue with his Colonel's uniform. Cormack doubted if they were the first such party to pass this way and, in any case, the soldiers seemed apathetic, knowing that it was only a matter of time before the war ended; the last thing they wanted to do was to stir up unnecessary trouble.

Nevertheless, while Woodward brought the car to a halt, Cormack rapidly checked his Browning pistol and replaced it inside his tunic. The checkpoint was situated outside a dilapidated farmhouse, which was presumably where the soldiers were quartered. A young Lieutenant stepped forward, saluting smartly, and took the papers from Woodward. He glanced at them briefly before he spoke to Cormack in the back, his voice respectful but firm.

"I'm afraid I must ask you to leave the car for a few moments, Herr Colonel."

140

"What the devil for?" Cormack snapped.

"Please, Herr Colonel. I have my orders."

Cormack glared at the Lieutenant but the officer stood his ground. "Oh, very well, but this had better not take long."

"Just a few moments, Herr Colonel, no more than that."

Cormack emerged from the car, followed by Marianne, who looked around her condescendingly, the image of a bored mistress.

"I'm afraid I must ask you for Fraulein Kotze's identification papers, Herr Colonel," said the Lieutenant apologetically.

"What the devil for?"

"Standing orders, Herr Colonel."

"Your name, Lieutenant?" Cormack demanded icily.

The officer snapped to attention. "Lieutenant Holtzmann, Herr Colonel."

"Well, Lieutenant Holtzmann, would you kindly stop wasting my time? The travel documents are in order, are they not?"

"Indeed they are, Herr Colonel, but-"

"But nothing. Just stamp the damned things and let us continue our journey, which, as you can see, is a priority assignment."

"Is there some problem, Lieutenant Holtzmann?" asked a voice behind Cormack; he turned and saw a tall Major walking unhurriedly around the Mercedes, looking interestedly at the several dents in the bodywork. At the Major's throat was a Knight's Cross with Oak Leaves, while he had an impressive row of campaign ribbons on his chest; Cormack groaned inwardly. This was no reserve unit officer, this was a fighting man, a different proposition altogether to the others they had encountered along the road north.

"And who are you, Major?" Cormack snapped.

The Major saluted, but it was the Army and not the Nazi salute, Cormack noticed uneasily. "Major Treischer at your service, Herr Colonel-?"

"Beitzen. Would you be so kind as to tell your Lieutenant here to stop wasting my time with trivial matters?"

"What's the problem, Holtzmann?" asked Treischer, quite unperturbed by Cormack's glare.

"The young lady, Herr Major. She has a passport, but no Reich identification papers."

"None at all?"

"No, Herr Major. As your instructions said-"

"Quite right, Lieutenant." Treischer turned back to face Cormack and shrugged. "You see, Herr Colonel, I have my orders, which are to allow nobody through without the necessary papers, which I

141

regret Fraulein Kotze-" he smiled apologetically at Marianne, "-has not got."

"Dammit, Major, I'll vouch for Fraulein Kotze," said Cormack. "She's my personal stenographer."

"Your stenographer, Herr Colonel," said Treischer with no inflexion at all in his voice; nevertheless, his implied meaning was only too clear. "Nevertheless, I still cannot let her through without the proper documents - or authorisation."

"Can I speak to you in private, Herr Major?" asked Cormack glacially.

"Certainly, Herr Colonel," said Treischer equably. "We'll go inside, shall we?" Without waiting for an answer, he led the way up the path to the farmhouse door, which led directly into a large kitchen. Inside, a radio operator was sitting in front of a large wireless transmitter which had been set up on the table; he shot to his feet when they entered. "Just leave us for a few minutes, will you, Bruck?" Treischer asked quietly.

"Yes, Herr Major."

It was increasingly evident to Cormack that Treischer was a good officer; he issued orders quietly but with absolute assurance - and he had his men well trained. Even the young Lieutenant had stuck to his guns in front of a superior officer, knowing that his CO would back him up - Treischer was exactly the sort of officer Cormack had been hoping to avoid. As Treischer turned to face him, Cormack could see the lines of weariness on his face, but his eyes were alert and intelligent. "What did you want to say to me that you didn't want my men to hear, Herr Colonel?"

Cormack slammed his fist down on the table. "Don't you dare talk to me like that, Major! You're talking to a superior officer, you know - kindly remember that!"

Treischer smiled faintly, infuriatingly. "I'm fully aware who I'm talking to - Herr Colonel." His voice was laden with irony. "And I repeat that I am merely carrying out my orders."

"You're not, Treischer - you're exceeding them!"

"Then take that up with Colonel Bergmann in Rostock. Until I receive instructions to the contrary from him, Fraulein Kotze stays here." There was no mistaking the contempt in his eyes now. "Of course, you and your sergeant are quite free to proceed, but you will have to leave your - ah - stenographer behind." Treischer shrugged. "I doubt if that is a new experience for members of the SS, is it - Herr Colonel?"

"How dare you! I'll have you court-martialled for that!"

Treischer shook his head again and grinned tiredly. "I'm afraid that, given the present circumstances, that possibility does not especially concern me, Beitzen." All pretence at military protocol in his manner had disappeared now. "Even in the unlikely event of one being convened before we're all captured or killed, how would you explain Fraulein Kotze's presence in a military vehicle? So forget these threats, will you? They don't impress me one little bit - but then, neither do you," he finished disgustedly.

Cormack stared at him and it was almost like looking into a mirror. It was not so much that there was any physical resemblance between himself and Treischer, but that he could see his own attitude reflected in Treischer's treatment of someone he evidently despised; if the positions had been reversed, Cormack felt that he would have acted exactly the same way as Treischer.... At least, he hoped he would.

Slowly, he walked over to Treischer and glared into his eyes. "So I don't impress you, Major?"

"No, you don't, quite frankly. You and your kind are running for safety and comfort while the real fighting men are dying all around you."

Cormack nodded slowly, as if conceding the point. "Very well - if that is your attitude-" He began to turn away but then pivoted back, smashing a venomous two-handed blow into the side of Treischer's head. Treischer reeled backwards and fell heavily onto the flagstones. Cormack stepped forward, taking out the silenced Browning with a weary, resigned sigh. He lined it up on Treischer's head and began to squeeze the trigger....

A second passed. Then another, and still he did not fire, but simply stood there, motionless, staring down at his victim. He couldn't do it. He couldn't shoot Treischer.

Already, the German was up on his knees, shaking his head groggily, yet still Cormack did nothing, although the gun was still pointing at its target. He couldn't let Treischer live - he was too dangerous an opponent, could reveal too much afterwards....

With a sigh, Cormack bent forward and brought his left hand chopping down onto the back of Treischer's neck with carefully controlled power; Treischer slumped forward and lay still, his eyes closed. Cormack looked down at him a moment longer then crossed quickly to the window. There were six Germans in view and he guessed there would be others nearby - they would not have a decorated Major commanding a mere half dozen men, surely? Marianne and Woodward were still standing by the Mercedes with Holtzmann about two yards away; he was the closest to them. Cormack surveyed the scene for four or five seconds and replaced

143

the Browning inside his tunic. With a final glance at Treischer, he went out of the door, pulling it shut behind him, and strode rapidly down the path, an expression of fury on his face.

"Get those priority documents out of the car, will you?" he shouted angrily to Woodward.

"The priority documents, Herr Colonel? Are you sure?"

"Just do it before we end up wasting more time, damn you!"

Woodward sprang to the door like a scalded cat and opened it to reach inside; when he stepped back, he was cradling a machine pistol. He spun round, lined the barrel up on the nearest soldier and squeezed the trigger, the impact of the bullets hurling the astonished German backwards. Cormack drew out the Browning and shot Holtzmann twice in the chest before pivoting round to shoot the soldier behind Marianne. Woodward traversed the Schmeisser, his body jerking to the recoil as he cut down two more Germans. Cormack swung round and fired his fourth shot at the last soldier, hitting him in the shoulder an instant before Woodward's final burst of fire ripped him apart.

The entire incident had lasted less than three seconds; Marianne was standing dumbfounded, staring incredulously at Holtzmann, who had crumpled onto his knees in front of her, his eyes wide in baffled incomprehension. Cormack grabbed her and practically threw her into the back of the car. Woodward jumped into the driving seat, pressing the starter while Cormack, acting almost unconsciously, wrenched three ammunition clips from the nearest soldier's belt and leaped into the back seat after Marianne, falling heavily against the back of the seat as the car surged forward.

Woodward spun the wheel and pressed his foot to the floor, the rear of the car slewing out to one side before it straightened out as he corrected for the skid. The next moment, they were accelerating away, with Cormack peering intently through the rear window for any sign of pursuit. There was none, to his surprise; Treischer's men must have been spread out over the countryside. Or, perhaps, after all, there were no other men....

"My God," Marianne suddenly groaned beside him; he looked at her, startled. "You killed them all, didn't you? All of them - you really don't believe in half measures, do you?" She laughed nervously, but there was a harsh edge to it.

"We had to, Marianne," said Cormack gently. "We had no choice."

"I know you didn't," she said shakily and took a deep breath. "I know you didn't. It's just-" She broke off and wiped the back of her hand impatiently across her face; there were tears glistening on

144

her cheeks.

"Are you all right?" asked Cormack; she glanced at him, surprised by the soothing tone of his voice and nodded firmly.

"Yes. I'll be all right in a minute. I - I'm just not used to this sort of thing." And what about that Gestapo agent you knifed? an inner voice demanded. Was that any different to this?

"None of us are," said Cormack softly, almost to himself. He stared out of the window for several seconds then said quietly, "Tony?"

"Yes?"

"I didn't kill Treischer."

Startled, Woodward glanced at him in the mirror. "You didn't? I thought you had when you came out on your own."

"I know. But I hadn't." Cormack sounded infinitely weary.

Marianne's eyes were flickering from one to the other, confused. "What difference does that make, anyway? We escaped, didn't we?"

Woodward nodded agreement, but a shade too vigorously. "They'll know we're here anyway, so it doesn't really matter, does it?"

"Don't be so bloody stupid, the pair of you!" Cormack hissed. "He got a good look at all three of us!" He paused and let out his breath in a long sigh; when he spoke again, his voice was tired, defeated. "He's no fool, that Treischer. He knows which names we're travelling under and what we look like, so he can have the whole bloody local Gestapo combing the town for us." He shook his head slowly. "I should have killed him."

There was a fearful, ominous silence that seemed to stretch out interminably before Marianne asked hesitantly, "Then why didn't you?"

Cormack's reply was almost inaudible. "I couldn't. That's all there is to it - I just couldn't."

He stared bleakly out of the window and shook his head as if in disbelief at his own folly. "I liked the poor sod too much."

CHAPTER 11.

Fitzgerald looked up from the file he was reading when he heard the knock on his door. "Come in," he called.

To his surprise, it was Philby, who was smiling apologetically. "Am I disturbing you, Miles? I just wanted a quick word with you."

"Certainly, sir - if you'd like to take a seat?"

"Thank you." He settled himself down. "I was just wondering if the Emerald pick up had gone according to plan last night."

Fitzgerald shook his head regretfully. "I'm afraid it didn't, sir. The Mosquito we sent in didn't come back and we don't have any idea what happened to it - the crew were instructed to observe radio silence throughout and so we didn't realise anything untoward had happened until it became overdue."

"I'm sorry to hear that," Philby replied with evident sincerity in his voice. "And no word of your team either, I take it?"

Again, Fitzgerald shook his head. "None at all. I'm afraid we have to assume the worst - they had a radio with them and would surely have sent us some sort of message if they had escaped whatever happened to the Mosquito - but they haven't."

Philby nodded. "I see. Mightn't they be deliberately maintaining radio silence themselves?"

"It's possible, I suppose," Fitzgerald conceded. "Cormack hasn't used the radio at all so far, to be honest."

"Cormack? Is he the leader of the rescue team?"

"Yes, he is."

"What sort of man is he? Is he capable?"

Grudgingly, Fitzgerald nodded. "He was in the Marines before he was seconded to SOE in '41. He's been behind enemy lines several times and his record is pretty impressive - he was the one who brought back the Liechtenstein radar two years ago."

"I see," Philby said again, a note of respect in his voice. "In other words, he's escaped from tight situations before and might well be able to do so again."

Fitzgerald shrugged. "He might, I suppose, but-" He broke off; he had been about to say that Cormack and Woodward had only been selected because of their expendability, but that would hardly be prudent in the present circumstances. "I don't hold out much hope, to be honest," he finished lamely.

"Don't be so pessimistic. This - Cormack, isn't it?"

Fitzgerald nodded.

"This Cormack - you say he's resourceful? Good at surviving in tight corners? Plenty of initiative?"

"All of those, yes."

"Then is he the sort of man who would deliberately not broadcast a message and just go it alone?"

Fitzgerald thought for a moment then nodded. "Judging by his record, yes, he might well do that."

"So he could still be at large and making his own way out?"

"He could be, yes."

"There you are!" Philby beamed. "Don't give up hope - 'Emerald' could still be a success. Don't write it off just yet." A thought seemed to occur to him and his expression became more serious. "Although it does pose a bit of a problem as regards your transfer, I suppose. We can't really put it through until this operation has been settled one way or the other, can we?"

"I suppose not," Fitzgerald admitted reluctantly.

"Unless we can put some sort of time limit on it," said Philby thoughtfully. "Look, if we assume that Cormack is still at large, what alternatives does he have? He can hardly stay where he is, can he? The Russians will nab him if he does."

"True." Fitzgerald swivelled round in his chair and looked at the wall map behind him. "He could try to break through to the Americans on the Elbe, I suppose. Our own forces are too far away at the moment, really.... Or there's the Baltic coast."

Philby nodded encouragement. "Didn't we have some sort of escape route for shot down air crew up there?"

"Yes, we did. It went through - Rostock, I think it was."

"Would Cormack know about it?"

"No, he wouldn't.... but Woodward probably would."

"Woodward?"

"The second member of the team. He's a pilot, so I imagine he'd know about it."

"So they might head that way.... Is the escape route still running?"

Fitzgerald shook his head. "Not for a while - there hasn't been much need for it recently, I don't suppose."

"But it could be activated?"

"I should think so. Certainly, its organiser is still sending back information to us."

"He's an agent as well?"

"Oh yes. He's been sending us material for two - three years now."

Philby nodded. "I think I've heard something about him. Fellow called Strauss? Strassner - something like that?"

"No.... I think you must be thinking of someone else. Our man's called Vogler - no, Voeller, that's it. Voeller."

Philby leaned back in his chair. "There you are then.' If Cormack can get out, either to the Americans or through Rostock, we'll know about it within - what? Two days?"

"I would think so."

"Well, how does this sound? If nothing's been heard within forty-eight hours, I'll suggest to Cathcart that you officially terminate 'Emerald' and then you can transfer to us. Reasonable?"

Fitzgerald smiled. "Sounds very reasonable, sir - Kim, I mean."

"In that case, I'd better leave you to get on with it, hadn't I? I've one or two things to sort out myself, anyway." He rose to his feet and left without another word; Fitzgerald was so preoccupied by his forthcoming transfer that it did not occur to him to wonder why Philby suddenly seemed to be in such a hurry.

ROSTOCK: 1200 HOURS.

Cormack looked nervously around before crossing the road to the derelict building that was Number 28. The door was cracked and blistered, presumably by flames from the explosion that had half destroyed the house and he had to force it open. Inside was a darkened hallway that seemed to have escaped serious damage. Slowly, he moved forward, his senses alert for the least sign of danger; almost without realising it, he had taken his gun out from inside the creased civilian jacket he was now wearing - the SS uniform had become a positive liability.

The kitchen was at the far end of the hall and Cormack paused for several seconds in front of the door, allowing his eyes to adjust properly to the gloom before opening it. A powerfully built man was seated at a table inside, facing him, seemingly quite unperturbed by the gun that was now levelled at his chest. "Who are you?" he asked calmly.

"My name is Fischer. I'm a friend of Max Ehrlich," said Cormack, giving the coded introduction Woodward had outlined to him. "Are you Voeller?"

"Yes, I am. Do come in."

Cautiously, Cormack approached the table, looking around the kitchen, but Voeller was evidently alone. Slowly, he brought the gun down and met the other man's steady gaze.

"Are you British?"

Cormack nodded. "Yes."

"But not in the RAF - I've never seen any aircrew carrying a silenced gun before."

Despite himself, Cormack grinned, as much out of relief as anything. "No, not the RAF," he agreed.

"So how did you know the number?" Two hours before, Cormack had telephoned the number Woodward had dredged up from his memory for contacting Voeller and this rendezvous had been arranged.

"I've got an RAF pilot with me."

"And you want to get out to Sweden?"

"That's about it, yes."

"Forgive my bluntness, but why bother? The war will be over in a matter of days - why not just hide out somewhere until then?"

"We'd still be on the wrong side of the lines."

Voeller nodded slowly. "I see. You're as worried by the Russians as you are about the Germans." It seemed to confirm a conclusion he had already arrived at in his mind. "How many of you are there?"

"Two others."

"Where are they?"

"A patch of waste ground next to the docks on the eastern side of the river."

"I know it - out towards Petersdorf. Do you have any papers?"

"Yes. Two sets, but one set will be useless now." Thanks to me, he thought bitterly.

"Very well. I'll see what I can do, but I can't promise anything in less than thirty-six hours. I would think you'll have to hide out until tomorrow evening at any rate."

"You can't do anything earlier than that?"

Voeller shook his head. "I don't know if the vessel is in harbour tonight - or if the skipper is still willing to work for me. In any case, we have to get various documents sorted out - sailing papers, for example."

"Fair enough," Cormack conceded. "Let's just hope the Russians don't get here first. Oh, one more thing - have you notified London that we've made contact yet?"

"No, but I generally don't, anyway."

"Good. Don't tell them anything this time either - right?"

"As you wish." Voeller looked thoughtfully at Cormack but said nothing. He rose to his feet and Cormack realised for the first time just how big a man he was; he had to be six foot three or four at least. "You'd better take me to your friends, Herr Fischer, and then we'll see about finding you somewhere to stay tonight."

As he followed Voeller out of the building, Cormack felt himself beginning to relax for almost the first time in the last four days. Voeller was so obviously capable, so clearly knew what he was doing that he inspired a quiet confidence in Cormack; like himself, Voeller was a professional. For the first time since he had seen the Mosquito explode into flames - was it really only thirteen hours ago? - Cormack began to believe that they might yet escape.

Woodward looked out of the window at the windswept estuary of the Warnow, which was about a hundred yards away across a desolate strip of wasteland that was littered with piles of rubbish and rusting hulks of metal that might once have been girders but were now twisted and bent beyond recognition. It was a bleak, depressing vista, but ideal as a hiding place because it was obvious that nobody ever came here; the old workmen's shed in which Woodward and Marianne were sheltering had not been used for months - years, possibly. It was a fair bet that, before the war, this area had been set aside to allow for expansion of the dockyard facilities - down at the shore, there were still the remains of concrete foundations - but six years of blockade by the Royal Navy had meant that even the existing docks over to Woodward's left had not been fully utilised.

"Any sign of him?" Marianne asked; she was sitting on a rickety table behind him.

"No." Woodward turned away from the window. "He's only been gone an hour."

"I just hope to God nothing else goes wrong."

"Oh, we're not doing too badly, Marianne - we've got this far, after all. We're almost on the last lap now."

She shook her head. "Don't count your chickens, Tony. I've just got this awful premonition that we're not out of it yet."

"All right, Marianne, I'll accept that we're not home and dry yet but if anyone can get us out of here in one piece, it's Alan."

"Oh, come off it, Tony," she protested. "I know you respect him, admire him, even, but he's no superman. In fact, I think he's more scared than the two of us put together. I mean, why didn't he kill that officer at the checkpoint? He could betray all of us."

Woodward stared at her. "That sounds pretty callous, Marianne."

"I suppose it does," she admitted. "But he hasn't shown any mercy to anyone else so far, so what was different about this one?" she asked, an edge of bitterness in her voice. "He posed a greater threat to us than any of the others, yet Cormack let him live."

"Don't you think he doesn't realise that? Why do you think he was so angry with himself?"

"It was too late then, wasn't it?" She took a deep breath. "When I first met him, I thought he was a cold-blooded bastard and I remember thinking that this was precisely the sort of man that was needed - you know, calculating, ruthless, that sort of thing. He isn't like that at all. I saw him when we almost got caught at the pick-up - he nearly went to pieces there, didn't he, Tony?" She sighed wearily. "I thought he could get us out of here, but, by the look of it, he's going to crack up before we get much further."

Woodward shook his head firmly. "He won't crack up, Marianne."

"How can you say that? He's a bundle of nerves as it is!"

"And that bundle of nerves, as you put it, has got us out of Berlin and all the way here - don't forget that!" Woodward exclaimed heatedly.

She held out her hands in a placatory gesture. "Tony - I'm not criticising him - or you. I just want to know that he can get us through this."

Woodward went back to the window and looked out at the estuary again, his eyes following a seagull as it glided past. When he spoke, his voice seemed far away. "I was the same as you when I first met him, Marianne. I thought he was a nasty piece of work altogether, a real East End rowdy - but that was when I thought that a bit of cloak and dagger work would be exciting and romantic. A bit of a lark - that sort of thing, which perhaps gives you an idea of how valid my opinions were at the time. I just didn't realise what operating behind enemy lines could do to a man." He glanced at her and smiled apologetically. "Or a woman. Christ knows how he put up with me - I nearly ballsed up the entire operation the minute we landed in Holland. I watched him kill a German soldier - he slit his throat, right in front of me, and I began to realise what his kind of war - this kind of war - was all about. I remember wondering how anybody could be so cold-blooded as that. I thought he was the biggest bastard I'd ever met.

"That was before he saved my life."

"Go on," she said, almost in a whisper.

"I was picked up by the Gestapo - and he got me out again. Walked right into Gestapo headquarters and rescued me, when he could have run for it - but he didn't. Then, to cap it all, he pulled off the bloody mission when we all thought he'd get the hell out of it. And I'll tell you this, Marianne, although it didn't strike me until after it was all over - for most of the time, he was even more on edge than this, but he still went ahead and stole that damned plane." He smiled faintly in reminiscence and turned back to her. "You see, Marianne, I think it's when he's most under pressure that he works best - don't ask me how or why, but I'm pretty sure it's true. Manoeuvre him into a corner and he'll fight like hell, but give him time to think about things and he's liable to hesitate - especially if it involves killing," he finished quietly.

Marianne stared at him for several seconds and shook her head slowly, wondering again what sort of man Cormack was when he could evoke such a response from the normally flippant and irreverent Woodward. "I hope you're right, Tony. I really do." She sighed. "It's just-"

"Hold on," said Woodward urgently; he was back at the window. "Someone's coming.... It's all right, it's Alan. He's got someone with him."

Voeller had to duck his head to get through the door, his eyes widening in momentary surprise when he saw Marianne. "Right," he said briskly. "I'm not going to ask who you are or what you're doing here - I've already formed the impression from Herr Fischer here that you won't tell me anyway. May I see your papers, though?"

Cormack nodded at Woodward, who handed over his civilian documents; Voeller examined them closely and nodded. "They aren't genuine, I take it?"

"No, they're not," Cormack agreed.

"They're very good forgeries, all the same, good enough to fool most checkpoints." He turned to Marianne. "And you, fraulein?"

"I only have this passport." She handed it over to him; he raised his eyebrows, but said nothing as he scrutinised it. "This looks genuine," he said.

"Courtesy of the Nazis themselves," Marianne said bitterly.

Again, Voeller made no comment on her cryptic remark, simply returning the passport to her. "Bearing in mind the - ah - trouble you apparently had on your way here, it would be safest if you were to remain out of sight, I think." He looked around the interior of the shed. "Unfortunately, this isn't safe - not at night. There are

152

regular patrols through here during the night, with guard dogs, so you'll have to stay at my home tonight, while I try to arrange your boat journey. I'll come here and collect you at five thirty - all right?"

"Right," Cormack nodded.

FRANKFURT-ON-ODER: 1900 HOURS.

Rindt forced his eyes open as he was roughly shaken awake; looking up, he saw the face of Pavel, one of the two guards who had followed him everywhere since he had arrived in Frankfurt that morning. The minute that Hentschel and he had passed through the Russian lines, they had been hustled into a waiting jeep and driven straight here; Rindt had been struck by their evident priority in that they had been passed through the various checkpoints without any delay at all. He had not seen Hentschel at all since their arrival, which was unsurprising since he had been subjected to an intensive interrogation session that had lasted for several hours. The nameless inquisitors had seemed vaguely disappointed by his willingness to answer every question without hesitation or evasion - but what else could he do? They had not had to threaten him with what they might do to Inga - he knew only too well that he had to co-operate and so he had felt no guilt or remorse as he had betrayed his country's secrets, giving names, dates, locations - everything. From the moment that Hentschel had told him to leave Berlin with him, Rindt had known that it would come to this, as surely as night followed day. And so he had held nothing back, had told them all they had wanted to know until they had brought him here to his cell. To be fair, he admitted, it was a damn sight more comfortable than he'd expected in that the bed even had a mattress and a blanket, but it wouldn't have made any difference if they had given him a bed of nails - he would still have gone out like a light, the way he had felt. And now they were waking him up....

Cursing, he looked at his watch and discovered that he had been asleep for barely an hour and a half. Was this part of their interrogation technique? It probably was, he decided - the Gestapo used sleep deprivation methods themselves and their methods were based on those used by the NKVD, whose prisoner he undoubtedly was at the moment.

"Come on. Wake up. Colonel Semyonin wants to see you," said the guard in appalling German. He gestured at a bowl of water on the chair; Rindt nodded and sat up on the bed, swinging his feet onto the floor. After he had scooped a few handfuls of water onto his face, he felt slightly more human - and they had provided a towel for him. This was certainly not in the Gestapo handbook....

"Follow." Pavel went to the door. Mystified, Rindt pulled on his tunic and followed him. They went along a corridor and up two flights of stairs to an oak-panelled door; Rindt suspected that they were on the premises of what had once been a law firm, but he had no time to look around before Pavel stopped in front of a door and knocked briskly.

A voice called out in Russian and Pavel opened the door, ushering Rindt in ahead of him. There were two men in the room; sitting behind a large teak desk was a diminutive man in a Colonel's uniform who was presumably Semyonin, but was the other man that Rindt noticed first, simply because his presence here was so unbelievable.

"Dear God in Heaven...." Rindt whispered.

And yet it was true. Sitting there, smoking a cigar and clearly quite at ease with a Russian Colonel in the NKVD was Heinrich Mueller - the head of the Gestapo.

It was Mueller who spoke first, with a faint smile on his face at Rindt's evident discomfiture. "You seem surprised to see me, Rindt."

Still Rindt said nothing, but continued to stare disbelievingly at Mueller - what in hell was going on? Gradually, everything began to fall into place. "So that's it...." he murmured. "You're working for them.... For the Russians."

Mueller smiled and nodded briefly. "Precisely."

Rindt shook his head incredulously. "Bloody hell.... No wonder we never...." he said, almost to himself as the implications began to sink home. "You were absolutely safe, weren't you? Nobody in their right mind would ever suspect Gestapo Mueller, would they? And even if they did, you could easily arrange for their disappearance." In his mind's eye, Rindt could see it all. How many Russian agents had been able to operate safely simply because Mueller was ensuring their continued freedom? He would have had access to every counter-intelligence operation that had been mounted by the RSHA - all he had to do was either to block or delay it, or simply warn the intended victims. Time after time, Rindt recalled, there had been occasions when suspected Russian agents had simply disappeared, almost from under their noses, or where a prolonged surveillance of a suspected safehouse or dead

154

letter drop had revealed precisely nothing. Promising looking investigations that had suddenly been terminated or where the personnel
concerned had been transferred elsewhere.... or Russian agents who had actually been arrested but had then somehow died under interrogation without revealing anything.... It was all so easy to see now. "Dear God, Mueller, how long have you been working for them?"

"You can hardly expect us to tell you that, Rindt," said Semyonin, rising to his feet and coming round the table.

"No, I suppose not.... but it explains a lot," said Rindt, an expression of chagrin on his face.

"Indeed?" said Semyonin interestedly. "Such as?"

"Why we have never made any real progress against Russian spy cells in the last eighteen months. How Hentschel came to be so well informed about my being appointed to the Leck investigation - obviously, he got it from the horse's mouth. And also why I was chosen anyway, now I come to think of it," he said slowly, nodding emphatically. "Of course that was it! You needed someone you could trust, didn't you, Mueller? Someone who would be involved in the investigation but who would not betray you if he began to suspect anything."

Mueller nodded. "Exactly, Rindt."

"And that was why Inga couldn't get out of Danzig," Rindt said bitterly. "So that I could be blackmailed - you're a bastard, Mueller!"

The other man's eyes glinted. "You can't talk to me like that, Rindt. Just remember where you are and who you're dealing with!"

Rindt bit back the angry retort that was on his lips. Mueller was right, damn him - he dared not do or say anything that might antagonise the Russians. He nodded slowly and forced himself to relax, but not before Mueller caught one last glimpse of the expression in his eyes before Rindt carefully removed it; it had been one of pure, undiluted hatred and Mueller knew that he had made an implacable enemy, one that would have to be dealt with, sooner or later....

"In any case, all this is wasting time," said Semyonin, with an irritated look that encompassed both of them. "You see, Rindt, we have had you brought here for a particular purpose. We want you to perform a further service for us."

"I thought so," said Rindt softly. "I didn't think you'd brought me out of Berlin just for the good of my health. Or for what I might know - you could have got all that from Comrade Mueller here."

Mueller's eyes flashed angrily at Rindt's use of "Comrade", but Semyonin merely looked amused. "Indeed. Briefly, Rindt, the situation is this. We think we know where Marianne Kovacs might be and so we'd like you to continue your original assignment - to bring her to us." Semyonin's voice was mild, almost tentative, as if he were making a suggestion that Rindt could refuse if he so wished, but Rindt was not deceived for an instant; there was a calm authority about the Russian that boded ill for anyone who stood in his way.

"And how am I supposed to do that?"

"We believe that she might be in Rostock. The British apparently have an RAF escape route through there to Sweden, run by a man called Voeller - there is a very good chance that they will use this method of escaping."

Rindt looked thoughtfully at Semyonin. "You seem remarkably well informed, Colonel."

"That is neither here nor there. What we want you to do is to go to Rostock, find her if she's there and bring her back. How you do that is entirely up to you - General Mueller has given me a glowing report of your abilities."

Rindt looked from one to the other incredulously. "You're not serious, are you? How the devil am I supposed to carry out something like that? And why, for God's sake? Is she that important?"

Semyonin nodded imperturbably, as though he had expected Rindt's outburst. "I'll answer your second question first. Yes, she is that important. She must be, if the British have gone to the trouble of sending in a rescue squad - they would hardly have done that unless she was in possession of vital information and so we would like to know what that is. And as regards carrying out the operation, perhaps I should point out that we will not be sending you in alone. You'll have one of our Action Teams with you - four men, all experienced at working behind enemy lines, who will be able to give you all the help you will need."

And to keep an eye on me, no doubt, thought Rindt. "Why me, for heaven's sake?"

"Surely that is obvious, Rindt," Mueller snapped. "You will not have to adopt a cover identity, nor will you have to use forged documents. You will simply be carrying out your original assignment, using genuine documents that have been signed by myself and Bormann - do you think anyone will question those orders?"

No, they wouldn't, thought Rindt; the documents would give

him almost unlimited authority and freedom to do virtually as he pleased. Considered from a viewpoint of professional detachment, the idea made sense - and it had the added bonus, from the Russian point of view, that if anything were to go wrong, then they would not be risking one of their own agents; almost certainly, the "Action Team" to which Semyonin had referred would be expendable. Unfortunately, when one was the equally expendable agent, it was difficult to remain objective about the situation....

"And if I get her out? What then?"

"The original promise still stands," said Semyonin calmly. "Your wife will be returned to you."

Returned to you - as if she were a piece of furniture, thought Rindt bitterly, but he said nothing; it would have been utter folly if he had.

"We're sending you in tonight," Semyonin continued. "We'll give you a full briefing just before you go, but, first, there's someone we'd think you'd like to see next door." He nodded at a connecting door, just behind Mueller.

Dumbly, Rindt stared at the two men, scarcely daring to hope, despite Semyonin's words; he made no move towards the door until Mueller smiled almost conspiratorially at him. "Go on, Rindt. You won't have much time with her, so I shouldn't waste any of it."

Rindt did not hear the last part of this; he ran to the door, hurled it open.... and there she was, sitting on a chair with two woman guards behind, her eyes widening in amazement and incredulous joy as she saw him.

"Alex!" She leaped to her feet and rushed towards him, into his arms; he pulled her to him, holding her tightly then they were kissing and sobbing and calling each other's names all at once in a frenzy of delight and relief.

"Oh God, Inga, I've been so worried about you!"

"Alex, Alex.... Just hold me tight.... Oh God, I love you! I've missed you so much!"

"And I love you, Inga.... I love you." He could see the tears glistening in her eyes, could feel his own cheeks were wet, but he did not care. All that mattered was that Inga was here, in his arms.... "Oh, Inga, darling! I thought I'd never see you again. I thought I'd lost you!" He was sobbing uncontrollably now.

"It's all right, darling. I'm here now." She reached up and tenderly wiped away his tears, before her own control broke down and she cried out, "Don't leave me, Alex!"

"Oh, God...." he whispered. Rostock. Marianne. The thoughts burst into his mind with an explosive force and he suddenly remembered Mueller and Semyonin behind him. "It's all right," he murmured. "Everything's going to be all right.... I promise you." Who was he trying to convince - Inga.... or himself?

As if she too had recalled that they were not alone, she moved away from him a little, glancing nervously at the two men through the doorway. "Are you all right?" she asked awkwardly. "Are you well?"

"Well enough," he replied, his voice stilted. "You?"

"They've looked after me well enough," she said, now looking worriedly at her two guards.

"Your mother?"

"They're looking after her in hospital. They let me visit her every two or three days."

Rindt forced a smile. "They can't be feeding you properly - you've lost weight."

"You always said I needed to."

Dear God, thought Rindt despairingly, it's as though we're two teenagers on our first date! Why can't they just leave us alone together for a few minutes? Is that too much to ask?

"You're looking thinner yourself, Alex."

"I haven't had your cooking, have I?"

No, it was all right after all, he decided; their eyes were telling each other what they really wanted to know, regardless of what their mouths were saying. I love you, I love you, he told her as he stared intently at her and said, "Do you have all you need? Clothes - that sort of thing?"

"Yes. They let me take most of my things from Mother's flat." I want you to make love to me, her eyes told him in that blatantly inviting look he remembered so well; he pressed her hungrily against him and kissed her, vaguely aware of Semyonin saying something to the women guards.

"Right," said Mueller's voice, breaking into the tiny world they had created for themselves for those few seconds. "That's enough for now, Rindt."

"Just a few moments longer!" Inga pleaded. "Please!"

The office door opened in response to a barked order from Semyonin and Pavel came in with another guard; they moved towards Inga and Rindt.

"That is all the time you're permitted," said Mueller harshly. "And be thankful you've had that much."

"Alex!" Inga cried as the women guards seized hold of her; Rindt clung on to her, kissing her one last time before they wrenched her out of his grasp. Inga struggled momentarily then relaxed, realising the futility of offering any resistance. The guards took her to the office door, but her eyes were on his face all the time.

"It's all right, Inga," Rindt called to her. "We'll be together again, I promise you. And soon!"

"I love you!"

"And I love you!"

Then the door was closed behind her and she was gone. Rindt closed his eyes and drew in a great lungful of air. You bastards, he thought viciously; I bet you really enjoyed that, you sadistic.... He took another deep breath before he could trust himself to speak; now, more than ever, he had to curb his tongue.

"Thank you," he said quietly, almost sick with self-loathing. "For letting me see her."

"That's all right," said Mueller. "And you'll see her again once all this is over."

"In the meantime, some rest," said Semyonin, his manner brisk, businesslike. "Your final briefing will be at 2300, so you'll have about three hours in which to get some sleep. I suspect you'll need it."

Rindt nodded and was then escorted out by the guards. Once he had gone, Mueller stared thoughtfully at the closed door and said quietly:

"Will you keep your promise? About his wife, I mean?"

Semyonin hesitated before answering; it was difficult to decide precisely what Mueller's status was at the moment. A high ranking prisoner, or, as 'Spartakus', a top level NKVD agent? Moscow Centre had not clarified the situation at all, but it was safer to assume the latter.... He shook his head in reply to the question. "Of course not. Why should we? From what you say, he is an extremely able man - we can use him again and again if we have his wife. She is his Achilles heel - he is deeply in love with her, I'm afraid." There was a note almost of wistful regret in his voice.

Mueller glanced sharply at him but thought better of making any comment. "Just as I suspected. What will you do? Grant him these meetings with her every time he completes an assignment?"

"Something like that, I would imagine." Semyonin also looked at the door and added softly, "Rindt is no fool. I suspect he knows all this already." His voice tailed off and he shrugged suddenly. "But what else can he do?"

CHAPTER 12.

ROSTOCK, TUESDAY MAY 1ST: 0400 HOURS.

"Captain Cormack?" The soft voice, coupled with the gentle shaking of his shoulder, brought Cormack reluctantly awake. It took him a few seconds to remember where he was - on the sofa in Voeller's living room - then he looked up at the pale outline of Marianne's face.

"What is it, Marianne?"

"I can't sleep. I need someone to talk to."

Cormack looked up at her, surprised and glanced across at the shadowy outline of the armchair where Woodward was slumped; she divined his unspoken comment.

"It's you I want to talk to, Captain, not Tony."

Again, Cormack stared at her then shrugged. "Fair enough," he murmured. "Go ahead."

"Not here," she whispered. "I don't want to wake Tony up. In my room?"

"All right." Cormack reached out for the threadbare dressing gown that Voeller had lent him and pulled it on. She led the way into the spare bedroom that she had been given and closed the door before going over to the window to draw the blackout curtain. In the moonlight, he could see that she was wearing a pair of Voeller's pyjamas that were several sizes too big for her. She sat down on the bed.

"Do sit down, Captain."

He looked around and saw that the bed was the only place to sit; he hesitated momentarily before sitting down next to her. "Just one thing, Marianne - you don't have to call me Captain."

"So what do I call you? Alan?"

"If you like," he said, his voice completely devoid of expression.

She stared appraisingly at him for several seconds. "Can't you just relax - Alan? Take that barrier down for a few minutes?"

"Look, what was it you wanted?" he said abruptly.

"As I said - I couldn't sleep." She sighed. "I felt absolutely shattered when I got into bed - I thought I'd go out like a light. But I can't. I keep thinking about what might happen tomorrow. I'm scared stiff and I don't mind admitting it." She laughed nervously.

160

"So I suppose I'm looking for some reassurance - which is why I wanted to talk to you - Alan."

"For reassurance? Me?" The thought seemed to amuse him. "Then you've come to the wrong person, I'm afraid. Reassurance is more Tony's line."

"Alan - without being nasty to him, what does Tony know about it? If it was something to do with flying that I needed to be reassured about, then I'd talk to him, but it isn't." She shook her head slowly. "Maybe reassurance isn't the right word anyway. Maybe it's just the truth I want - straight from the horse's mouth. Are we going to be all right?"

Cormack blew out his cheeks. "I wish to hell I knew the answer to that myself, Marianne. All I can tell you is that Voeller's been doing this sort of thing for three years now and he's been doing all right so far. There's no reason to think that it's all going to go wrong now."

"Yes, but won't they be looking for us after what happened at the checkpoint?"

Cormack nodded. "Bound to be. On the other hand, Rostock's a fair sized place and, probably, a lot of the Gestapo will be more interested in saving their own skins than in looking for us. And they've only got the one day to find us - don't forget that."

"Then why were you so worried about not - er - about not dealing with that officer?"

Cormack smiled humourlessly. "Nice way of putting it - 'dealing' with him. I don't know, really. He could pass on our descriptions, which would make life awkward if we have to go through another checkpoint, but that's not critical, in all probability. I suppose I was annoyed because I should have done it and I hadn't."

"As a professional, you mean."

"Exactly. If I had killed him, it would have been one less thing to worry about."

"But one more thing to add to your conscience?" she said, very softly.

He glanced sharply at her and nodded slowly. "Yes. You could put it that way, I suppose." He laughed bitterly. "But what's one more killing, when all's said and done?"

Neither of them said anything for several seconds then Marianne broke the silence. "So you think we've got a reasonable chance tomorrow?"

"Fifty-fifty, I'd say."

"Is that the truth? You're not just trying to cheer me up?"

"No," he said quietly. "I wouldn't do that to you. You had the guts to tell me you're scared and so you deserve the truth." He shrugged awkwardly. "I think if I were in your place, I'd want someone to tell me exactly what the situation was as well, you see."

"Thank you for that - Alan."

"Sorry I couldn't be more - reassuring."

She shook her head. "As I said, if that was all that I'd wanted I'd have gone to Tony. So - fifty-fifty, you reckon? An even chance?"

"Something like that."

"It depends on which way you look at it, I suppose," she mused. "An even chance of escaping - or an even chance of being killed or caught." She laughed nervously. "I'm not sure I feel any better, actually, knowing that." Suddenly, she stood up and hugged herself, as if she were shivering. She went over to the window and looked out into the night. "I've just got this awful feeling, Alan, a horrible premonition that something's going to go wrong...."

"Don't be so silly, Marianne." Almost without realising it, he stood up and went to stand behind her. "We all feel like that sometimes - Good God, I ought to know, the number of times I've thought that, but I'm still here."

She turned to face him and smiled tiredly. "Now you're being reassuring. That isn't exactly a logical argument, is it?"

"And neither's yours."

"No, I don't suppose it is." She took a deep breath. "I don't know, Alan.... I'm still scared."

"And what's wrong with that? I'll let you into a secret - so am I." He smiled faintly. "On second thoughts, though, I don't suppose that's any secret at all. It must be pretty obvious by now."

"Then why do you do it? What are you doing here if it scares you so much?"

He looked away from her and did not answer for some time. Eventually, he said, "You tell me, Marianne. I've been asking myself that question God knows how many times lately. I thought I'd finished with all this for good - but here I am."

"You still haven't said why." she persisted, her voice soft.

"I was strong-armed into it to some extent."

"You mean you knew that Tony wouldn't have a chance on his own?"

He stared at her, surprised. "How did you know?"

"It wasn't difficult. Tony is very sweet and all that, but - well - he's a pilot, not an undercover agent. His being here didn't make

162

any sense at all until I realised that there's a kind of bond between you two. He really admires you, you know."

Cormack was plainly embarrassed. "Can't think why."

"Maybe saving his life had something to do with it?"

"And he saved mine as well," he said simply. "We're quits on that as far as I'm concerned."

"So is that it? You couldn't let him come here on his own?"

"That's part of the reason, yes, but there's more to it than that," Cormack admitted slowly. He grinned sheepishly. "Maybe there was an element of the knight in shining armour bit."

She shook her head incredulously. "I'm sorry, Alan - if Tony had said that, I'd have believed it, but not you - and I don't mean to be nasty. You've got more sense than that."

"I don't know whether I've been insulted or complimented," he said dryly. "No, it wasn't so much the rescuing the damsel in distress as - oh, I don't know - anger at what they were doing to you." He looked out of the window. "You see, they were just going to leave you here, but somebody decided something had to be done, so they picked Tony and me - two old crocks, really - and told us to pull you out. We were expendable, you see."

"And so was I, then," she whispered.

"Exactly. They're bastards, all of them - and I couldn't let them do that to anyone, no matter who it was. I've been behind enemy lines and so I know something of what you've gone through. And if I were in your position, I'd want to know that someone was going to try and get me out." He shrugged awkwardly. "You said Tony admired me - fair enough, but hasn't it occurred to you that what you've been doing is far more admirable than anything I've done?"

She stared at him. "No, it hasn't."

"Well, believe it. And those bastards were going to ditch you - I couldn't let them do that. Not after everything you've been through. I suppose there are some things you can't walk away from, no matter how much you might want to."

Slowly, Marianne shook her head. "So that's why you weren't worried about the ODESSA papers. You really are a surprising man, Alan."

"Me? Hardly."

"Allow me to be the judge of that, will you?" Her eyes were fixed on his with a curious intensity, but it was some time before she spoke again. "Alan?"

"Yes?"

"Will you stay here with me tonight?"

Somehow, he did not seem surprised by the question; it was as if

163

the shared confidences had brought them closer together and made such a suggestion almost inevitable. "If that's what you'd like," he replied, gently.

"I just don't want to be alone, you see. Not tonight."

Cormack nodded and stepped forward, putting his arms around her and pulling her close to him. "Then you won't be," he said softly, speaking into her hair.

Her arms were round him now and she rested her head on his chest. "The last man I spent the night with was Fegelein. And before that was Goebbels. And before that...." Her voice tailed off and Cormack knew that she was talking to herself, not to him. She looked up at his face. "So - as this could be my last chance, I'd rather go to bed with someone I like - can you understand that?"

He nodded. "Yes, I can." She had the strange impression that he was suddenly far away, in another time and place. "I know exactly what you mean." His voice was wistful, sad.

Gently, she slid out of his arms and took off the pyjamas with swift, impatient movements. In the moonlight, her body seemed to glow, but as he felt himself responding to her, Cormack remembered how Lena had stood naked in the darkness, exactly like that, and how she had given herself to him so completely.... A chill gripped him; was it all happening over again?

Marianne seemed to sense his hesitation and came to him; she opened out his dressing gown and pressed herself against him. "Come on, Alan. Lie down with me and let's see what happens."

At first, they just lay in each other's arms, saying nothing until, presently, Cormack kissed her gently, his tongue probing into her mouth. She returned the kiss, running her fingers through his hair as she began to relax. And now she could feel his hands on her body, caressing her with feather light touches, arousing her; the thought came to her that she had not intended this, not at all, but now that she was here with him, it seemed like the most natural thing in the world for it to be happening.... and when had she last really made love anyway? Fegelein, Goebbels, all those others she had had to give herself to.... Cormack touched her, so very gently; she moaned softly and pulled him to her with a sudden fierce eagerness that was almost frightening in its intensity; it had been too long, far too long....

0500 HOURS.

The sky was just beginning to lighten in the east when the sentry on duty at the checkpoint saw five figures approaching along the

Stralsund road. As they approached, he could see that they were all in SS uniform and that the leading man was a Colonel; hurriedly, he ran round the back of the personnel carrier parked next to the road, opened the passenger door and called, "Herr Lieutenant!"

The Lieutenant's eyes snapped open, startled. "Eh?" he grunted before he managed to focus on the soldier. "Yes, Preuss?"

"You'd better come quickly, Herr Lieutenant. It's the SS-"

"Oh, bloody hell. Right, I'm coming." The Lieutenant grabbed his helmet and scrambled out of the cockpit, jumping down next to Preuss. As he walked towards the barrier, which was nothing more than a pole resting on two oil drums, he watched the approaching men. Even in the early morning light, he could see that the Colonel was not in a happy mood. That's all I need, he thought....

The Colonel came striding purposefully forward, reaching inside his tunic for a sheaf of documents which he handed to the Lieutenant without saying anything at all. The Lieutenant saluted awkwardly and looked at the papers, noting the other man's name first: Colonel Rindt. His eyes widened involuntarily at Mueller's signature at the bottom of the front page.

"I require transport," Rindt said curtly, knowing that the Lieutenant would expect nothing else from the Gestapo. "Our own vehicles were damaged by landmines about ten kilometres back. We've had to walk here." His tone of voice left no doubt that he regarded the entire incident as a personal insult. "Is that the only vehicle you have?" he continued, pointing at the personnel carrier.

"Er - yes, Herr Colonel."

"Typical. Still, I suppose it will have to do - I'm damned if I'm going to walk any further. If you have any equipment on it that you need, you'd better get your men to remove it, Lieutenant."

The Lieutenant drew a deep breath. "With respect, Herr-"

"I do hope you're not going to be troublesome, Lieutenant," Rindt interrupted in an almost bored voice. "Look at those orders again - signed by General Mueller, countersigned by Reichsleiter Bormann himself. Now are you telling me that your commanding officer outranks them?"

"No, of course not, Herr Colonel."

"Good. Then do as I say, will you?"

The Lieutenant hesitated for only a moment longer then nodded urgently. "Preuss! Schwarz! Get all our equipment unloaded from the carrier!" he called.

Rindt smiled thinly. "Thank you, Lieutenant. You are too kind." He took the documents back from the Lieutenant and saluted.

"Heil Hitler!"
"Heil Hitler!"

Within five minutes, the personnel carrier had been emptied. Rindt climbed up into the passenger seat, nodded to his driver and raised his gloved hand in an almost regal acknowledgment to the Lieutenant as the carrier moved off.

The Lieutenant, still seething from his cavalier treatment, watched it go, thinking murderous thoughts about Rindt: fucking Nazi bastard.

The personnel carrier drew up outside the Gestapo headquarters building at just before six a.m. and by the time the clocks were chiming the hour, Rindt had already telephoned Krieger, the senior Gestapo officer, at his quarters, ordering him to report in at once. When he put the telephone down and saw the frankly apprehensive expressions on the faces around the lobby, the thought came to him that, under different circumstances, he might almost have been enjoying the situation.... He turned to the young SS-Lieutenant behind the desk; like the equally youthful officer at the checkpoint, the man's face had blanched when he had seen Rindt's orders.

"Right," Rindt said briskly. "Muehlmann, isn't it?"

"Yes, Herr Colonel."

"Right, Muehlmann, while we're waiting for Major Krieger to put in an appearance, we'll make a start on my investigations. I need information on a man called Voeller." He spelled out the name. "I want the records checked immediately."

"Yes, Herr Colonel." Muehlmann hesitated then said, "There may be more than one, so if you could tell me his Christian name?"

"If I knew that I would have told you, Muehlmann," said Rindt silkily.

"Yes, Herr Colonel. At once."

"And see about some food and coffee, will you, for me and my men? We've had a very tiring journey." As Muehlmann hurried away, Rindt looked over at the four Russians who had been parachuted in with him last night. He had met them at the briefing just before they had been driven out to the airfield; only one of them - Vassiliev - spoke any German worth talking about, but this was not critical as they were posing as members of the 14th Galician Division of the SS, which was composed entirely of Ukrainian recruits and so nobody would question their lack of German. Semyonin had told him that they were experienced in working behind enemy lines, but Rindt disliked having to rely on complete strangers whose primary allegiance lay elsewhere. He had barely succeeded in memorising their names - Andreyev, Petrov, Ivanov and Vassiliev - although he doubted if they were genuine; these surnames were probably as common in Russia as Schmidt or Braun would be in Germany. Furthermore, apart from Vassiliev, who was wearing a sergeant's uniform, he wasn't quite sure which one was which. Hardly the most auspicious start to an operation....

It didn't matter, he reminded himself. They were there simply to follow his orders, to give him assistance if he needed it - that much had been made clear to him; he hoped that their instructions had been just as specific.

Krieger arrived at just after six-thirty, looking first harassed, then suitably chastened when he saw the orders; Mueller had been right, Rindt thought irrelevantly as he motioned Krieger to sit down in his own office. Nobody had dreamed of questioning them.

"Right," said Rindt, opening his briefcase and passing over a photograph of Marianne Kovacs which he presumed Mueller had removed from Gestapo HQ in Berlin before going over to the Russians. "We're looking for this woman and it is a matter of the utmost priority. We believe that she might be attempting to leave the country via Rostock and will probably be travelling with two armed enemy agents. I want an all out search instituted for her. Copies of this are to be sent to all of your checkpoints and she is to be arrested on sight. Is that clear?"

"At once, Herr Colonel," said Krieger eagerly then hesitated as a thought struck him. "There is one thing, Herr Colonel. Yesterday morning, there was a shooting incident at an army checkpoint south of Rostock. Two men and a woman shot their way through and escaped into the city."

"And what steps have you taken to find them?"

"Er - to be honest, we haven't really done very much, I'm afraid, Herr Colonel." Krieger spoke rapidly to forestall the threatened explosion on Rindt's face. "You see, it was an Army checkpoint and they said the men were in SS uniform."

"I see," said Rindt slowly; of course the Gestapo would not be too diligent in following it up, not when some of their own men might be involved. "Then start taking steps, Krieger. These are probably the very ones we are looking for. I want them found."

"At once, Herr Colonel!" Krieger shot to his feet like a scalded cat and was halfway to the door when Rindt said:

"You say they shot their way through. Were there casualties?"

"Er - yes, Herr Colonel. In fact, there was only one survivor, a Major Treischer. He's in the military hospital."

Rindt stared at him in disgust. Probably half a dozen men had died and Krieger had done nothing about it, simply because their killers had been in SS uniform. Talk about protecting your own....

"I'll go and talk to him." It's about time someone did, he thought bitterly.

0800 HOURS.

"Was this the woman, Major?" Rindt asked, holding out Marianne's photograph to Treischer, who was sitting up in bed, his head swathed in bandages; they were keeping him under observation for twenty four hours in case of concussion from the blow to the head. Treischer took the photo and studied it carefully.

"Yes. That's her."

Rindt let out a huge sigh of relief; it was only then that he realised he had been holding his breath waiting for the answer. "You're sure?"

"Of course I am," Treischer replied with ill-concealed dislike, a hostility that was undeniably directed at the SS uniform; Rindt ignored it.

"What name was she travelling under?" He reached into his pocket and took out a small notebook.

"Maria Kotze."

Rindt noted it down. "And the two men?"

"The officer was a Colonel Beitzen, but I can't remember the other one's name - he was a Dutchman. Vandamm, Vandemeer, something like that."

"Can you describe them?"

"Beitzen was tall, with dark hair and blue eyes. In his early thirties. He looked pretty fit."

"No visible identifying marks?"

"No."

"The Dutchman?"

"Tall and slim. Brown hair, blue eyes. Middle or late twenties."

Rindt carefully noted these down. "One more thing, Major. Was there any particular reason why this Beitzen left you alive, but killed everyone else in your unit?"

Treischer glared at him. "How the hell should I know? The bastard knocked me unconscious - by the time I came round they

168

had gone and all my men were dead."

Curious though, thought Rindt, staring at his notebook. Why leave someone behind who could give their descriptions? It didn't fit; these men had certainly been ruthless enough so far.... He shrugged impatiently. The question was irrelevant; all that mattered was that Marianne Kovacs was here - in Rostock.

CHAPTER 13.

GESTAPO HEADQUARTERS, ROSTOCK: 1030 HOURS, TUESDAY, MAY 1ST.

Rindt strode into Krieger's office to find the Major's desk covered with folders and documents; behind the desk, Krieger looked up at him, startled, and was halfway out of his seat before Rindt stopped him.

"Never mind that. What's all this?" He indicated the jumble on the desk.

"Er - there are over forty Voellers in Rostock, Herr Colonel, and-"

"Forty," Rindt echoed hollowly. "And these are all their files, I take it?"

"Yes, Herr Colonel. However, you did give Muehlmann one or two indications what you had in mind so I took the liberty of weeding some of them out. If they're under twenty or over-"

"And?" Rindt interrupted.

"We've narrowed it down to six fairly likely candidates. The others-"

"Who are these six?"

"They're all involved in transport, one way or another," Krieger explained, gathering together the relevant folders.

"Any in the dockyard? Or the harbour authority?"

Krieger hesitated then nodded. "One, Herr Colonel." He thumbed hurriedly through the files and passed one to Rindt, who glanced at the name on the title page: Kurt Voeller. Quickly, he read through it, nodding once or twice before he returned it to Krieger.

"A distinct possibility, I'd say," Rindt observed.

"Are you sure, Herr Colonel?" Krieger replied tentatively, leafing through the dossier. "Both of his sons won Iron Crosses on the Russian Front."

"But both posthumously," said Rindt thoughtfully. "Who does he blame for their deaths - the Russians, or us? Just because they died for the Fatherland, it doesn't mean to say that his loyalty is as great, does it? And he's not a Party member, either. He's a widower - both sons dead...." he mused. "No ties...." He turned to

Krieger. "I want his house placed under immediate surveillance and I want someone sent to the dockyard as well. If he's there, I want him watched - but discreetly."

"Certainly, Herr Colonel. And the others?" Krieger pointed at the remaining five folders.

"Put them under surveillance as well," Rindt replied. "And as many of the others as is feasible." Far better to take no chances, he decided; one of these men had to be the man they were all looking for - Marianne as well as himself. Once he found Voeller, Marianne would not be far away.

WARNEMUNDE: 1200 HOURS.

"So that's the boat we're going in?" asked Cormack dubiously, looking down at the fifty foot fishing vessel moored to the end of the wooden jetty. To say that it was dilapidated would have been an understatement; the paint was flaking off the hull and wheelhouse and the deck was littered with uncoiled ropes and netting. On the stern the words *Anna Luise* were just visible above the boat's port of origin, Lubeck.

"I'm afraid so," Voeller replied apologetically. "Don't let her looks deceive you - she's seaworthy enough."

"I hope so," said Cormack, unconvinced. He looked around at the other fishing boats in the small harbour and had to admit that the *Anna Luise* was in no worse condition than several others. The harbour was next to the naval base, separated from it by a high wire mesh fence topped by barbed wire; Voeller had explained that there were several E-boats and motor launches based there, as well as a depot ship, but that there were no larger warships at all. The fishing port was much the same as one would find almost anywhere, a small harbour with an artificial breakwater that had apparently been damaged in an air raid at some stage and never repaired; there was a ten yard gap in it, like a missing tooth, about half way along its length.

"Come on," said Voeller, gesturing at the ladder leading down to the ANNA LUISE's deck. "Olbricht should be aboard."

"What about his crew?"

"There are normally only two others - his son and a man called Plotz - and they will be in the bierkeller at the moment, most likely." Voeller led the way down the ladder and stamped heavily on the deck, calling out, "Helmut! Are you there?"

171

There was a delay of several seconds before a gaunt figure appeared from behind the wheelhouse. As Olbricht came nearer, Cormack could see that his face was tanned and weatherbeaten; he was about fifty, Cormack decided, and looked as tough as old boots. "Kurt," he said, grinning, as he shook hands with Voeller; they were clearly old friends. Olbricht looked enquiringly at Cormack.

"A friend of mine, Helmut. Herr Fischer."

"Another one? In that case, we'd better go below then." He led the way aft and down a hatch behind the wheelhouse into a small, stuffy cabin whose furniture consisted of a bunk, a chair and a table. Olbricht took the chair, leaving Voeller and Cormack to sit on the bunk. "So you want to go to Sweden, Herr Fischer?" he asked Cormack, bluntly.

Voeller nodded. "He does, Helmut. And tonight."

"Tonight? Impossible."

"Nothing's impossible, and you know it." Voeller reached into his jacket and took out a bulky envelope which he passed to Olbricht. "Your sailing clearance forms are in there, properly signed and stamped."

The older man smiled ruefully. "I should have known. It will cost you."

"Doesn't it always? That's in the envelope as well."

This time, Olbricht chuckled good-naturedly. "Just like old times, eh, Kurt?" He turned to Cormack, gazing at him appraisingly. "How many of you are there, Herr Fischer?"

"Three altogether," Cormack replied. "One of us is a woman." There was a very faint, almost imperceptible smile on his face; he could still remember the way she had looked - relaxed and at peace - as he had slipped out of bed early that morning. It had certainly been something to cherish, the way she had made love.... With an effort, he dragged his mind back to the present; Olbricht was staring accusingly at Voeller.

"A woman?" he demanded. "How the devil am I supposed to explain her away if we're stopped?"

"Oh, come off it, Helmut," said Voeller crisply. "You and I both know that the fishing boats round here use women in their crews all the time."

"Not on my boat," Olbricht retorted.

"Look - do you want the money or not?" asked Voeller, reaching out for the envelope.

Hastily, Olbricht snatched it up. "I didn't say I wouldn't take her, did I?" He turned back to Cormack. "I'll be sailing at ten o'clock exactly - you and your companions will have to be aboard by then or we'll miss the tide. You'll have to pose as crew members if we're stopped by any patrol boats."

"I'll give you the necessary papers before you go," Voeller interrupted.

"What happens to your normal crew?" Cormack asked Olbricht.

"My son will sail with me, but Willi Plotz can have the night off. Don't worry - they won't say anything."

Cormack nodded slowly. It was evident that both Voeller and Olbricht had things well in hand, so why did he still have this feeling of disquiet? "Right," he said. "Ten o'clock?"

"Yes. If you're late, I'll have to sail without you. I don't want the harbour officials asking why I didn't put to sea after I'd got all the authorisations."

"We'll be there," Cormack promised. He rose to his feet, followed by Voeller. Olbricht remained where he was, looking from one to the other, thoughtfully, then he nodded briefly in farewell.

It was only when they were walking away along the quayside that Cormack asked, "Are you sure you can trust him, Voeller?"

"Olbricht? With my life. Don't let all that business about him taking money fool you. He only gets paid more or less what he would have got for a night's fishing anyway, so he's hardly being greedy. I think he rather enjoys smuggling people out - it enables him to thumb his nose at the authorities."

"I hope you're right."

"Well, let me put it this way. He's taken more men out for me than any other skipper over the past three years and he hasn't betrayed me yet. I hardly think he's going to do so now. On top of that, nobody knows the waters around here like he does - he knows where all the minefields are, for instance, and where he can come close inshore to avoid being spotted."

"Fair enough," Cormack conceded, then a thought seemed to strike him. "You mentioned minefields - what about coastal batteries, if the alarm's sounded?"

Voeller shook his head. "There aren't any. There used to be up until a year ago, then all the guns were removed and transferred to the Russian Front. They've never been replaced."

Cormack nodded; it made sense in that Rostock was in little danger of being attacked from the sea, but it still came as a welcome bonus. "We'd better get back to the others and give them the glad tidings."

1230 HOURS.

Rindt took a sip of coffee, grimacing at its taste - even by ersatz standards, it was pretty vile - and was about to return to Kurt Voeller's dossier when Krieger came in, walking rapidly.

"Herr Colonel?"

"Yes?"

"We've just had a phone call from Hausen at the dockyard, Herr Colonel. Kurt Voeller has not reported in for work today - or yesterday. There is no sign of him."

"Isn't there?" Rindt asked, sitting up. "Is he at his home?"

Krieger shook his head. "If he is, he has not stirred at all since the surveillance team arrived."

Rindt stood up and paced over to the window, his head bent in thought. It could be nothing - but he doubted it. Marianne had arrived in Rostock yesterday morning and Voeller had not been seen since then.... it had to be more than coincidence. There was a simple way to find out, of course, but it would mean showing his hand and if she hadn't made contact with him yet, it might scare her off. But then if she had contacted Voeller and he didn't act now....

He turned abruptly. "Raid the house."

1300 HOURS.

Marianne came into the living room to find Woodward standing at the window, looking out into the street; he turned when he realised she was there. "Hallo, Marianne. Feel better for your beauty sleep?"

She looked suspiciously at him; how much did he know, or guess? "Much better, thanks. Where is everybody?"

"Alan and Voeller left earlier on to go and fix up the arrangements for the boat tonight. They said they'd be back at about one. Any minute, in fact."

She glanced at the wall clock. "Good God, is it as late as that?"

"It is, I'm afraid."

"I hadn't realised. You should have woken me."

"Why? There's nothing doing at the moment. There's some coffee in the kitchen if you want it."

"Thanks." She went through to the kitchen; Woodward moved over to the doorway so that he could carry on the conversation. "Did they say where they were going?" she asked.

174

"Alan and Voeller? No, they didn't."

"Not even to you?"

"No - and I didn't ask. I don't have to know, after all - it's safer all round."

She looked at him levelly. "It looks as though some of Alan's rubbed off on you, Tony."

Woodward nodded slowly. "I suppose it has." He sighed. "It's a filthy business, really, isn't it?"

"I know. I suppose someone has to do it. That's what I've had to keep telling myself, anyway. The problem is, it's like lying down with pigs and expecting not to get up smelling - you become tainted yourself. You do things that you feel ashamed of and you have to justify them somehow. Sometimes it's not easy." Her voice was far away. "Sometimes you just have to do something - I don't know - something genuine or decent, just to prove you're still human." She looked at Woodward. "Maybe that's why Alan didn't kill that officer."

Her use of Cormack's first name was not lost on Woodward; he nodded a little sadly. "Probably. Deep down, a long way down, he's as soft as anything, I think."

"I know," she said quietly, staring into infinity. "Tony?"

"Yes?"

"Who was Lena?"

So that settled it, Woodward thought. If Cormack had mentioned Lena to her, then the relationship between them had changed dramatically since yesterday. "Lena? I'm not really sure if I should tell you."

"Please, Tony. I'd like to know. Was she important to him?" She hesitated then asked, almost inaudibly, "Is she still important?"

Woodward thought for a moment before he said, "Yes, I suppose she still is, in a way. But not in any way you need worry about. You see, she's dead now." He took a deep breath. "And he was there when she was killed."

"Oh, God...." she whispered.

"It was right at the end of the Holland operation," Woodward continued, his voice far away. "She was shot while we were taking off. Another ten seconds and she'd have been all right - we'd have been airborne, you see. I didn't know it had happened until we landed. I opened up the hatch and found Alan still holding her in his arms...." He looked intently at Marianne. "When did he tell you about her?"

"He didn't. Not directly." It had been that first time, when they had both been in a frenzy of passion; he had called out

175

"Lena...." almost despairingly. It hadn't happened after that and there had been something in that cry, a sense of loss and pain, that had stopped any feeling of jealousy on her part; she had guessed the truth, or at least part of it.

"You're very fond of him, aren't you, Marianne?" Woodward asked gently.

She looked at him, startled, and nodded. "Yes. I think I am."

"Ah well," said Woodward philosophically, a rueful grin on his face. "Can't win them all, I suppose. Some blokes have all the luck. Anyway-" He broke off, his expression suddenly changing; he seemed to be listening to something.

"What is it, Tony?"

He didn't answer; instead, he turned and strode rapidly into the living room to peer out of the window. "Oh no...." he groaned; two Kubelwagens were pulling up in the street outside and already, SS troopers were piling out, heading for Voeller's gate....

"The Gestapo!" he hissed, scooping up a pistol from the sideboard. "Out the back door!"

Marianne was already on her way, wrenching open the door into the back yard; through the back gate was an alleyway. Woodward followed her, hearing a peremptory hammering on the front door behind him. How the hell had they known? Had they picked up Cormack or Voeller?

Just as Marianne reached the back gate, it was sent crashing back on its hinges by a burly trooper, who looked at Woodward, saw the gun in his hand and knocked Marianne to one side, bringing up his machine pistol one-handed. Woodward fired, the bullet taking the trooper in the chest and hurling him backwards into the alley, dead before he hit the ground; Woodward stretched out his hand to pull Marianne to her feet and ran out into the alley.

He came skidding to a halt.

Five troopers were standing in a semi-circle facing them, each one with a machine pistol pointing unwaveringly in their direction. Slowly, Woodward let the pistol drop to his side and raised his arms.

They were taken back into the house and told to stand facing the wall, feet apart, their hands stretched out in front of them against the wall; they were then searched thoroughly. There was a cold-blooded detachment about the troopers that chilled Woodward; they didn't even seem all that interested in Marianne while they were searching her. These were professionals....

176

A third car pulled up outside and, several seconds later, a tall SS-Colonel entered the room. Marianne's eyes widened in amazement. "Alex!" she gasped. "What are you doing here?"

Rindt ignored the question. "Where is Voeller?" he asked Woodward.

"Flight Lieutenant Anthony Woodward. 908167. And that's all I'm saying."

"I doubt that. Where is Cormack?" Rindt asked: he had been given the name during the final briefing the night before.

Woodward's eyes widened momentarily in evident surprise, then he shook his head. "Who?"

Rindt nodded, as if he had expected no other answer. "Marianne? Do you have anything to say?" His voice sounded stilted, artificial, as though he were acting a role he did not much enjoy, Woodward observed.

Marianne was still staring incredulously at Rindt. "How did you get here, Alex?"

"Marianne.... It's I who should be asking the questions, not you," Rindt reminded her. "Where are the other two?"

She shook her head firmly. "I don't know what you're talking about."

He moved closer to her and spoke in a low undertone so that only she could hear him. "Look, Marianne, I've got a job to do and I'm going to do it. Don't make me send you for interrogation." He was almost pleading with her, she realised with a slow surprise.

"Alex.... I don't understand.... Why are you doing all this?" She was staring at him in utter bewilderment; Alex Rindt had never been a Nazi, so why was he so relentlessly pursuing them from Berlin to Rostock? A thought struck her. "You haven't left Inga behind in Berlin, have you?"

It was as if she had struck him; he recoiled visibly and a shutter seemed to drop behind his eyes. "Very well," he said, turning away from her. "You've left me no choice. Muehlmann, have these two taken back to headquarters, but they are not to be questioned until I return. I'll wait here for a while to see if the others come back here." He glanced at both Woodward and Marianne to see how they would react to this, but their expressions were inscrutable.

Rindt shrugged in apparent indifference. "Take them out."

"What's happened?" asked Voeller anxiously.

"Nothing," snapped Cormack. The two of them were standing

177

with their backs pressed against the wall of the street's end house; every so often, Cormack peered around the corner to see what was happening at Voeller's house. The moment they had entered the street, five minutes before, they had spotted the two Kubelwagens outside the house and had ducked back out of sight; since then, a Mercedes had arrived and an SS-Colonel had gone inside. Cormack estimated that there were probably at least ten Germans in there at the moment.

"Where's the car?" he asked Voeller suddenly. "Where did you hide it?"

"Just around the corner from here - in a lock up. Why?"

"If they were going to Gestapo HQ, are there several routes they could take or only one?"

"There are two or three, but only one likely one."

"Right. Take me to the car."

Voeller hesitated, then nodded. "This way."

Marianne and Woodward were bundled unceremoniously into the back of one of the Kubelwagens, with a trooper sitting next to Woodward holding a Schmeisser machine pistol. In front was a driver and the Lieutenant Rindt had called Muehlmann, who gave the order to move as soon as he climbed in. Muehlmann was making no attempt to conceal his triumphant expression - in fact, he was positively gloating over his success, Woodward decided, but that did nothing to dispel the utter despair that had descended on him. He tried to give Marianne an encouraging smile, but it was more like a death's head grimace than anything else.

In any case, Marianne seemed engrossed in thought, her forehead creased in a frown of puzzlement. "Do you know that Colonel?" she asked Muehlmann.

"Silence!" Muehlmann barked, as she had expected, and Marianne nodded briefly, her face still registering her perplexity. And Woodward could see why; how the hell had he known where to find them? Not that it mattered much, anyway, now.... Except that they hadn't got Cormack yet and it was down to Marianne and himself to make sure that they didn't.

The Kubelwagen had made two left turns by now and was presumably heading back the way it had come; how long would the journey be? Probably fifteen minutes at the most, Woodward decided, and they would be inside the Gestapo headquarters. It would be too much to expect Cormack to come and get him out of such a place a second time, so if nothing happened before then....

The driver let out a startled shout that snapped Woodward out of his brooding reverie in time to see a Mercedes coming out of a side road to the left. Its engine was roaring and it was coming straight at them, but at the last moment it swerved and side-swiped the Kubelwagen on the front wing. For a split second, as the Kubelwagen slewed to the right and its occupants were thrown to one side, the barrel of the Schmeisser was no longer pointing at Woodward; he grabbed it and wrenched it out of the guard's grasp as the car slammed squarely into a wall. Woodward was hurled forward into the back of the passenger seat, but he kept hold of the weapon.

Everything seemed to be happening in slow motion now. The Mercedes had skidded to a halt ten yards away and Woodward could see Cormack already scrambling out, a Schmeisser cradled in his arms as Woodward jabbed the machine pistol's butt at the trooper's face, smashing it into his jaw; the guard reeled back as Cormack moved round to give himself a clear field of fire. Woodward clubbed the trooper a second time as Cormack opened up, the bullets shattering the windscreen and side window before ripping through the front of the car.

Muehlmann pushed the door open and dived out, reaching inside his uniform for his gun as he scrambled away; he loosed off a quick shot at Cormack over the car's bonnet, then reeled back, clutching at his face, which had suddenly dissolved into a scarlet mass of blood as the second burst of fire from the Schmeisser scythed into him. He fell onto his back, shrieking in agony, his heels drumming on the pavement in an obscene death rattle; mercifully, the screams came to an abrupt halt, as though sheared off, and he lay still, lifeless.

Woodward struck the trooper a third time before he turned the Schmeisser around and held it on the hapless guard, who was, however, clearly too dazed to put up any resistance. Cormack stepped forward and yanked open the driver's door, pulling the driver's body out on to the pavement; he untipped the seat and peered into the back. "You two all right?"

Woodward nodded. "Fine. Bit shaken up, that's all."

"Come on then - don't hang about."

Marianne's face was deathly white as she clambered out but she threw off Cormack's helping hand and ran to the Mercedes unaided. Woodward emerged, shaking his head disbelievingly. "You know, this is getting to be a bit of a habit, Alan, you rescuing me-"

"Save it, Tony," Cormack snapped. "Just grab some of those ammo clips and get in the car, will you?"

179

Woodward bit his lip; Cormack was right, of course - this was no time for flippancy. "You're the boss - but, just for the record - thanks."

Following Voeller's instructions, Cormack drove the car onto a patch of waste ground on the outskirts of Warnemunde, finally coming to a halt in a disused warehouse. Wearily, they climbed out and stretched their legs, but without speaking; none of them had said much since leaving the scene of the ramming incident. It was as if each one had realised how close it had been - if Cormack and Voeller had returned to the house five minutes earlier or later, or if Muehlmann had chosen a different route.... They had been lucky, there was no doubt about that, but how much longer would their luck hold?

"Right," said Cormack quietly. "Discussion time. What the hell do we do now?" He looked at each of the others in turn, but when none of them answered, he went on, "All right. Let's take it a step at a time. First - what were the Gestapo doing at the house?"

"Marianne knew the senior officer," said Woodward. "Didn't you?" he asked her.

She nodded. "Alex Rindt. I knew him in Berlin - but I haven't a clue how he came to be here."

"Never mind that," said Cormack flatly. "What matters is that he is here, and so it has to be you he's after, Marianne."

She nodded again. "It certainly looks like it," she agreed. "But how did he know where to find us?"

"He was told," said Cormack slowly. "Nothing else makes any sense at all. It can't have been coincidence that he just happens to be in Rostock and that he just happened to know about you, Voeller. He knew where we'd be."

"But how?" asked Woodward. "If the Gestapo already knew about the escape route, why haven't they arrested Voeller before now?"

"Because they didn't know, that's why." Cormack's voice sounded infinitely weary. "Rindt is getting his information from somewhere else - he has to be. Probably the Russians, via our own leak back in London."

"You can't be serious, Alan," Woodward protested.

"Why not? This is the second time we've had someone waiting for us - as if they've been tipped off. The first time we know it was the Russians, so-"

"Alan's right," said Marianne suddenly. "And I think I know

why. When I asked Rindt about his wife, he reacted very strangely. That's what I couldn't understand about his being here. Although he's in the Gestapo, it's not really through choice - he was transferred several years ago - and he isn't a fanatical Nazi either. So why would he be following us like this? But his wife went to Danzig several weeks ago, so if she was taken prisoner by the Russians.... He's devoted to her, you see."

"So that's it," said Cormack grimly. "Blackmail. They probably got him out of Berlin and sent him here. This source in London almost certainly told the Russians all about you, Voeller - so Rindt was told as well. So we have to assume that Rindt knows whatever London knows."

"In other words, he could be waiting for us when we go to meet Olbricht," said Voeller slowly.

"Does London know Olbricht's name?" asked Cormack.

Voeller shook his head. "No. I've never mentioned any names to them."

"But Rindt's no fool," Marianne said. "Even though he might not know about Olbricht, he could still deduce that we're going to use a fishing boat and put the harbour under surveillance."

"Granted," Cormack agreed. "That's our problem. We have three alternatives. One - we carry on as planned and meet Olbricht at ten, even though there's a distinct possibility that Rindt will be waiting for us. Two. We try to head westwards by land until we reach the British or American lines. Three. We hide out here until the war's over, which will only be a matter of days now."

"Forget the third one," said Woodward. "According to the briefings we were given, the Russians will be here first anyway - and that's assuming the Gestapo don't find us in the meantime."

"Fair enough." Cormack nodded.

"And Number Two's not really on either," said Marianne. "What papers we had are still in the house, so we'd be trying to travel - what? A hundred miles? - without any papers at all."

The others nodded reluctantly. "So we're back to Number One?" said Cormack slowly.

"Looks like it," said Woodward. "Hobson's Choice, really, isn't it?"

"Unless anyone has any other ideas?" asked Cormack. There was a heavy silence; Cormack shrugged. "Then we go ahead as originally planned."

"And hope Rindt hasn't out-guessed us?" said Marianne.

"Exactly. A fifty-fifty chance, I'd say," said Cormack quietly. "Not bad odds for a gambler."

Who are you trying to convince? thought Woodward, looking at Cormack quizzically. Us - or yourself?

But he said nothing; there was, really, nothing left to say, anyway.

CHAPTER 14.

ROSTOCK: 1400 HOURS, TUESDAY MAY 1ST.

Rindt stormed into Krieger's office, slamming the door back onto its hinges with such force that it rebounded back, nearly catching Krieger behind him. Krieger stared apprehensively at Rindt, who had come to a halt in front of the window, glaring down at the street below; Krieger dared not say a word in case it produced another furious outburst. Rindt seemed determined to the point of obsession to capture these enemy agents and had been in an explosive temper ever since the radio message had come through, describing how the two British agents had been rescued. And how Muehlmann and his driver had been killed, yet Rindt had not seemed to consider that at all....

Rindt took a deep breath and turned to face Krieger. "Very well," he said, clearly trying to keep his voice under control. "No use crying over spilt milk, is it? Let's see if we can sort out where they've gone."

"Yes, Herr Colonel," said Krieger meekly.

Rindt walked across to the wall map of Rostock and the Warnow estuary and gazed thoughtfully at it. "Now, if Voeller is running an escape route to Sweden, how would he go about it?"

"Well, he works in the dockyard," Krieger said hesitantly. "He might be able to put people aboard neutral ships, especially those running a regular route from here to Malmo or Trelleborg. It would be easy enough to bribe crew members."

Rindt nodded. "Good point. Do we have any such ships in harbour at the moment? Or any neutral vessels at all?"

"I - I don't know, Herr Colonel," Krieger admitted.

"Then find out, dammit!"

"Yes, Herr Colonel-"

Rindt shook his head: this wouldn't do at all, he thought - he had to get a grip on himself! "Wait a moment, Krieger. I haven't finished yet. Now, supposing we're wrong and Voeller isn't going to use a neutral ship, how else would he do it? A fishing boat, perhaps?"

"It's possible, Herr Colonel. There's a fishing harbour at Warnemunde and-"Rindt looked back at the map, locating

Warnemunde. "Are they still fishing, these boats?"

"I believe so, Herr Colonel."

"I see." Rindt thought for a moment and said, "Very well. This is what I want you to do. Check with the port authorities and find out if there are any neutral ships in port at the moment. If there are, I want them placed under discreet surveillance - and I mean discreet, do you understand? I don't want these agents frightened off."

"Yes, Herr Colonel. Will you want these vessels searched? We could use some Customs pretext."

Rindt nodded. "Yes. Do that."

"What about Warnemunde, Herr Colonel?"

"I'll deal with that myself," Rindt said almost absently. "I want some civilian clothes for myself and my squad. Fisherman's clothes."

"Yes, Herr Colonel." The surprise was evident in Krieger's voice; Rindt was on the point of explaining that, again, he did not want to scare off the British agents by having Gestapo uniforms all over the place, before he realised that it was not necessary - Krieger would obey orders, no matter what he felt about them privately. A prime example of the Germanic desire for order, he thought inconsequentially....

"Have a squad of men ready here if I ask for assistance, Krieger."

"Yes, Herr Colonel."

WARNEMUNDE: 1800 HOURS.

Rindt paused for a moment in the doorway and looked around the smoky bierkeller, which was little more than a large room with a bar down one side, the peeling wallpaper a relic of some long forgotten attempt at decoration. He was struck by the timelessness of the scene; the customers seemed totally unconcerned that, within days, they might be under Russian rule. Life would simply go on as it always had. Fishing - today's catch - that was all that mattered here. Shaking his head impatiently - he had no time for such idle musings - he began to make his way over to the bar.

Although he was dressed in a similar fashion to everyone else, with a pea jacket over a heavy fisherman's sweater and corduroy trousers, he was aware of several pairs of eyes watching him suspiciously. Not half as much, however, as if he had decided to walk in wearing his full SS uniform, he decided wryly.... "A beer, please," he said to the barkeeper, who served him a stein of beer that looked distinctly flat to Rindt, but he made no comment. "I'm looking for a man called Voeller," he said to the barman. "Any idea where I can find him?"

"Never heard of him," the barman replied curtly and went off to serve someone else. Rindt realised that the man next to him at the bar was watching him amusedly and shrugged ruefully.

"Charming fellow," he observed.

The man nodded. "He's always like that. A miserable sod, to be sure, but his prices are cheaper than anywhere else."

"I can see why," said Rindt, after sipping at his beer; it tasted as flat as it looked.

The other man finished his drink. "You said you were looking for a man named Voeller?" he asked, looking meaningfully at his empty glass.

Rindt sighed and signalled to the barman. "Another beer, please."

"Very kind of you," the man said as if surprised by the gesture. He waited until his glass had been refilled - somehow, Rindt noticed, his drink seemed perfectly all right - then said, "Would that be Kurt Voeller?"

"Yes, it would. He works in the docks at Rostock."

"That's him." The man nodded. "What do you want with him?"

"Some help. My bloody boat's broken down and I was told that if anyone could repair it, he could."

"He probably could at that. You're not from Warnemunde, then?"

"No. Stralsund," Rindt replied glibly.

"Haven't the Russians got there yet, then?"

"Probably there by now - that's why I was heading this way. I'd rather surrender to the British."

"Don't know why you're bothering. It won't make much difference to us up here - Russians, British, what's the difference?"

"Perhaps that's so, but I'd still like to talk to this Voeller."

"That's up to you, friend. I can't actually tell you where to find him, but I know someone who can." He looked down at his glass again; to Rindt's amazement, it was already empty. Resignedly, he ordered another drink; the man nodded appreciatively and continued, "A man called Olbricht - he's the skipper of the *Anna Luise*. Go along the waterfront about two hundred metres and you'll see an old wooden jetty. The *Anna Luise* is moored at the end of it."

1830 HOURS.

Rindt paused at the top of the ladder and looked around carefully; there was nobody in sight. Nodding to Vassiliev, he descended the ladder and headed aft, followed by the Russian. Andreyev, Petrov and Ivanov were in nearby hiding places, ready to sound the alarm if necessary, but there was no sign of life, either ashore or on the boat.

"Herr Olbricht?" Rindt called, tapping on the hatchway behind the wheelhouse. Almost immediately, the hatch was pulled back and he saw the pale outline of a face peering up at him.

"Yes - what is it?"

"Herr Voeller sent us, Herr Olbricht."

Olbricht gestured in disgust. "You weren't supposed to be here for another three hours yet. What the hell is Voeller playing at?"

"I don't understand," said Rindt in a puzzled voice. "We were told to come straight here. Is something wrong?"

"Oh, you'd better come down now you're here." Olbricht stepped back; after a glance at Vassiliev, Rindt clambered down the ladder. When he reached the bottom, he took out a silenced Walther pistol and turned to face Olbricht. The older man's eyes widened as he saw the gun.

"What the devil-?" He broke off as Rindt moved forward into the pool of light from the flickering kerosene lamp. "Who are you?"

"Never mind who I am," Rindt snapped. "Who were you expecting?"

"Nobody. Are you the Gestapo?" There was a look of dogged defiance on Olbricht's face; Rindt sighed and called up the hatch to Vassiliev,

"Come down here, will you?" He looked impassively at Olbricht. "So - who were you expecting?"

"Nobody."

There was the sound of footsteps on the deck above their heads and, moments later, Vassiliev climbed down the ladder. He pulled the hatch closed and slid the retaining clips home.

"Right, Olbricht," said Rindt quietly. "I'll ask you once more - who are you waiting for?"

Olbricht said nothing, but seemed to jut his chin defiantly at Rindt. Vassiliev took two steps forward, his face expressionless

186

and, without any warning, he drove his fist into the fisherman's solar plexus. Olbricht gasped and bent almost double, clutching at his stomach and fighting to draw air into his lungs. Slowly, he sank onto his knees and, with a sweeping back-handed blow, Vassiliev hit him again, sending him sprawling on the deck. Vassiliev glanced at Rindt, who shook his head; the Russian stepped back with obvious reluctance.

Rindt watched, his features carefully impassive, as Olbricht pulled himself up onto his hands and knees, holding on to the bunk's blankets. "Well?"

"I don't know anything!" Olbricht protested feebly, his voice a hoarse croak.

Without waiting for any signal from Rindt, Vassiliev stepped forward and kicked Olbricht viciously in the ribs; Olbricht cried out and fell sideways, rolling onto his back. Before Rindt could stop him, Vassiliev brought the heel of his boot down into Olbricht's stomach; there was a smile of enjoyment on the Russian's face now.

"That's enough!" Rindt hissed. Vassiliev glanced at him, evidently surprised, but Rindt shook his head firmly. Pushing Vassiliev aside, Rindt crouched down next to Olbricht. "Look," he said, his voice patient, reasonable. "Why bring all this on yourself? Just tell me what I want to know and we'll leave you alone."

"Go to hell!" Olbricht moaned.

"Olbricht," Rindt said, his voice more threatening now, "I'll give you one more chance. Who are you waiting for?"

Olbricht shook his head slowly. "Not going to tell you."

Rindt sighed and was about to nod to Vassiliev once more when there was the sound of footsteps on the deck above; Olbricht's eyes widened and he was about to call out when Rindt clamped his hand across his mouth. The Walther pistol in Rindt's hand was aimed at Olbricht's temple. "Not a sound," Rindt hissed. "You hear?"

"Father?" a voice called from above the hatch. "Are you down there?"

Rindt nodded to Vassiliev, who slid back the retaining clips and pushed back the hatch; a slightly built youth began to climb down the ladder then stopped dead, staring at them in amazement. Vassiliev reached out and grabbed him, yanking him down into the cabin and throwing him onto the bunk.

"Your son?" Rindt asked Olbricht, although the question was superfluous; quite apart from the way the youth had called him

187

"father", there was no mistaking the resemblance between Olbricht and the newcomer. At a nod from Rindt, Vassiliev stepped forward and slapped the youth across the face, a swingeing open-handed blow that raised a livid red weal on his cheek. Olbricht stared helplessly at his son, his face a picture of sullen despair.

"Right, Olbricht," said Rindt softly, fighting down an almost overwhelming feeling of self-loathing at what he was doing. "This makes it simpler, doesn't it? I don't need to tell you what happens if you don't co-operate, do I?" He took his hand away from Olbricht's mouth.

Olbricht shook his head in defeat. "No, you don't," he muttered dejectedly.

"Who are you waiting for?" Rindt asked again.

"I don't know their names."

"How many of them are there?"

Olbricht looked fearfully at his son, still sprawled on the bunk; Vassiliev was glaring down at him, as if eager for any excuse to hit him again. "Three altogether."

"Is one of them a woman?"

Olbricht nodded weakly. "Yes."

Rindt closed his eyes and let out his breath in a great sigh of relief; he turned to Vassiliev. "Stay here with them - I'll send one of the others to stand guard on him with you. I'll be back in a few minutes." He looked at Olbricht briefly. "And don't lay a finger on either of them - we might need them later on. Understand?"

"Yes." Vassiliev nodded reluctantly.

Rindt went to the hatchway ladder, slid back the bolts and climbed up on deck; slowly, he walked towards the bow, his head bowed in thought. Sometime before ten o'clock, Marianne would be arriving aboard with Voeller and the two British agents - and he already had good reason to respect their abilities; he could not afford to underestimate them. Ideally, he would have liked to take Marianne prisoner without having to use anyone but the Russians, so that it would then be a lot easier to spirit her away afterwards, but it was very much a case of putting all his eggs in one basket if he did that - and it would be four against five, leaving little margin for error. On top of that, the Russians were an unknown quantity as far as Rindt was concerned - how much could he rely on them not to let the British escape? All he knew about them, really, was that Vassiliev liked beating people up.... how would he cope with someone like Cormack, the British leader, who was clearly highly resourceful?

Reluctantly, Rindt shook his head; he could not afford to take the chance. His first priority had to be Marianne's capture - or recapture, he admitted grimly - and the only way he could be certain of achieving that was to have as many men as possible waiting for the agents when they arrived.... He would need reinforcements. Capture Marianne first, then see about getting her away to the Russians.

He would have to telephone Gestapo headquarters.

1930 HOURS.

Rindt held up his hand and signalled the Mercedes to a halt, climbing into the back to sit next to Krieger. "Where are the men?" he asked without preamble.

"In two personnel carriers - I've left them in Florianstrasse."

Rindt nodded. "Good. You've brought the map?"

"Yes, Herr Colonel." Krieger reached inside his tunic and produced a map of the Warnemunde harbour area, which he unfolded and spread out on his lap.

"Right," said Rindt. "The *Anna Luise* is moored here at the end of this jetty." He indicated the position on the map. "I want men stationed here, here and here - but for God's sake keep them out of sight and tell them to wait for my order to move."

"Yes, Herr Colonel."

Rindt looked pensively at the map and said slowly, "I want a sentry on patrol just here." He pointed to the quayside next to the jetty.

"There, Herr Colonel?" Krieger queried.

"There," Rindt said firmly. "I've been thinking about these agents. Whoever is leading them is no fool. He will be expecting us to be here, I suspect, and if we are nowhere to be seen at all, he might well be suspicious. One sentry will make him think that we are maintaining a general watch on the harbour, but will not be so threatening that he will be frightened away. And he won't be expecting us to have any sentry there at all if we are lying in wait for him."

Krieger nodded doubtfully. "I see, Herr Colonel. But what will happen to the sentry himself?"

Rindt looked directly at Krieger, his expression unfathomable in the gathering dusk. "I don't think you appreciate how important these agents are, Krieger. There must be no more slip ups -

189

the sentry will just have to take his chances."

"Yes, Herr Colonel."

"Now, just remember this, Olbricht," said Rindt quietly. "If you co-operate, your son will come to no harm at all. The minute those agents are under arrest, your son will be returned to you. But if you do or say anything to warn them, or if their suspicions are aroused by the slightest degree - in short, if we do not capture them, then - well, do I have to say any more?"

Olbricht shook his head. "No, you don't," he said wearily. "I'll do what you want, don't worry."

"Good." Rindt nodded and turned to Vassiliev, who was standing silently at the foot of the hatchway ladder. "Get one of the others to stay with him," he murmured, nodding at Olbricht.

Vassiliev nodded. "I'll send Andreyev along. You don't trust the old man, I suppose?"

"Oh, he won't be any trouble," said Rindt, looking back at Olbricht. "You see, I know exactly what he's thinking," he added softly. And what he's going through, he thought as he climbed the ladder, sick with self-disgust; what he was doing to Olbricht was identical to what had been done to him and what made it worse was that, over the last few days, he had realised just how ruthless one could be, just how low one could stoop, given the right incentive. But did the end justify the means? Would he ever be able to live with himself again - or with Inga, knowing what he had been obliged to do to ensure her safety?

With a sudden chill, the realisation came to Rindt that, whether Inga was returned to him or not, nothing would ever be the same again. Something precious had been lost forever - and through no fault of his own, that was the damnable part of it....

He shook his head angrily and strode across the deck; this was no time for such introspection. He climbed up the ladder to the jetty and looked carefully around to make sure that there was no sign of the Gestapo troopers. Finally, he nodded to himself, satisfied. The trap had been set and all that remained was for it to be sprung.

2130 HOURS.

Voeller signalled urgently with his hand, motioning Cormack, Woodward and Marianne to a halt before peering cautiously around the next corner. The waterfront was deserted, as he had expected it to be; it was rarely patrolled, even by the Gestapo. He nodded to the others then led them along the darkened front, until they were about fifty yards from the wooden jetty where the *Anna Luise* was moored, but this time it was Cormack who motioned them into the cover of a darkened doorway.

"You two wait here," he murmured to Marianne and Voeller. "Tony and I'll go and take a shufti." He saw the look of protest on Voeller's face and went on, "Now do as I say, Voeller - this isn't your field." Reluctantly, Voeller nodded as Cormack turned to Woodward. "Stick close behind me, Tony."

"Right."

Cormack looked both ways along the front and headed for a pile of packing crates twenty yards away, crouching down behind them before he looked around again. Moments later, he was taking cover behind another crate that was only thirty yards from the landward end of the jetty; seconds later, Woodward had joined him. Slowly, carefully, Cormack peered over the top of the crate and took stock of his surroundings, staring intently into every pool of shadow in turn to try and detect the least sign of movement, keeping his eyes fixed on the same point for a minute or more at a time.

Nothing. No sign of movement at all. By now, his eyes were thoroughly accustomed to the darkness and he could not see any indication that anyone was lying in wait for him. Perhaps Rindt had not made the connection between Voeller and the fishing harbour.... And perhaps pigs can fly as well, he thought contemptuously. There was someone out there; he knew it as certainly as if he had see him with his own eyes. But where the hell was he?

There. A figure moved into view from behind what appeared to be a pile of oil drums and moved rapidly towards the jetty. Despite himself, Cormack smiled faintly in the darkness, a smile of relief. At least now he knew....

"Stay here," he murmured to Woodward. "Watch for my signal."

Yet again, Cormack looked around then flitted silently over to a small shed right on the edge of the quay - probably a paint store. Cautiously, he peered around the corner; the other man was only ten yards away now. Cormack bent down and picked up a pebble. Aiming carefully, he lobbed it into the air so that it would land beyond the sentry.

The noise the pebble made was not loud but it evidently startled the guard; he spun round, away from Cormack. In utter silence,

Cormack rushed him from behind, his hand chopping into the back of the sentry's neck; his victim sprawled forward on the quayside. Cormack dropped into a crouch and pivoted around, ready to ward off any attack from a second guard, but the night was utterly still. Slowly he straightened up, forcing himself to relax and signalled to Woodward to join him.

"Just the one sentry?" whispered Woodward.

"Looks like it. Let's get aboard that bloody boat."

They made their way slowly along the jetty, looking around them all the time, until they were five yards from the end, when Cormack flattened himself full length on the wooden boards, gesturing at Woodward to do the same. With the utmost care, Cormack pulled himself forward until he was peering over the jetty's edge, down at the *Anna Luise*.

There was nobody on deck at all; Cormack twisted his head round and gave a thumbs-up sign to Woodward before scrambling over to the nearest ladder and climbing down it. He made his way aft, until he reached the hatch down into the cabin, where he knocked quietly.

Almost immediately, the hatch was opened and Olbricht climbed up on deck beside him; he had evidently turned off the lamp in the cabin, because there was no light at all spilling out from it, so that his face was just a dark smudge to Cormack. "Where are the others?" he murmured.

"Not far away. Is everything all right?"

"I think something's stirred them up," said Olbricht nervously. "They've got sentries all over the harbour."

Cormack nodded. "I know - I've just had to deal with one."

"Well, get the others on board and we'll cast off."

"Right." Cormack looked up at Woodward, who was standing at the top of the jetty ladder. "Go and get Marianne and Voeller, Tony - and be quick about it."

Woodward raised a hand in acknowledgment then disappeared. Cormack turned to Olbricht and said, "Better tell your son to get the engine started - I want to get moving as soon as they're aboard."

"Dieter isn't coming with us this time," said Olbricht; Cormack glanced sharply at him, hearing the strained note in the other man's voice. The thought came to him that Olbricht had been on edge ever since he had emerged from the cabin.

"Why not?" he asked abruptly.

"I don't want to risk him - not if the Gestapo have been alerted,"

Olbricht replied tensely.

Fair enough, thought Cormack; it certainly helped to explain Olbricht's obviously frayed nerves. "Right - get the engine started anyway, will you?" He turned away, heading toward the ladder and so he missed Olbricht's momentary hesitation; by the time he glanced back from the foot of the ladder, Olbricht was already on his way down to the engine compartment.

Once he was on the jetty, Cormack unslung his Schmeisser and watched the quayside carefully for any sign of danger, but there was nothing. So why did he have that feeling once more that there was someone else out there? Because that sixth sense was nagging at him again, telling him that something wasn't as it should be - but what, for Christ's sake?

He tensed as he saw a movement, but relaxed a moment later, realising that it was only Woodward, Marianne and Voeller running silently towards the jetty. Within thirty seconds they would be aboard and they could get the hell out of here....

The engine. Why hadn't Olbricht started the engine yet? Oh, dear God, that was it - for the last half minute or more, Cormack had been subconsciously waiting for the engine to cough into life and it hadn't.... He spun round and hurtled down the ladder, jumping the last six feet onto the deck and ran aft, seized by a sudden certainty: this was it, this was where it all went wrong.

He skidded to a halt at the engine hatch and stared at Olbricht in astonishment; the skipper was just standing there looking at the engine with a kind of weary resignation. Cormack looked into the compartment, but could only see blurred outlines. "What the hell's the matter?"

Olbricht said nothing, but simply shook his head tiredly. Cormack's hand dived inside his jacket and took out a pencil torch; he flicked it on and shone it on the engine.

"Oh, bloody hell, no...." he murmured; he did not have to be an expert to see that the engine had been sabotaged. Fuel lines had been disconnected, electrical leads yanked out and piston rods shattered; there was no chance at all that they would ever get that engine to start.

"They wrecked it," said Olbricht, almost inaudibly. "And they took Dieter...."

Cormack did not wait to hear any more; he leaped up on deck and sprinted towards the jetty ladder. As he passed the wheelhouse, he caught a glimpse of movement out of the corner of his eye before Andreyev came lunging out at him. Cormack barely had time to see the glint of a knife blade in the Russian's hand before Andreyev attacked, whipping his arm across in a vicious slash that would have sliced Cormack's chest open had it made contact but Cormack reacted almost instinctively, chopping down with his left hand at Andreyev's wrist. The Russian gasped in pain and the knife fell from his suddenly nerveless fingers, but it still had not struck the deck when Cormack unleashed a straight fingered blow into Andreyev's stomach. The Russian twisted aside, avoiding the worst of the blow and called out:

"Olbricht - the flare!"

A split second later, Cormack's fist slammed into the side of his head, sending Andreyev sprawling on the deck. Cormack pivoted round, reaching inside his jacket for his Browning pistol as he saw Olbricht standing by the wheelhouse with what looked like a gun in his hand; Cormack aimed and fired in a single motion, the bullet hitting Olbricht in the chest. It was too late; Olbricht's finger tightened convulsively on the trigger of the flare pistol and the wheelhouse erupted into flames as the flare smashed into it. Olbricht reeled backwards, clutching at his chest then sank onto his knees, staring incredulously at Cormack before he toppled forward and lay quite still.

Cormack spat out an oath at the sight of the leaping flames; the fire was rapidly taking hold and would sound the alarm as effectively as the flare would have done anyway. He turned once again and lunged towards the ladder, but then he saw Andreyev lifting himself onto one knee, taking something out from inside his jacket; Cormack loosed off another rapid shot and Andreyev was thrown backwards as the bullet took him in the chest, but Cormack barely noticed as he grabbed the ladder and scrambled up it. As he reached the top, he saw the others, standing stock-still only yards away, their faces registering complete bewilderment. Cormack gestured frantically at them. "It's a trap!" he yelled. "Get out of here!"

The others hesitated, but only for an instant, then, almost as one, they turned and began to run back the way they had come. If they could get back onto the quayside, find some cover, thought Cormack, they might still escape.... from the trap he had led them into, for Christ's sake! He had walked right into it.... The landward end of the jetty was suddenly very close - they might just make it....

The night was shattered by a sudden burst of automatic fire and the bullets slammed into the jetty no more than five yards in front of them, sending up a line of wooden chips; they came skidding to a halt as they were abruptly transfixed by a searchlight beam, from somewhere over to the left.

"Oh, shit...." Cormack muttered, his shoulders sagging in despair and defeat. Standing on the quayside, clearly visible now in the blinding glare and no more than twenty yards away was a line of SS troopers, each one holding a machine pistol aimed unwaveringly at the four of them.

CHAPTER 15.

Cormack slowly lowered his Schmeisser to the wooden planking, taking care not to look at the others. He did not want them to see the despair that he knew must be written on his face. Almost as soon as he had done so, he heard a muttered order and two of the troopers began to run along the jetty towards the *Anna Luise* Cormack could see that the fire aboard her was spreading rapidly.

For almost a minute, nobody moved and then Rindt walked slowly into the searchlight's glare. He looked thoughtfully at Voeller and nodded to himself as if recognising him before going to confront Cormack. "Captain Cormack, I believe?"

Cormack's eyes widened momentarily in surprise before he nodded tiredly. "That's me," he said dully.

Rindt stared at him intently and seemed on the point of saying something but he turned away and called out, "Get the cars. I want the prisoners searched and then taken to Naval Headquarters immediately."

"Naval Headquarters, Herr Colonel?"

"You heard, Krieger. Now get on with it!"

The prisoners were shepherded together into a single, dejected group as three Kubelwagens were driven into the light. At a word from Rindt, the troopers formed a double line, between the prisoners and the cars, a channel through which they would have to pass and which made escape a suicidal impossibility. Cormack bit his lip, fighting off despair; Rindt certainly knew his business.

"Captain Cormack," Rindt said briskly. "Get into the first car, please. Flight Lieutenant Woodward - the second car. Marianne and Voeller in the third."

It was entirely professional, Cormack noted as he climbed into the car; Rindt was not making the same mistake as he had done earlier. Divide and rule. Cormack found himself wedged between two troopers, each one poking the barrel of a machine pistol into his ribs.

They needn't bother, Cormack thought emptily; he wasn't going to try anything.... not now. This was it, the end of the whole operation; the thought registered, but only in a far offway, as if it applied to somebody else. He supposed, vaguely, that he ought to be planning something, some last attempt at escape, but it all seemed too much effort.... Far easier just to accept things, let Rindt do what he damn well liked.... I've had enough, Cormack thought and leaned back in the seat, letting out his breath in a long sigh, almost of relief....

The convoy pulled up at the E-boat base gates, but was passed through after only a brief glance at Rindt's documents. A few yards further on, the Kubelwagen rounded a corner and Cormack caught his first glimpse of the harbour in the moonlight.

They were approaching from the northern end and it was immediately obvious that it was mostly artificial. Two concrete breakwaters almost completely enclosed the harbour: the southern one was nearly five hundred yards long and extended out diagonally from the shore for almost a quarter of a mile in a north-easterly direction before curving suddenly round to the left so that it almost met up with the northern arm, which was only about fifty yards long. Linking the two moles was a metal swing-bridge that spanned the base's only entrance, which faced north-east. Inside the harbour were a number of patrol launches, three or four larger E-boats and a single large ship that looked like a converted freighter; Cormack surmised that it was the depot ship Voeller had mentioned. Two short wooden jetties protruded out from the quayside and the furthest had an E-boat moored at its end, where a party of men were loading crates aboard as though making ready to sail; Cormack found himself noting all these details without really knowing why.... Some last vestige of professional interest, he supposed, but it didn't really matter.... Nothing did.

Directly opposite the depot ship was a large building that Cormack assumed was the Naval Headquarters but they drove straight past, finally coming to a halt at the landward end of the furthest jetty. Rindt opened his door before the car had stopped moving, leaped out and gestured impatiently at the troopers beside Cormack. "Out," he said curtly; Cormack sighed and followed the troopers out. Looking behind, he could see the others also emerging from their cars, still covered by the Schmeissers being held by the troopers.

A naval officer came striding towards them, executing a casual salute as he went up to Rindt. "Herr Colonel?"

"Yes?"

"May I have a word with you, Herr Colonel? There seems to be something of a problem-"

"Problem? What do you mean?" Rindt glanced over at Cormack and took the officer by the arm, leading him out of earshot. It was evident from the way Rindt was gesticulating impatiently that the officer had brought bad news. He shook his head in exasperation and strode back towards his prisoners. "Keep an eye on them!" he snapped at his sergeant. "Wait here for my orders."

The sergeant saluted smartly as Rindt climbed into the leading Kubelwagen and snapped an order to the driver. The car moved off, executing a U-turn before heading back the way they had come with a squeal of tyres.

Woodward looked over at Cormack, but he seemed lost in a world of his own, staring dejectedly down at the ground; he looked utterly defeated, spent. Slowly, it dawned on Woodward that Cormack had come to the end of a very long road; he had carried them this far, but he had finally run out of strength, willpower, whatever - he had given everything he had and there was nothing left.... It's up to me, thought Woodward, taking a deep breath. Let's see how much I've learned from him....

Slowly, he turned and moved towards Voeller. He nodded at the E-boat. "Could you manage the engines on one of those?"

Voeller looked at him, startled and then at the guards, but they showed no inclination to stop their prisoners talking. He nodded slowly. "It isn't difficult - you can run the engines from the wheelhouse. But -"

"Don't say anything. It's the only chance we've got. Marianne?"

Marianne looked around; she had been watching Cormack, her concern for him written in her eyes. "Yes?"

"When they take us to the E-boat, I want you to stage some sort of diversion. Will you do that?"

She glanced at Cormack again. "Yes, but-"

"Silence!" the sergeant bellowed at them.

Woodward looked at him, an aggrieved expression on his face and nodded acquiescently. As he turned away, he muttered to Marianne, "Watch for my signal."

Rindt glared at the naval officer behind the desk; Rear-Admiral Wellemeyer was proving to be just as stubborn as he had feared. The Navy had always had fewer Nazi Party members than either the Army or the Luftwaffe and correspondingly less respect for an SS uniform at the best of times, and now, with the Third Reich on the edge of defeat it was only too evident that Wellemeyer felt himself under little obligation to co-operate with Rindt at all. By keeping him waiting for over ten minutes at the beginning of their meeting, Wellemeyer had made it clear that he had no intention of allowing any of his vessels to be used by Rindt. Under normal circumstances, Rindt would have agreed with him whole-heartedly but these were not normal circumstances, not for Rindt.... "Look, Admiral, I made all the necessary arrangements with Captain Lutze - are you now telling me you're cancelling them?"

"Captain Lutze had no right to act without proper authority. He should have checked with me first."

"And what would you have told him if he had, Admiral? Are you disputing my authority? Or these?" Rindt pointed to the documents lying on the desk between them, the ones bearing Bormann's and Mueller's signatures.

"They make no mention of your commandeering one of my E-boats, Rindt! That isn't included anywhere as far as I can see."

"Of course they don't, Admiral! But they give me absolute carte blanche into the investigation concerning Das Leck, don't they? And they also empower me to take her to the proper authorities for trial and execution - so I have to get her to Flensburg immediately."

"There's no mention of Flensburg here-"

"Oh, for God's sake, Admiral! I have to take her to the supreme military authority, who is now Admiral Doenitz in Flensburg. I can hardly take her back to Berlin, can I?"

"Perhaps not - but dammit, Rindt, what possible difference is it going to make now whether she's executed or not?"

"I have my orders, Admiral," said Rindt stiffly. "I'm carrying them out to the best of my ability, regardless of my personal views. Can you say the same?"

Wellemeyer sighed and went over to the window that overlooked the harbour. "Come here, Rindt," he said quietly; Rindt went over and stood next to him. "Three E-boats. That's all I have left here now. A week ago I had ten. Last night I had five and now I only have three. And in two hours' time, I'm sending all three of them to sea to try and lift some wounded troops from the shore about thirty kilometres to the east of here. That's all we've been doing for the past month, evacuating wounded soldiers. For every one we take aboard, we have to leave God knows how many behind - and you want me to send a third of my available vessels in the opposite direction, just so that you can shoot a spy?" There was no anger in Wellemeyer's voice, just an infinite weariness - and an undertone of unwavering determination that filled Rindt with heavy despair; there was nothing he could say or do that would make Wellemeyer change his mind. And he was absolutely right, of course, to make such a stand.... But it was no longer a matter of right and wrong, even if it ever had been.

Rindt moved stealthily backwards, reaching inside his tunic to take out a silenced automatic pistol. There was no other way, not any more....

Aiming carefully at the base of the other man's spine, Rindt squeezed the trigger, twice. Wellemeyer was hurled against the window frame as the bullets ripped into him. He clutched frantically at the curtain and fell heavily to one side, taking the drape with him so that it covered the lower half of his body as he sprawled on the floor. His eyes stared accusingly at Rindt for what seemed like an eternity as his mouth desperately tried to form one last word, or to shout, then his head lolled lifelessly to one side.

Rindt stood gazing numbly down at his victim, his face ashen. Not only was he a traitor and a blackmailer, he was a murderer as well now.... "I'm sorry," he whispered. "You left me no choice...." But still the dead eyes accused him; he shook his head violently and snatched up the desk telephone.

"Get me.... Number Two Jetty," he said after a glance up at the harbour map on the wall. "Hello? Get me Sergeant Vassiliev, will you?" There was a pause before he heard Vassiliev's voice answer,

"Sergeant Vassiliev here."

"This is Colonel Rindt. Proceed as planned. I shall be there in three minutes." He slammed the phone down and hurriedly gathered up the documents, replacing them in their leather wallet before going over to Wellemeyer's body. Without looking at the dead man's face, he hunted rapidly through his pockets until he found a bunch of keys. He stood up, keys in hand and looked quickly around the office; after a moment's thought, he took the telephone off its hook and crossed to the door.

A moment later, he was in the corridor, locking the door behind him.

Vassiliev nodded to himself as he replaced the receiver and turned to the troopers guarding the prisoners. "Right. C Detachment remain here, the rest of you dismiss. Report back to Captain Krieger at headquarters."

The naval officer who had spoken to Rindt earlier came over. "What's happening, Sergeant?"

"We're to proceed with the original orders, Herr Lieutenant. I've to get these prisoners on board." He nodded at Woodward and the others, who were now only being guarded by two troopers:

Petrov and Ivanov.

"I'll need official confirmation, of course," said the officer.

"Of course, Herr Lieutenant," Vassiliev echoed, standing aside to let the officer use the telephone. He called out, "Get those prisoners on board." Behind him, he could hear the Lieutenant trying to get through to Wellemeyer, but Vassiliev knew that it would be in vain: the fact that it had been Rindt who had telephoned and not the Admiral had told Vassiliev what had happened. As Rindt had done, he reached inside his uniform and took out a silenced automatic, looking round to make sure nobody was watching them. The SS troopers were all climbing into the Kubelwagens, paying no attention at all; it should be safe enough....

"What do you mean it's engaged?" the officer demanded. "Damn! Look, try and get through to him, will you? This is urgent."

Vassiliev grinned to himself and relaxed slightly; it looked as though he wouldn't need to use the gun after all, thanks to Rindt. He looked along the jetty and saw that the prisoners were nearly at the end. Just a couple more minutes, he told himself, and then Rindt will be back with the documents, ready to browbeat the young E-boat captain into sailing.... They were nearly there.

And then it all began to go wrong.

As they approached the end of the jetty, Woodward could see more of the long, sleek shape of the E-boat coming into view; he glanced over his shoulder and saw that the cars containing the SS troopers were driving off, which meant that there were only the two troopers and their sergeant guarding them now. Not bad odds, if you ignored the fact that they were armed.... He looked across at Cormack, hoping that he had shaken off his trance like state, but he was still walking slowly along, his eyes staring dully into infinity. For God's sake, Alan, snap out of it!

"Keep moving!" the nearest guard hissed; Woodward shrugged and turned back. Marianne was alongside him now, her eyes following him, waiting for his signal.... It had to be now.

He nodded and she stumbled forward, crying out as she fell awkwardly on the wooden planks; she clutched at her ankle, her face contorted with pain. Her cry seemed to bring Cormack out of his brooding reverie; he stared at her, his face confused as Woodward crouched down beside her. What the hell was going on? He took a step towards her and the guard behind him prodded him with his gun barrel.

"Stay where you are!" the trooper barked.

"But-" Cormack began and then his eyes met Woodward's and, at last, he realised what Woodward was doing. You mad, crazy bastard, Tony, he thought disbelievingly. You'll never get away with it.... He hesitated a moment longer and then, taking a deep breath, he yelled excitedly, "You don't understand! I've got to see how she is!"

The sudden commotion distracted the trooper standing over Woodward and Marianne; he looked round and Woodward exploded into action, lunging upwards and swinging his fist into the guard's stomach with venomous force. As the trooper doubled up, Woodward grabbed the Schmeisser and wrenched it from his grasp, but the second trooper was already bringing up his own weapon, his finger tightening on the trigger.

In a blur of motion, Cormack's hand chopped down on the guard's wrist; the guard bellowed in pain and Cormack's foot lashed out, sending the machine pistol spinning out of his grasp. Woodward now had the Schmeisser cradled in his arms, ready to fire. "Down!" Woodward yelled; Cormack and Voeller dived flat as Woodward loosed off a two second burst that ripped into the two guards. One pirouetted around, arms outstretched, while the other was driven across the jetty by the impact of the bullets; he seemed to poise on the edge like a diver before he slowly toppled over.

Woodward pivoted round to face Vassiliev, who was sprinting along the jetty towards them, the young officer behind him. Completely unaware of the savage grimace on his face, Woodward loosed off a long burst of fire that cut down the two men. Out of the corner of his eye, he saw Cormack scoop up the other Schmeisser, taking an ammunition clip from the second trooper's belt.

"What the hell are you up to?" yelled Cormack.

"We're going to take the E-boat!" Woodward shouted, grinning exultantly; he strode to the end of the jetty, angling his own machine pistol down at the E-boat, six feet or so below. There were perhaps half a dozen faces peering up at him, their expressions a mixture of bewilderment and fear as they saw the Schmeisser.

"We're coming aboard," Woodward called out. "I'll kill anyone who doesn't do exactly-" Someone was running towards the aft gun, but the Schmeisser stuttered viciously into life once more. The man threw up his arms and disappeared over the side without a cry.

"Don't be bloody stupid! Do you all want to die?" He gestured at a seaman in the bows. "You - be ready to cast off!" He turned to Cormack. "Can you get down there and make sure they don't try anything else?"

"Sure," Cormack replied, a faint smile on his face. "You're crazy - you know that?" He shinned down the ladder and took up a position in the wheelhouse, covering everyone there; Voeller suddenly appeared next to Woodward, staring incredulously at him.

"Get down there and get that engine started!" Woodward snapped.

Voeller stared at him a moment longer and then suddenly sprang for the ladder as though galvanised into action; he disappeared through the engine room hatch as Marianne reached the E-boat's deck; moments later, he reappeared, grinning and making a thumbs-up gesture to Woodward. "They're ready to go!" he shouted.

"Right!" Woodward glanced back towards the shore. The SS cars had turned, hearing the gunfire and were approaching the end of the jetty, fifty yards away. About a dozen more soldiers were running along the quayside; Woodward estimated that they had perhaps thirty seconds at the most. "Come on, Voeller - get that bloody engine going!"

As if in answer, the E-boat's powerful diesels exploded into life, a deep-throated roar that was like music to the ears.... "Cast off!" he yelled, and scrambled down the ladder; the E-boat was already moving away from the jetty, the mooring lines splashing into the water alongside.

"Let's go!" Woodward shouted.

Rindt heard the gunfire as he reached the main staircase and, almost without thinking, he broke into a run, descending the stairs two or three at a time and slammed the double doors back on their hinges as he burst through the front entrance. He skidded to a halt at the top of the steps and looked over towards Number Two Jetty, about two hundred metres away; he could just make out the four figures on the jetty - and the prisoners were boarding the E-boat! Woodward was standing on the pier, aiming his gun down at the vessel and, as Rindt watched, he began to climb down the ladder.

"You stupid bastards!" Rindt shouted, his fists clenched in rage and frustration. Horrified, he watched as the E-boat moved clear of the jetty, with a series of splashes alongside as the crew jumped overboard - presumably under orders from Cormack or Woodward. They were going to get away.... Damn them! He looked frantically around and his eyes focused on the swing bridge across the harbour entrance, only seventy or eighty metres away along the northern mole. There was still time....

"Follow me!" he yelled to the Navy sentries. "The bridge!" He gestured at three or four other soldiers milling confusedly around and began to sprint towards the breakwater.

Woodward crouched down on the E-boat's stern, squeezing the Schmeisser's trigger as he raked the end of the receding jetty; two German soldiers danced grotesquely as the bullets scythed into them, but there was no flicker of expression on his face. Turning back in time to see the last crew member go over the side, he called, "That the lot?" Cormack raised a hand in confirmation and nodded.

Voeller was at the wheel, steering the E-boat directly at the entrance and rapidly picking up speed. "Take the aft gun!" Cormack yelled to Woodward and turned to Voeller. "Just take her straight out, quick as you can, right?"

"Right."

Cormack clapped him on the shoulder and nodded to Marianne, who was standing in the rear of the wheelhouse, her face pale in the moonlight; she smiled back at him as he moved forward to the bow 20mm gun. He slid into the chair and swivelled it round, to face the shore. He lined up the gun on the moored E-boats at the next jetty and opened fire, sending a line of tracer shells arcing over towards them. There was a crackle of automatic fire from the quayside, but he ignored it - at that range, a hundred yards or more now, they were welcome to try their luck as far as he was concerned. Woodward joined in with the aft gun and little bright flashes peppered the other boats' hulls and upperworks as the E-boat swept past; suddenly, the nearest vessel burst into flames.

They were past the other jetty now with the Naval HQ and depot ship passing abeam; Cormack kept the gun firing, raking the quayside and then the depot ship as the E-boat raced past. He swore as a line of tracer shells came plunging towards them from the ship. At the same moment, a searchlight suddenly exploded into life from the mole ahead, bathing them in its blinding glare. The E-boat heeled as Voeller put the helm over first one way then the other, avoiding the tracer shells but still the searchlight beam held them transfixed like flies in amber. Cormack traversed the gun and fired again, aiming at the single eye of the light; there was a sudden bright flash and the beam died. The diesels were roaring now, driving the E-boat through the water at more than twenty knots and the entrance was coming rapidly closer....

Cormack cursed and ducked reflexively as a fusillade of bullets slammed into the E-boat less than six feet away; he looked round and saw half a dozen men racing along the mole towards the bridge, firing as they went. Grim faced, Cormack swung the gun round and opened up again, pumping shell after shell at the running figures, cutting them down one by one. They were nearly there now; Voeller was slowing down, momentarily, as he steered at the narrow gap under the bridge.

And then the gun jammed.

Rindt threw himself flat as the E-boat's gun opened fire, but the man next to him was not so quick to react; he screamed and was thrown to one side, half his chest ripped away. In an almost unconscious action, Rindt stretched out his hand and grabbed the soldier's Schmeisser before scrambling behind the cover of three oil barrels. He looked rapidly around and saw that three men were already down, while the rest were frantically trying to find cover as the E-boat kept up its murderous fire. And there was nothing they could do to stop it, Rindt realised despairingly; the AA guns at each end of the bridge could not be depressed sufficiently to fire at the escaping E-boat as it went past. But there had to be something he could do.... He couldn't just let them go!

And then the rhythmic thumping of the E-boat's bow gun ceased; Rindt launched himself into a low crouching run that took him to the nearest soldier, lying motionless a dozen metres away. He unclipped the stick grenades from the dead man's belt, ran towards the bridge and threw himself flat to the ground as a machine pistol opened up from the E-boat. Then he was back on his feet, running towards the bridge. He had four grenades - if he could lob them into the wheelhouse, wreck the steering....

Ahead of him, two AA gunners were shooting at the approaching vessel with their rifles then a Schmeisser opened up from the E-boat, cutting them both down. Rindt swore as he skidded to a halt behind the AA position's sandbags; he was on his own and the E-boat was only twenty metres away now, its guns silent as it made its final approach. Obviously, they thought they'd killed everybody....

Its engine throttled back, the E-boat swept under the bridge as Rindt took half a dozen quick steps to the end of the breakwater, arming two grenades as he went. The long, menacing hull slid past below him and he caught a brief glimpse of Cormack in the bows before the wheelhouse came into view from under the bridge.

Now....

And as he was in the act of raising his arm to throw the grenades, Rindt distinctly heard Marianne's voice cry, "Look out!" Cormack spun round, his finger tightening on the Schmeisser's trigger as he saw Rindt. The burst of fire lifted Rindt bodily off his feet and hurled him backwards; the grenades curled aimlessly through the air and dropped into the water at the base of the mole, exploding harmlessly.

Rindt fell in an untidy sprawl on the quay, gasping in agony; it was as if his stomach were on fire. He clutched at his midriff, feeling a warm, wet stickiness and, raising his head with an effort, saw that his torso was a mass of blood. God only knew how many bullets had hit him, but that was suddenly unimportant.

With a convulsive twist that made him cry out in pain, he rolled himself onto his side, so that he could see the E-boat, which was already fifty metres or more away, the bow rising up out of the water as it picked up speed. There was nothing to stop them now; there were no shore batteries and no vessels fast enough to catch them.... They were escaping.... and Marianne was on board.... Rindt realised, distantly, that the image of the E-boat was blurring, slipping out of focus, fading into a red mist, but there was no pain, not any more, only the dreadful, unbearable knowledge that he would never see Inga again.... That he had finally lost her.... He tried to speak her name, but no sound came out. Inga.... For the last time, he pictured her face in his mind, smiling at him, loving him....

Then his head lolled back and tears trickled from eyes that were now staring sightlessly up at the stars.

Cormack made his way unsteadily aft to the wheelhouse, to where Marianne was still staring back at the breakwater. It was disappearing into the darkness as they raced towards the open sea; Voeller had opened up the throttle and the E-boat was rapidly gaining speed.

"It was Rindt," Marianne said wonderingly. "He threw his life away trying to stop us.... Why, for God's sake?"

"I don't suppose we'll ever know that," said Cormack quietly, unconsciously slipping his arm round her shoulders.

"But what was he trying to do? Stop an E-boat with a grenade?"

Cormack sighed and when he replied, his voice was far away. "Just because you've lost, that doesn't mean you throw in the towel. I don't think there was anything else left for him anyway - especially if they were using his wife to blackmail him. He had nowhere to go, nothing to go back to - what else could that poor bastard do but go on to the end?" He shook his head wearily and when he spoke again, his voice was so soft that Marianne had to strain to hear him. "That's what we all have to do, when it comes right down to it. Just keep going.... No matter what."

For a few moments longer, he stared into the darkness astern, seemingly unaware of Woodward as he came forward from the aft gun and then, as if deliberately obliterating the land from his mind, he turned and faced the bow, towards the sea. Somewhere out there was Sweden....

"Let's go home," he said quietly.

If you have enjoyed this book and would like to receive details of other Walker Adventure titles, please write to:

Thriller and Adventure Editor
Walker and Company
720 Fifth Avenue
New York, NY 10019